Five Nights at Freddy's™

TALES FROM THE PIZZAPLEX

#4 SUBMECHANOPHOBIA

Five Nights at Freddy's™

TALES FROM THE PIZZAPLEX

#4 SUBMECHANOPHOBIA

BY

SCOTT CAWTHON
KELLY PARRA
ANDREA WAGGENER

Scholastic Inc.

Photo of TV static: © Klikk/Dreamstime

Library of Congress Cataloging-in-Publication Data available

ISBN 978-1-338-85141-0

10 9 8 7 6 5 4 3 2 1   23 24 25 26 27

Printed in the U.S.A.   131

First printing 2023 • Book design by Jeff Shake

TABLE OF CONTENTS

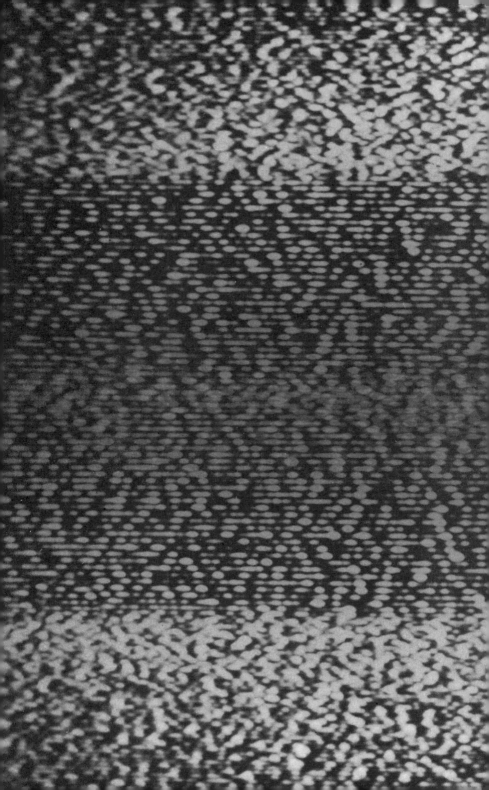

SUBMECHANOPHOBIA

GRAND REOPENING!

FREDDY'S FANTASY WATER PARK IS NOW OPEN!

BUY ONE TICKET, GET THE SECOND HALF OFF.

FAMILIES WELCOME!

BAM, BAM, BAM.

"Hey, kid, you're not supposed to be here."

Bam, bam.

"Don't hit the glass, *please*," Caden Wykowski called from a few feet away beside the main center of attraction—what the owner called—Freddy's Sea Life Mechaquarium. It was the only place in Freddy's Fantasy Water Park that held underwater animatronics. Caden had marveled when he first saw the large swimming mechanical underwater creatures: a sea dragon, two sea serpents, a few sharks, assorted fish, a mermaid, and a vintage scuba diver. The tank also displayed a faux undersea scene with coral, plants, and sea shells.

The little kid must have snuck through the maintenance section to see the animatronics up close. Guests were only supposed to see the mechaquarium from the outer attractions.

"Why won't the dragon look at me?" the kid whined. "Look at me, dragon!" The little guy wore red swim trunks, a yellow Freddy's Fantasy Water Park T-shirt, and flip-flops, and likely had wandered off from his chaperone.

"Because the dragon's not *real*, kid. It's an animatronic

Now, go on back to your family. They're probably wondering where you are."

"This place sucks!" The kid slapped the glass again.

"Hey!" Caden stalked toward him. "That's enough."

The kid spat out his chewing gum on the glass and
spun around and shot Caden straight in the chest with a
clear plastic water handgun—twice—stopping Caden in
his tracks, then ran off toward the doorway that he wasn't
supposed to enter in the first place.

Caden sighed, wiped a hand down his wet work polo,
and watched the big wad of pink gum slowly slide down
the tank's glass. He took out a rag from his pocket, leaned
down, and wiped off the wad. Then he huffed air on the
glass and tried to clean the surface the best he could.

"Hey, there, Wykowski! How's it goin'?"

Caden quickly straightened when he heard Martin
Copper's voice. Martin was the owner of Freddy's Fantasy
Water Park and his new boss.

Caden gave a nod, clearing his throat. "Ahem—good,
Mr. Copper."

Martin smiled and waved a dismissive hand in the air
as he made his way to him. "Call me 'boss,' will ya?"

Caden tried not to stare at his wide grin. "Um, sure, boss."

Martin Copper was an ordinary middle-aged man, of average height and build with thinning salt-and-pepper hair. The only eye-catching trait about him was his smile, which he'd apparently spent *a lot* of money on. His teeth were large, bright ivory, and capped straight to perfection. When he grinned, it was hard to ignore those pearly whites.

"Walk with me, Wykowski," Martin commanded, and Caden strolled with him along the narrow pathway around the circular tank. The sea serpents, one faded purple and the other pale pink, slid by Martin as he walked by, their snakelike bodies writhing beside the glass. Roy, his coworker, had nicknamed them Marco and Polo because they often hid in obscure spots in the tank.

"They can be kinda creepy sometimes, eh?" Martin said.

Caden nodded with a forced smile, looking away from the animatronics toward the surrounding water park.

The crowd was sparse for a Friday, but they'd just re-opened a week ago. The water park was structured like a giant wheel around the mechaquarium. To the north was the main entrance and the park's office. To the west were Bonnie's Sea Ponds, with two kiddie pools and the main diving pool. To the south was Freddy's Treasures and Eatery, and the pier to get on Chica's Fairy Boats. To the east were Foxy Island's Water Slides, and tucked in between the clear-tubed water slides and game area were the employee lounge and maintenance workshop.

Chica's Fairy Boats flowed along the small stream that separated the water attractions from the mechaquarium. At the moment, the boats were filled with a few kids who were squirming to get as close to the animatronics as possible. Caden knew that Martin discouraged this. The animatronics were pretty worn down with chipped paint, rusted spots, and a few broken pieces that you couldn't really notice unless you were up close. The water park had been popular years ago but had been closed for years until Freddy Fazbear's Mega Pizzaplex opened two towns over. Martin was hoping to coast off the success of the Pizzaplex, but he hadn't put any money into renovating the place. It was Caden's job to try to keep the prized attractions up and running.

Which was turning out to be harder than he had anticipated.

Managing the mechaquarium was the only job with decent wages he could manage in Meadow Brook without some extra schooling. School hadn't been a pleasant experience for him, and he'd always learned best by working with his hands.

Martin sniffed and pulled at his nose. "I know I told ya already, but I need the tank kept clean, Wykowski. Spotless." Martin talked with his hands. When he was making a point, he'd stab the air or slice in front of him as if wielding an axe. Caden wondered if he knew how intense he seemed. "This mechaquarium is the bread and butter of the whole park. I need it to have a *big* comeback." He bared his teeth and pointed to a copper-colored tooth on the side of his mouth. "I gotta pay off this dental work. Real *copper*, ya get it?"

Caden nodded. "Nice. Um, yeah, Mist—boss. I check the water chemical levels every night and make sure everything's running smoothly along with the other pools."

"Good, good. And when an animatronic breaks, ya gotta fix it right away. No messing around. When the attractions close, the people don't come, and I lose money. And if I lose money, no jobs for anyone. Get it?"

Caden nodded at the finger pointed in his face. "Understood. I'll fix it right away, boss."

"I hired ya 'cause of your mechanics background stuff. You took those shop classes in high school, right?"

"Yep, took the hands-on mechanic courses, and I had that summer job where I worked on the mini animatronics at Penguin Pizzeria. I'm good with fixing things. My Grams always said so." Caden glanced into the tank, scanning the swimming animatronics, and scratched his head. He realized he couldn't see the mermaid. *Uh-oh.*

As if Martin had read his thoughts, he stopped walking and stared into the tank. "*Wait a darn minute.* The mermaid? Where's the mermaid?" He leaned his flat forehead against the tank's thick glass and looked down. Caden followed his gaze. There at the bottom of the mechaquarium, laying on a rock, was the mermaid. Her arms were crooked. Her eyes were wide open, with one socket pitch-black as one eyeball was missing. Her mouth was agape as if she had drowned.

"The mermaid's down. I repeat, Wykowski, the mermaid is down!" Martin shook his head, rubbing a hand on the back of his neck. "Shut it down and get her fixed, gosh darn it." Then Martin stormed off in a tizzy, waving his hands around in the air. "The more times I close it, the more money I lose," he muttered. "Get her fixed, Wykowski!"

"Sure, boss," Caden spoke quietly. "Not a problem. Right away."

"I can do this," Caden quietly muttered to himself as he climbed up the ladder to the enclosed platform that surrounded the top of the mechaquarium. "I am fearless." His Grams always told him that using positive affirmations could help him get through tough situations. It had helped while growing up, but he was discovering the words to be inadequate for his new job.

"I am brave." He looked across the park and spotted Roy, closing down Chica's Fairy Boats and offering free coupons to visitors to play games. Caden reached for the wet suit hanging on a hook and realized his hand was shaking. He curled his hand into a fist and opened it, then grabbed the wet suit used for diving into the mechaquarium. He licked his dry lips and tried to get his breathing under control as he felt his air starting to thin.

He shut his eyes and shook his head. "I can breathe fine. I can do this." He stripped down to his swim trunks, and pulled on the snug suit and zipped it up. "I'm not a little kid anymore."

He was nineteen and on his own, with Grams's bills piling up. She'd raised him since he was six, and it was his responsibility to take care of her house while she stayed in the nursing home. It was the last thing she'd told him when she was being taken away in the ambulance for accidentally hurting herself after an episode of early-onset Alzheimer's. It was important to her to keep her home, and he wasn't about to let her down.

He needed this job. So he needed to be able to *do* the job.

He walked over to the mechaquarium controls and shifted the power lever. The hum of electricity clicked off. Then he pushed the button to pull back the blue tarp across the top of the tank. He heard the slow hum as the mechanical cover retreated. The strong chemicals in the water floated up into the air.

Caden slipped his feet into the diving fins, hefted on the heavy air tank, hooked his tool pouch to the carabiner on his suit, and slipped the goggles onto his head. He gazed down into the water and saw the shadows of the unmoving animatronics floating below him. A tremor radiated down his back. His feet felt heavy, as if they were glued to the platform. He lifted his legs one at a time to get them moving, then rolled his stiff shoulders.

Whenever he shut down the animatronics' power, the sea creatures stopped in different areas of the mechaquarium. Some were floating at the top, some in the middle, and others sank to the faux seafloor.

This would be only his second time inside the tank. The first time, he'd ducked under the water and swam above the animatronics, too scared to get close to them. He wasn't all that sure he could go farther down to the bottom. But this time he had to. *Had to.*

Hopefully this was just a motor issue. The main operating system of the motors was simple, just a bit of wiring and a reset button that could be pressed in the tank. If anything was seriously wrong, the animatronic would have to be hauled out to be fixed. He was pretty sure Martin would flip out if another animatronic needed to be removed from the tank, though.

Caden sat down on the edge of the platform, slipping his fins into the water. "I can do this. Everything will be fine. *Please let everything be fine.*" He pulled the goggles down over his eyes, put the breathing regulator into his mouth, and before he could stop himself, slid into the cold water. The chill of the water hit him first as he sunk straight down—

Right in front of the face of a shark's wide-open mouth with huge, sharp, rusted teeth.

Caden's eyes widened as a wave of panic slammed into him.

His heart hit against his chest, and he momentarily forgot where he was. All he saw was the terrifying mechanical shark, and black oblivion waiting down its throat. He waved his arms erratically, trying to get away. He whirled and slammed into the vintage scuba diver, tangling with its arms.

It was grabbing him. *Holding him!*

Ahhhh! His mouth opened with a scream, releasing the breathing regulator. Water gushed down his throat. He shoved up toward the surface, burst through the water, scrambling to the edge, and pulled himself out of the tank.

He rolled over onto the side, choking out water and gagging. His chest felt like it was going to burst open and his body shook with tremors. He ripped off his goggles and took a moment to control his breathing as the blur of terror slowly faded away. Water dripped into his eyes and he blinked. He suddenly realized where he was and what he was doing.

He was at his job at the fantasy water park.

He was diving into the mechaquarium to fix the mermaid.

There was nothing that could hurt him in the aquarium.

He was safe.

"Ah, man," he muttered to himself as he closed his eyes. *"Stupid, stupid, stupid."*

Ever since he was younger, Caden suffered from submechanophobia.

The fear of machines while underwater.

After Caden's parents were lost at sea during a second honeymoon, Caden had entered therapy. When he went to live with Grams and went back to school, everything seemed fine. For a time. He was making his way back into a normal life until the one fated day that he referred to as:

The Second Grade Field Trip Gone Totally Wrong.

It turned out, his parents' death had left him with an unshakable fear of underwater machines. He didn't even know for certain what had happened to his parents, but his brain had decided that underwater mechanics were involved, and that fear had never gone away. After the field trip incident, he was teased for the rest of his school years. No matter how well he did on the field or how nice or how quiet he was, his classmates had never forgotten. And they, in turn, never let him forget.

For years, Caden wanted to leave, to run away, but he couldn't just leave Grams. So he'd stuck it out, and he'd found ways to cope.

Maybe he had even hoped, wished, dreamed that one day his parents might come home to him.

And he was still terrified and he didn't understand why. During his episodes, it was as if all common sense was ripped out of him and he became this pile of fear and helplessness. His therapist, Dr. Marks, thought he possibly had imagined his parents' plight so vividly that it had caused the phobia. But Dr. Marks had also said it was just a clinical guess.

Just a guess.

It was hard to cure something when you had no idea what it stemmed from in the first place.

Though therapy hadn't given him the answers he needed, it had taught him a few techniques to endure his phobia.

He'd learned to avoid the fear.

Avoidance wasn't always the best way to solve a problem, he knew, but it was the only thing that helped. That was why he loved building and fixing things. When he dug into a project, it distracted him from the harder times in his life.

Caden sat on the edge of the platform until he calmed down, slowly breathing in and out. He plotted out a pathway to the mermaid at the other side of the tank that would allow him to avoid all the other mechanical sea creatures. That would be his clear path in and out.

With a plan in place, Caden forced back his fear and slipped into the water before he could change his mind. He spotted the huge green sea dragon a few feet away as he sank. It was the largest of the animatronics, with scary metal spikes down its back and tail. Caden's pulse fluttered as he dived down straight for the mermaid. His adrenaline spiked, and he wanted to rush, to hurry, and to get out and away from the animatronics.

Stay calm, he told himself. *Hold steady.*

Diving wasn't meant to be done fast. He had to pace his breathing and regulate pressure. And try to clear his mind.

Strangely, whenever he went underwater, an odd static noise filled his head. You would think it would be silent under the water. But it seemed that the white noise was just another thing he didn't understand about his phobia.

As he swam farther down, he could feel his gut tighten. He eyed the long-tailed sea serpent, Marco, staring at him from a few feet away. The animatronic was powered down, but the eerie way the sea serpent stared directly at him made Caden feel like he was being stalked. Watched. For a second, he thought he noticed a flicker of yellow light in its eyes.

The power is off, he reminded himself as he finally reached the mermaid, whose eyes he thankfully could not see. He unsealed the compartment panel on the mermaid's back and tightened a loose wire. He flicked the button to reset the machine, and her arms suddenly waved around. Caden flinched, hitting the aquarium glass with his air tank.

The panic came clawing back.

When the mermaid settled back down, he forced the anxiety away and moved again. He gazed at the tank wall, making sure he hadn't damaged it. He closed up the mermaid, slid the screwdriver into his pouch, and swam as fast as he could to the surface. He swam as if someone was right behind him, ready to chomp his fins with sharp metal teeth. He couldn't shake the feeling that the sea dragon was watching his every move. Caden yanked himself up on the platform, pulled off all his equipment, and hurried to the power lever, dripping water onto the platform.

"Come on, work." He pulled the lever up to power on and turned to look at the tank. The animatronics' eyes lit up, and slowly they began to swim around the mechaquarium.

Caden gazed down at the mermaid as she swam at the bottom, moving her arms and tail around. Her faded red hair waved through the water.

His shoulders sagged with relief.

I did it.

He scrubbed a hand down his face and through his wet hair. Then he stripped down to his swim trunks, dried off, and started to organize his diving equipment. Martin hadn't told him how to care for anything, but Caden had always been a stickler for a clean shop and work environment. He'd researched how to take care of diving equipment and the proper ways to use it. Every tool, every piece of equipment, had a designated place so he knew where it was when he needed it.

He always refilled the air tank no matter how full it was. He wiped down the goggles and hung the fins and tool pouch on a section on the wall. He set the breathing regulator in a clean box. When he was dressed and everything was set to rights, he left to let Eva, the office manager, know that the mechaquarium and fairy boats were back in business.

Score one for Wykowski.

However, with how exhausted he felt, it didn't seem like much of a win at all.

"Hey, Caden!"

Caden swiveled around to see his coworker Roy walking toward him. Nearly a decade and a half older than Caden, Roy always looked like he had just rolled out of bed, with dark hair that always stuck up in crazy directions. His uniform was usually too small and wrinkled. You wouldn't know it by his appearance, but Roy managed to be an all-star employee at the water park. He knew how to run every game booth, cooked a mean hot dog on a stick, and was also the park janitor. When Caden had asked him how he managed to do it all, Roy told him he used to come to Freddy's Fantasy Water Park as a kid and loved every part of the park experience. This was his dream job.

"Yeah, Roy?" Caden swirled the water tube, checking the levels of chemicals in the kiddie pool at Bonnie's Sea Ponds before any of the little kids jumped in.

Roy flung a thumb over his shoulder. "Think Hank's down."

Caden expelled a weary breath and dumped the small tube of water back in the pool. Hank was the shark with the rust spot in the shape of a hammer on its tail. Hank the Hammer, Roy liked to call him. He'd named the other two sharks: Mac the Muscle, and Sly, the latter of whom always managed to sneak around the faux sea rocks and plants. Zeus was, of course, the sea dragon, Delilah was the mermaid, Frank was the diver, and Marco and Polo were the serpents.

"Got it. Thanks."

Roy scratched at the whiskers on his chin. "One job I couldn't land here at the park was the techie one. Not the best with puzzles. Don't think I could swim with the air tank, either."

Caden shrugged. "You do everything else here, Roy. You had to leave a job for someone else."

Roy grinned, showing yellow teeth, and expelled a snorting laugh that was unique to just him. "Yeah, guess I had to leave something for you to do. What I wouldn't give to have your job, though. Swimming around with Zeus and Delilah. Now that would be mind-blowing!"

Caden let out a nervous laugh. "Yeah . . ."

"Okay, buddy, you go do your thing. I'll make the announcement that the mechaquarium and fairy boats will be down for a bit. Get Hank back up and running with the rest of them."

"Thanks, will do." Caden gave him a thumbs-up, put away the water-testing kit, and took off toward the mechaquarium. He walked by a few patrons in the park. The day was slightly overcast, but the sun usually burned away the gloom at lunch. A couple of kids were holding bright balloons as they ran around. Parents were scolding the children not to run. A few seagulls were flying above, spying for dropped food, and the coo of pigeons could be heard along with the park music playing through the speakers.

"No way. Caden Wykowski, *you're* working here?"

Caden came to a halt. *Oh no.* Unfortunately, he knew that voice. He turned around to see his old classmate

Darryl Cunningham with Yasmine Mendoza and a little girl at her side.

It had been a year since they'd graduated, and Caden had hoped to never see his nemesis again. But it was hard to avoid anyone in Meadow Brook.

Caden gave a fake smile and combed a nervous hand through the top of his hair. "Darryl. Hey, Yasmine. How's it going?"

"Hi, Caden, we didn't know you worked here," Yasmine said, with a toss of her wavy black hair. "That's cool."

"Are you kidding me?" Darryl spat out. "A water park was the *last* place I thought Caden Wykowski would turn up." Darryl hadn't changed a bit. Honey-blond hair, slim, and well-dressed. But what you couldn't see from looking at him was his mean streak. Darryl had instigated many rounds of the name-calling, shoves, and beatings that Caden had suffered over the years. All because of Caden's stupid phobia that had only acted up on that one field trip.

Kids never forgot that kind of stuff.

Caden looked down at the little girl, who was sucking on a lollipop. "Who's this?"

Yasmine put a hand on her shoulder. "My little sister, Marie. We brought her to the park to see the sea creatures, but looks like you guys are shutting it down."

"Figures," Darryl said, with a sneer. "This place is such a dump. Why'd they even reopen? The Mega Pizzaplexes are so much better. I went to one by our school . . . It puts this place to shame." Then Darryl hocked a loogie and spat on the ground.

"Yeah, well," Caden said. "Hopefully it won't be closed too long. Just have to get in the tank and restart one of the animatronics." He looked at Marie. "Then you'll be able to see them swim around again, okay?"

Darryl's eyes widened, with a twist of his mouth. "Wait, what? *You're* the technician here? Holy cow. Now I really must be dreaming! You hear this, Yasmine? Caden gets in the actual water to fix the animatronics. Is there a puddle under your feet?" Then he snickered, his shoulders bunching up just like when he laughed at Caden in school. "We must have woken up in a different reality today. Wait till I tell the guys!"

Caden crossed his arms as frustration tightened his fists. "Yeah, well, people change. Got to start making a living. What are you doing these days, Darryl?"

Darryl straightened his shoulders and very slightly stuck out his skinny chest. "Came down for the three-day weekend from school. Yasmine and I both got into the same university. We're going to school to get *real* jobs after we graduate."

Caden shrugged. "Yeah, well, school's not for everyone."

"More like not everyone's smart enough. Right, Wykowski?"

Caden frowned at him.

"I was sorry to hear about your grandmother, Caden," Yasmine cut in, her brown eyes sincere. Yasmine was one of the kids who'd actually been nice to him, but she'd always hung out with Darryl and a group of jerks, so he always steered clear of her, too.

"Thanks, she's doing okay now. There are people watching her around the clock." He glanced across the park and pretended to see Martin. "There's the boss. Well, I gotta get back to work."

"Nice seeing you," Yasmine said, and Caden took off as fast as he could.

"Don't get eaten by the animatronics!" Darryl called

out, snickering. "And be sure to use the bathroom first! *Hahahahaha!*"

Caden just shook his head, seething with irritation.

Caden rubbed at his chin, studying the mechaquarium from the outside of the glass. It was definitely Hank the Hammer that was down. In fact, the animatronic was flipped over, floating in the middle of the tank, like a dead fish.

How the heck did that happen? he wanted to know. And how was he going to flip Hank over again?

He rubbed a hand down his face.

He took a couple of big breaths and climbed up the ladder to the platform. *Breathe in, breathe out.* Man, he felt a little nauseated about the idea of going back in again. His palms were even beginning to sweat.

But this was his job!

A job he probably wouldn't have taken if he had realized just how many times the mechanical critters would break down. But there weren't that many jobs for fresh-out–of–high school mechanics within driving distance of Gram's house. And so he'd taken what he could get and hoped that facing his deepest fears daily would somehow allow him to overcome the phobia.

So far, it was just making it worse.

He stepped up and onto the platform and walked over to the power lever to shut off the main power. He heard the vibration of the tank shift and settle to Off; then he pushed the button to open the tarp as he got his diving gear on.

He walked around the mechaquarium, trying to find the best pathway down to avoid the other animatronics. Unfortunately, this time the machines seemed to be spread out all over and at every angle. He would have to swim around at least one of them to get to Hank.

Great.

He blew out a frustrated breath. "Come on, I can do this. There's nothing to worry about." He figured the lesser evil was to swim through some random fish in order to get to Hank. Caden sat down on the edge with his gear on, slipped on his goggles, put in his breathing regulator, and slid into the cold water. He first swam above the other two sharks a few feet below him. Mac the Muscle was dark blue and the biggest of the three. Swimming over its large body sent a shiver down Caden's back. Sly was light blue and smaller, with beady eyes and a small tail. Hank was just plain gray.

Caden kicked down toward the school of fish and pushed through them. Each time he brushed against one, it was like being zapped with dread. He broke through the wall of fish, with his heart pounding, and swam over to Hank.

Unfortunately, with Hank upside down, Caden couldn't reach the panel on the back from here. He would have to swim under the shark to fix him.

Sheesh, it was like every time he got into the tank there was some other obstacle to overcome.

Caden swam under the shark and, like a scaredy-cat, jerked back out again. His breathing was rushed and erratic. The pressure of having the mechanical shark over him freaked him out.

Breathe in. Breathe out, he chanted in his head as he tried to calm himself. Caden looked out through the mechaquarium and noticed the visitors weren't paying much attention to the tank. Thank goodness. He caught something in the side of his vision and whirled around to spot Zeus the sea dragon a few feet away, with its mouth slightly open.

Where the heck had he come from?

Not only was the sea dragon the biggest animatronic, but it was also the scariest. Small clawed hands and feet were attached to the large body. Wings jutted from the sides of its reptilian body. Sharp teeth speared out from its huge jaw. Just looking at the creature from outside the tank could trigger one of Caden's panic attacks if he stared at it too long.

He didn't remember seeing Zeus anywhere near Hank. But he'd been so worried about getting to Hank, maybe he hadn't noticed before. Who knew? His mind was all over the place!

Just get the job done.

Quickly, he shifted under Hank, opened the panel with a screwdriver, and focused on problem-solving. He checked the wires. Fiddled with them, making sure nothing came loose, then pushed the RESET button. Hank shuddered and jerked its tail. Caden lurched back, waiting for the shark to settle back down, and then rushed to shut the panel and seal it closed. He turned to swim up to the surface but came to a stop.

Zeus was now floating right in front of him.

Caden swam quickly back from Zeus until he crashed into something hard. Caden checked behind him. He'd collided into a wall of sea rock. He jerked his attention back to Zeus. Somehow the terrifying sea dragon was even closer to Caden, sending a tremor vibrating through his whole body.

But how?

The power was off. There was no way the sea dragon

could move without the power on. It was all metal. If it were to move at all, it would only be because a cable had snapped and it had sunk to the bottom.

How did it get so close?

What the heck's going on?!

Caden watched the sea dragon.

It got even closer.

Oh no!

Caden looked around, scanning for a way out.

The dragon came to an abrupt stop right at Caden's head, pinning him to the wall.

The tip of its scaled snout was directly in front of Caden's face. The huge sharp teeth were close enough to chomp him.

Caden wanted to scream!

His chest was rising up and down. His back was glued to the sea wall. He tried not to suck in too much air and make himself dizzy.

He was going to die!

He was absolutely frozen with terror.

Someone help me!

Caden wanted to look anywhere else, but he found himself staring into the dragon's open mouth. It wasn't looking so good. Some of the teeth were broken off. The green paint on the scales had rubbed off on areas along its head. Black oil had stained the side of its mouth over the years, and in the dimness of the tank it reminded Caden of dried blood.

He didn't know how long he was frozen, pinned against the sea rock by the animatronic.

Caden finally noticed some type of dirty wiring hanging out of the bottom teeth.

Focus on the wire. Focus on the technical, he told himself. *I can fix this.*

Caden stared at the wire until the terror clawing at his insides eased a little.

His pulse fluttered, and his stomach felt like it was turning over in his gut.

Just fix it now so you won't have to fix it later.

For a moment, he couldn't move. So he started to picture the inner workings of the animatronics, reminding himself that they were indeed machines. Powerless. Hand shaking, he slowly reached out toward the wiring that floated in the water. The material was actually soft and malleable like . . . string. Caden pulled, but it was stuck between the teeth. He shut his eyes and yanked. Something had drifted out of the sea dragon.

He realized it wasn't a wire but a shoelace.

He'd pulled out a little kid's shoe that was covered with black oil from Zeus's huge mouth.

That night, Caden dreamed he was back in second grade on a field trip to an amusement park. He'd been assigned to a group with Darryl, Peter, Sally, and Tony, chaperoned by Mrs. Thompson. Once they got to the park, the beginning of the trip had been pretty fun. They rode a few rides and got to play games. Caden liked the spinning cups the best. His friend Darryl liked the big swings. They each had cotton candy and a hot dog. He couldn't wait to tell Grams how much fun he was having.

Next on the itinerary was a trip on the submarine ride. It wasn't actually a submarine but a boat that you stepped down into in order to see all the underwater sea life through the viewing glass as it sailed around a large pond.

Tinny music played through a speaker. Caden felt a little nervous stepping down into the glass boat. His stomach turned over like when it was upset. His palms began to sweat looking at the greenish, murky water surrounding the boat. He didn't feel good about being in the boat, but he had to stay with his group.

He wanted to go home.

The boat rocked below his feet. Fake kelp waved from side to side in the water, but the water wasn't very clear through the viewing glass. It was cloudy and speckled with dirt.

"This is so cool!" Darryl said, pointing all around. "Isn't it cool?"

The other kids agreed and *ooh*ed at the little fish that swam past the glass.

Caden didn't see anything cool about it at all.

Darryl grabbed Caden's arm and pulled him over to the glass. "Look, Caden, isn't it neat? It's like we're underwater! When I grow up, I'm going to live in a submarine! It's going to be so awesome. Do you want to live in a submarine, too?"

"Um . . ." Caden spotted something in the cloudy water through the glass. He squinted. He watched the kelp shift back and forth. Something was . . . *moving* as the boat drifted closer.

Caden felt his heart pound, he pointed toward the glass. "Um . . ."

His hand curled into a fist at his side.

A large whale animatronic popped out through long strands of kelp, its mouth opened super wide. Its teeth were blackened and brown. Its throat was deep and dark, and it was big enough to swallow Caden whole.

Caden's breath clogged in his throat.

Darryl pulled him closer to the glass, and Caden ripped his arm away and leaped back.

He held his breath for so long he thought he'd pass out. He let out his breath, then sucked in a big gulp of air and released the biggest scream he'd ever shouted in his life.

He screeched as if he were being attacked.

Tortured. Murdered. Like he was being eaten alive.

Mrs. Thompson, Darryl, and the other kids tried to calm him down, but all he saw was the mechanical whale that ignited pure terror within him.

Mrs. Thompson grabbed him by the shoulders. Her face was pale. Her eyes were wide. "Caden! Stop this right now!"

Caden jerked away, screaming. He knocked into some kind of emergency switch on the wall of the boat and a loud alarm sounded over the static radio, piercing everyone's ears. The kids slapped their hands against the sides of their heads.

The boat jerked and halted. The whale froze, mouth gaping, as the boat stopped.

Mrs. Thompson grabbed Caden again, blocking his view of the water. "Caden, please, stop! You're okay! Stop screaming! Please, someone turn off that alarm!"

Caden finally quieted. His entire body shook. His chest moved up and down with harsh breaths. His throat burned from screaming so loudly. Tears ran down his face and snot ran out of his nose. He slowly regained his senses, remembering where he was and what was happening.

What was happening was that Darryl was pointing at him. "Look! Caden peed his pants! *Hahahahaha!*"

The kids began to chant:

> *Caden peed his pants!*
> *Caden peed his pants!*

Caden looked down to see a puddle at his feet as he heard the kids laughing at him.

*   *   *

Hahahahaha!

Caden jerked awake in his bed, covered with a sheen of sweat. His sheet was stuck to his skin, so he peeled it off and sat up. He checked to make sure he hadn't literally wet his pants and then scrubbed at his face. Thank goodness he'd been better able to control his bodily fluids as he got older.

He looked at the clock. It was 3:03 a.m. His mouth was parched so he got up, stepped around the pile of clothes on the floor, and walked out of his bedroom and down the narrow hallway to the kitchen. He rolled his stiff neck and stretched his arms out, yawning. The old wooden floors creaked under his feet. Grams's place was a two-bedroom home, wallpapered with tiny pink flowers. Her furniture dated back to the seventies; the matching brown-and-orange couch and recliner sported knitted doilies. There were piles of newspapers and magazines on the floor and on the coffee table. Baskets of yarn and unfinished knitting projects were placed around the living room. Her kitchen counters were avocado green, which clashed with the yellow linoleum. Even the dishes in the cupboards were old.

Sometimes Caden felt like he lived in a museum.

Friends never came over to hang out, so he'd never felt embarrassed by the out-of-date decor. The truth was, Grams's house had been a comfortable and safe haven for him, away from the teasing kids and the feeling of being an outsider. When he stepped inside, the outside world faded away. Then the next day, he would have to step out again and face a different reality at school.

He'd made a couple of friends over the years, both new kids, but one had moved away and the other had joined in the teasing after a while.

Through the years at school, Caden had learned to disappear from his world. He'd found safe spaces in middle and high schools, mostly in the welding workshops or mechanics classes. Places he could duck away from Darryl and his posse, in between classes and after school, until the other kids cleared out and went home.

He'd never felt lonely.

Being alone had become second nature to him, just like working on things that needed to be fixed.

He opened the refrigerator and grabbed a chilled water bottle, twisted off the lid, and guzzled down nearly half the water. He shut the fridge and turned to look at the darkened house. Funny how being alone in the dark didn't scare him one bit, and yet being underwater with machines in broad daylight could reduce him to tears.

His thoughts drifted to the shoe he'd found yesterday. He'd wrapped the shoe in a plastic bag and tucked it away until the end of the shift and brought it home. He wasn't exactly sure why he'd held on to it, or why he hadn't turned it in. It was like a piece of a puzzle. He had to work out what it meant.

Caden walked to the front room and found the bag he'd left on the coffee table. He turned on a light, sat down, and pulled the damp shoe out of the bag.

The shoe was discolored but at one time could have been white. Now it was stained with oil and rust. It was small. Maybe from a kid in kindergarten or first grade. That was how old he'd been when his life had changed. When his parents had disappeared.

How could a little kid's shoe end up in a closed-off water aquarium?

Why would it be in the mouth of an animatronic dragon?

Did Martin Copper know about this?

"What's your story?" he murmured out loud.

Then he shook his head.

It's just a shoe.

He returned it to the bag, turned off the light, and went back to bed.

"Hi, Roy."

Roy was handing out two ice-cream cones to a couple of kids from the ice-cream booth. "Hey there, Caden, what's happenin'?"

"Just feeling like a cone." Free snacks was one of the few perks of this job.

"That sounds good to me, too." He grinned. "Chocolate or vanilla?"

"Chocolate."

"Coming right up!"

Since no one else was in the line for ice cream, Roy brought out two chocolate soft serves and they sat down on either side of a picnic table. It was the middle of the week so the park was slightly empty. He supposed the park would fill when kids got out of school. Caden had done all of his morning prep work and figured he would take some time to pick Roy's brain.

Roy licked his cone with gusto.

"Hey, Roy?"

"Huh?"

"So you used to come to the park before it closed down, right?"

"Yep. Biggest bummer when it closed. My favorite hangout spot."

"Yeah, you mentioned that. Why'd it close all those years ago, anyhow?"

Roy frowned. "Not sure. Couple of rumors went around town that Mr. Copper ran out of money. It was busy at the time, though. Always a packed park on the weekends. I mean, I loved the mechaquarium like the other kids. Must have rode Chica's Fairy Boats like a thousand times to get a closer look at the sea creatures." He snorted out his unique laugh.

"Did you or any little kids sneak over and look at the animatronics up close?"

Roy lifted his eyebrows and looked around to see if anyone was close by; then he grinned. "Oh yeah! I would always sneak through to the off-limits area and check out my animatronic friends. They were my friends back then, anyway. I'd talk to them, and it was like they would listen, you know. Kid imagination stuff."

"Sure. I know what you mean. What about the other kids?"

He shrugged. "They probably did, not that I'd seen anyone. Hard to resist, you know? Those animatronics, especially Zeus, were amazing to the little kids. They were scary and cool at the same time." Then he crunched on his cone and with a mouthful asked, "Why are you askin'?"

"Just curious." Caden frowned. He guessed it was okay to share about the shoe. "Found a little kid's shoe in Zeus's mouth yesterday."

Roy's mouth gaped. "What? You sure?"

Caden nodded. "Yep, the strangest thing. Can't imagine how it got in there. Unless a kid snuck up on the platform and threw it in there. But it wasn't done recently. The shoe was old and falling apart. It's been in there a while."

"*Wow.*" Roy stared out into the distance. "Wonder how it got in there? Never had the guts to climb up to the top as a kid. Hope nobody got hurt. Maybe someone threw it in as a prank or something."

"Yeah, maybe." Caden was glad he wasn't the only

one who knew anymore, but Roy's reaction had him a bit spooked. This *was* as serious as he thought. He raised his nearly finished cone. "Well, thanks for the cone, Roy. Got to get back to work."

"Yeah, see ya, buddy."

A little later that day, Martin strolled over to Caden as he was rinsing down the Foxy's Island Water Slides walkway area with a water hose. "Wykowski!"

Caden lifted his eyebrows. "Yeah, boss."

He crossed his arms against his chest. "What's this I hear about a shoe in the mechaquarium?"

Dang, Roy and his big mouth.

Caden scratched his head. "Yeah, um, I found it in there yesterday, then fished it out. You don't have to worry about it."

Martin pulled at his ear. "So the dragon had it?"

Caden nodded, turning off the water nozzle. "It was an old shoe. Looked like it had been there a while. Took care of it."

He squinted at him. "You got rid of it? Where is it?"

Caden finished rolling up the water hose. "Um, yeah, I got rid of it."

"Next time you find something, you tell me. I gotta know these things."

"Sure. Sorry, I didn't think it was a big deal, boss."

Martin rolled his shoulders. "It's not. But I want to know everything that goes on in the park, got it?"

Caden straightened from putting the hose away, rubbing his chin as he nodded. "How'd you think a shoe got in there, anyway, boss?"

Martin tossed his hands up. "How the heck do I know? Someone must have thrown it in years ago as a dumb joke. Teenagers were always pulling pranks around the park back then. Causin' me trouble. Darn headache, I tell ya. One of the reasons why I closed. I had to hire security to stop people from sneaking in during the shutdown. I'd put in extra locks, but they would just break through. It was a friggin' mess. Now Roy's my security when we're closed."

Roy really didn't have a life outside the park, Caden realized. "I was going to ask you, do you know anything about the animatronics moving when the power's off?"

Martin abruptly snickered, his teeth flashed brightly. "You're getting the creeps, aren't you?"

"The what?"

"I had techs years ago telling me the same thing. But it's just you guys getting spooked being in there by yourselves with them." He pointed a thumb toward the mechaquarium. "They don't move without power, and they sure as heck ain't gonna eat you, kid."

Caden's cheeks heated. "No, I know. I didn't mean anything like that."

Martin suddenly got serious as he pointed a finger at Caden. "Just keep me in the loop on everything, Wykowski. *Everything.* I want to make sure this park is safe and successful. Like I told you—"

"It's your bread and butter."

Martin jerked his head in a nod. "Right. Glad you're paying attention."

Caden felt a curious tingle at the back of his neck. "Sure, boss. I'll let you know everything." *Everything except that they* definitely *move without power.* "No problem."

Caden walked around the narrow pathway along the outside of the mechaquarium, checking on the animatronics.

There was Zeus, the three sharks, Delilah the mermaid, Frank the Diver, and Marco, the pale purple sea serpent. Where was Polo?

Unease turned Caden's stomach. He hadn't been in the tank since the Zeus incident and had no desire to go in again.

Caden walked around the mechaquarium, trying to find Polo. *Where are you, you sneaky serpent?*

He finally spotted the pale pink serpent, stuck between two sea rocks near the bottom. At first he thought it was just hiding, but as he moved closer, he saw that Polo was down. There was no movement and its usually lit eyes were dead.

Caden ran his hands through his hair and paced back and forth, his pulse fluttering with unease.

Wait. Then he stopped and looked around. *The park had a good group of visitors at the moment,* he thought. Maybe he'd just wait a little while. No one would likely notice *one* serpent was missing.

"*Caden Wykowski, call the front office!*" Eva's loud voice rang out through the speakers across the park.

Caden sighed. He felt like he was in high school all over again. He fished out the old flip phone Martin had given him and dialed.

"Yeah, Eva."

"Oh, hey, Caden. Roy wanted me to tell you, Polo's down. One of those sea serpents in the mechaquarium."

Of course. "Yep, will take care of it. Thanks, Eva."

"Sure thing, sweetie."

"Um, you can call me on this work phone, Eva, when you need something. The boss gave me one. Remember?"

She let out a laugh. "Oh yeah, I forget sometimes! I'll try to remember to call the phone. As they say, old habits die hard."

★ ★ ★

After the fairy boats were closed off, Caden shut off the power to the mechaquarium, and opened the tarp to the tank. He did his usual affirmations and breathing exercises as he put on the diving suit and the equipment. He walked around the tank several times, eyeing the clearest route to Polo.

Dang if that serpent hadn't gotten itself in a tight corner.

Caden figured if he kept close to the area that Polo lodged itself in, he'd be able to avoid the other animatronics. The closest ones to the serpent were Frank the Diver and Sly the Shark. Zeus was *way* on the other side of the tank. Now if it made its way all the way toward Caden *this* time . . .

He shook his head. No, the animatronics were powerless.

Nothing moved on its own.

What about Zeus?

He'd thought about this. A lot. And had decided that by swimming around and causing the water to flow, the dragon had just probably floated with the current. Simple explanation.

Caden sat down on the edge of the tank and sent out a quick prayer. He slipped the breathing regulator into his mouth and slowly dipped into the cold water, his mind filling with distant static. He sank down and then swam toward the area where Polo was wedged.

He avoided the diver. Its arms were floating out in front of it. Then Caden shifted to look at Sly. Of course, it appeared like the small shark was staring right at him again. Caden looked away and aimed for the rocks.

There was a small space between the tank wall and the rocks that Caden could reach an arm through in order to fix Polo. Some of the rocks had real moss on them, and Caden wondered if he was keeping the levels of the chemicals strong enough to kill fungi growth.

There were years of buildup of algae on the rocks and seashells. He'd advised Martin that the tank needed an expert cleaning, but his boss had shaken his head, worried about costs and downtime for the park.

Caden slipped his arm through the rocks and unscrewed Polo's panel with one hand. It took some stretching and maneuvering, but he finally managed it. He glanced up and eyed the animatronics.

Frank had somehow shifted and was now looking down at him. The helmet's glass was tinted so dark that there was no animatronic face that could be seen.

It felt like Frank was . . . spying on him.

Caden's pulse fluttered.

Just hurry, he told himself.

He checked Polo's wires by touch. Nothing felt loose. He stretched and flicked the reset button, snatching his arm back. Polo jerked so hard it hit the side of the rocks, breaking a piece of the scenery off.

As always, Caden froze in panic until the serpent settled down.

The piece of rock floated in front of him. But it seemed odd. Not like a rock at all. And rocks didn't float.

Caden grabbed for it.

It was weird, narrow, and discolored with algae. Curious, he tucked the rock into his tool pouch, but suddenly he felt . . . odd.

He blinked. His air supply had thinned.

Was he having a panic attack?

No, no, he was okay. He knew exactly where he was and what he was doing.

And then his air supply was just gone.

What the heck?

He always filled his tanks up. How could he have run out of air? He'd forgotten to double-check the air level before putting it on, but he knew he didn't have to. He made sure it was always full after every dive. He didn't have a pressure gauge because the last one had been broken and Martin wouldn't replace it.

He pulled the regulator from his mouth, shook it, and tried again.

Nothing.

He was definitely out of air.

He pulled the breathing regulator out of his mouth, pressed his lips together, and quickly closed up Polo. He looked up to see the diver was even closer.

Not again.

Caden shoved off the rocks below to get to the top. But he was stuck. He looked down. A rip in his tool pouch had caught on a rigid seashell. He yanked at the pouch as trepidation washed over him. He tried to unclip the pouch at his belt. But the panic was setting in and he couldn't do it underwater.

He needed air! He couldn't breathe!

Darkness started to cloud his vision.

He yanked fiercely and finally got himself free. He swam as fast as he could to the top. It felt like his chest was about to explode. He felt the diver's arm brush against him, and he shoved it away, kicking his legs.

He burst out of the top and sucked in air like a human vacuum. He gagged so hard it felt like something was clawing up his throat. His face flashed hot as a wave of dizziness seeped over him.

He gripped the side of the platform and pulled half his

body out, hacking and trying to breathe at the same time.

Then he coughed so hard he spewed chunks on the platform.

Caden took the rest of the day off. He told Eva what had happened, that his tank had run out of air, that he got caught on a seashell, and that he lost air for a short time.

Eva was the original office manager of the park before the first closing. She'd left her job at the jelly-packing plant to come back and work for Martin when he re-opened. Caden had learned in a short time that she liked boxed chocolates and strong coffee.

Eva adjusted her bifocal glasses. Her brightly dyed red hair was piled on top of her head in a messy bun. "Oh my gosh, Caden! You have to be more careful. You go home and rest. I'll let Martin know what happened."

"Thanks, Eva."

She shook her head. "I keep telling Martin we need more safety measures here. Maybe you shouldn't be diving by yourself. This shouldn't have happened."

Nerves began to tingle in his chest. "It's okay, Eva. I told Martin I could do this. I need this job. I can do it on my own."

"Okay, okay. Take care. You'll be in tomorrow, then?"

"Yes. Count on it."

"You're so responsible, Caden. You're a good boy. If I didn't have bad knees, I'd get up and give you a hug." She offered him her box of chocolates instead. "Here, have one. Chocolate always makes things better."

"I'm okay, thanks." He gave a small smile and left the office.

The smile fell away as he walked to his car. Caden was uneasy. He knew he'd filled the air tank the last time he'd used it. This time as he put away his equipment and filled the air tank, he'd checked the spare. It was nearly empty as well.

Could someone have let the air out on purpose?

But why?

Had someone been diving into the mechaquarium after hours?

His cell phone rang. Roy. News traveled fast around the park.

He didn't answer. He needed some time to think things over.

He thought about working on a project at home, his comfort zone, but instead he drove to the town bakery and picked up a couple donuts for Grams.

It was late afternoon, and she might be in the resident community area if she was feeling up to it. He'd come to find out that with her Alzheimer's she had good days and bad days. Days she was quiet and peaceful, and days that she wanted to bicker with anyone she came across. And then there were days that were somehow both good and bad.

When he entered her nursing room, Caden smelled cleaning chemicals and others smells better not described. Elderly individuals were rolling through the hallways in wheelchairs. Some walked with a walker. Others were sitting in chairs in the hallways, taking a nap.

He didn't find Grams in her room, so he strolled to the community room and there she was, sitting in her wheelchair and watching the other residents play a board game. Grams had been a crafter when he was growing up, always knitting or crocheting. But as her Alzheimer's set in, she'd lost interest in crafting.

Or had forgotten how to do it.

The last year, she'd begun to walk around the house,

rummaging through her old magazines and newspapers. She'd stare out the window, looking at neighbors walk by and claim people were watching her, spying on her, telling stories about her. She would mumble to herself and slowly lost interest in her projects. She was the one who told him to do something with his idle hands when he was little. To create, to fix, to build. It broke his heart to see her now, doing nothing when creating something had brought her so much joy.

He smiled. "Hi, Grams. How're you doing?"

Grams looked up. She frowned at him for nearly a minute, then smiled. "Caden, my boy. You came to see me."

"Yes, I got off early today and could make it during visiting hours." He rolled her chair over to a settee and sat across from her. "How are you feeling?"

She shrugged a thin shoulder. "So-so. My leg still hurts from when I broke it." Her blue eyes were wide. Her pale skin sagged on her thin face. She fingered her crocheted blanket on her lap with her gnarled, skinny fingers. "How are you? Did you find a job?" she asked him absently, not meeting his eyes.

So she remembered. "Yeah, I work at Freddy's Fantasy Water Park now."

She scowled. "That place is closed. Don't lie to your Grams."

He smiled. "It reopened a few weeks ago, and I just started. It's been good."

"Oh really?" she asked, but somehow managed to stare out at the room and seem disinterested. That was how most of his conversations were with her nowadays.

"I got your favorite, a maple donut." He reached into the bag and then handed it to her.

She licked her dry lips. "That looks good." She took

the donut and bit into it and chewed. "Do I still have my house?"

Caden took out a double chocolate. "Yes, everything is being taken care of. Don't you worry, Grams."

"How? Do you have a job?"

Grams didn't have much of a short-term memory. "Yeah, I got hired at the water park in town."

Then her eyes widened even more. "With the water animatronics? No, no, Caden, you can't work there. You can't."

"It's okay, Grams. I'm handling it."

"You don't like the things in the water. So scared since you lost your mom and dad. My Cynthia. I miss my Cynthia."

"Me too." He started on his donut to quench the sadness.

Grams pointed with her donut. "That water park, something strange about it. I remember."

Caden tilted his head. "What do you mean?"

"Story there. Strange one. Mystery."

Grams had been an avid gossip most of her life and had worked at the counter of an old hobby shop that had long ago gone out of business. She'd read the local paper every day and watched the late news each night. She'd go to all the community events and mingled with neighbors and townspeople, finding out the local gossip before most people.

"What kind of a story, Grams? What kind of mystery?"

She took another bite of donut, staring at the room. "Strange," she muttered again.

Caden tried again. "Grams, do you remember any stories about the water park?"

Grams didn't answer. "I'm tired now. I think I'll go take a nap. Can I take a nap?"

"Sure, okay. I'll get someone to help you." Caden asked a nursing assistant if she could help Grams back to her room to rest.

He watched Grams as she was wheeled away, wishing for the days when she was clear-minded and strong. He realized he would never have her that way again.

He exited the nursing home and got in his car. He sat for a moment, going over the day in his mind. He felt exhausted and the donut wasn't sitting well in his upset stomach.

Then he remembered the rock.

He dug it out of his pocket. It was thin and narrow. He rubbed at the built-up dirt with this thumb. He looked at the edges and saw they were slightly rounded.

He stared at it and stared. Something was off . . .

Then it hit him.

This wasn't a rock.

It was a small bone.

He sucked in a breath as the bone dropped from his fingers.

It was night at the water park, and it was much more crowded than usual. There were people walking around, families talking and laughing. People were eating pop-corn, pizza, and ice cream.

Yet, there were no lights on. Everyone was shadowed in the dark.

Kids were in line to ride Chica's Fairy Boats and others walked up the stairs to Foxy's Island Water Slides. People were playing games. Eerie carnival music streamed through speakers.

"What's going on?" he whispered. "Where are the lights?"

Someone bumped against him. The person wore a

Freddy Fazbear costume. The darkened, furry face stared at him. Caden jerked back and walked away through the crowd.

He looked at the center of the park, at the mechaquarium. It was the only attraction that was lit up with bright lights. All the sea creatures were swimming around.

Fast.

Usually they swam at a slower pace. But it was like these animatronics were alive. Thriving. Eager. Trapped in an aquarium that was too small for their energy.

Standing around the mechaquarium on the maintenance walkways were a bunch of little kids, smiling and pointing at the glass.

Hey, they aren't supposed to be there. The mechaquarium is off-limits.

Caden ran toward the maintenance entrance and saw all the kids surrounding the tank. The animatronics swam quickly next to the glass, staring at the children. The sea creatures' eyes seemed brighter than normal, as if they were possessed.

The sea dragon was the biggest, with the longest tail. The dragon's paint was bright green as if it was brand-new. Its huge jaw opened and snapped closed.

Many of the kids cheered, hitting the glass of the mechaquarium.

"Don't hit the glass," Caden called out. But no one listened.

Caden noticed a couple of little kids climbing up the ladder toward the platform.

"No!" Caden yelled at them. "You can't go up there! Get down." He rushed toward the ladder, but it was like the crowd of children grew bigger, blocking his way to the ladder. He tried to push through them, but they started to grab at his shirt and arms.

"I have to stop them. They could get hurt. *Please. Stop.*"

Then he saw Martin and Roy standing around the tank, staring at the animatronics. He saw Eva, too. They all watched as the little kids climbed up to the platform.

"Boss, Roy! Stop the kids! They're making their way to the top of the platform! They could get hurt!"

Martin and Roy simply grinned, pointing at Delilah and Frank the Diver inside the large aquarium. It was like they couldn't hear him. Roy let out his snorting laugh. Martin flashed his bright grin. Eva kept stuffing chocolates into her mouth.

Caden's head whipped up as suddenly little kids jumped from the platform into the tank, one by one.

Caden's eyes widened as panic crashed over him. "Oh no!" He shoved through the little kids, toward the ladder. His breaths were short and fast.

He had to stop them. Had to save them.

But the closer he tried to get to the ladder, the farther he seemed to be. It didn't make any sense. He watched as the animatronics started to speed toward the kids like animals after their prey. The sharks and serpents rushed toward the top of the tank as the little kids kicked and waved their arms at the top of the water.

The sea dragon reared back its head like a snake and darted between the sharks and serpents, biting into a child's leg.

Caden felt his face flash cold, then hot.

Red blood spilled into the water like a cloud of liquid.

The animatronics attacked the children. The sharks body-slammed the kids and then rushed back to bite them. The mermaid grabbed a little kid's arm and tore it off. The diver grabbed a child by the leg and pulled him under.

More blood spread through the water.

Caden shouted in protest, tears stinging his eyes.

Someone grabbed him, turning him.

It was his mother and father.

Their faces were pale and discolored. Bloated.

They were dead.

Caden jerked awake, screaming.

His heart pounded a mile a minute. He was shaking.

He shoved off the covers and sat up.

"No, no, no."

The next morning, the house phone rang. Caden blinked groggily as he tied his shoes. "Who could be calling this early?" he murmured, then yawned.

He'd tossed and turned the rest of the night, afraid to go back to sleep after the nightmare. His eyes felt heavy. He'd taken a shower already, but it hadn't woken him up much.

He pushed off his bed and walked to the phone in the kitchen and answered. "Hello?"

"I'm calling for Stella Barns."

Caden ran his hand through the top of his hair. "Um, she's in a nursing home."

"Are you next of kin? Her guardian?"

"Um, yeah. I'm her grandson."

She proceeded to tell him that Grams needed a ton of verification papers to continue her medical insurance.

Caden wrote everything down on a notepad, trying to concentrate. "Wait. When do you need this by?"

"Well, she missed the deadline, so we need them faxed or emailed ASAP or we'll discontinue her coverage."

"No, please . . . Can you grant her an extension? I'll get them to you as fast as I can. I promise. It's been a crazy month."

She agreed to one more week, and Caden thanked her and hung up the phone. "Great."

Important papers. He looked around the kitchen, but he knew that wasn't where Grams kept her important stuff. He walked down the hallway to her bedroom and opened the door. The room smelled musty from being closed up for a month. Not only that, but newspapers and magazines were stacked in several areas of the room. Along with spools of yarn and knitting needles.

Her bed was made with a burgundy knitted blanket. Her pillows were still fluffed and smoothed out. He went to Grams's dresser that was piled with papers and envelopes. He hoped he could find her important papers in all of her chaos. He looked in the mirror and noticed dark circles under his eyes. His brown hair was getting a little long, and he needed a haircut. He scraped at his jaw. He didn't really have much facial hair yet. He just looked tired from a bad night's sleep. He decided he would grab some coffee on the way to work.

He pushed aside past medical statements on the surface of her dresser, even some old articles from years ago. Why Grams kept all these he didn't know. Then he started to read the headlines.

BEAR ATTACK IN MEADOW BROOK
TRIPLETS BORN ON ST. PATRICK'S DAY!
LOCAL COUPLE LOST AT SEA

Caden hesitated. He lifted the picture with the headline, seeing his mom, dad, and himself in a grainy family photo. They looked happy and peaceful. He rubbed at his stinging eyes. He often wondered how his life would have been if his parents had made it back from that boat trip or had decided not to go at all. He would have been raised by two loving parents. His life would have been happier.

He wouldn't have been such an outsider his entire life. But most of all, he would have had his mom and dad.

It was the next headline underneath that one that caught his eye.

MISSING LOCAL BOY

Five-year-old Jason Butterfield had gone missing from his home over twenty years ago. The family had gone to Freddy's Fantasy Park that day and returned home, but the next morning the little boy was just gone.

The parents were distraught. They had no idea if he was taken in his sleep or if he'd run away. His bedroom window had been left open.

Jason had been last seen wearing a blue sweatshirt. Blue jeans.

And white tennis shoes.

Caden was suddenly wide-awake.

As Caden made his daily rounds at the park, his mind was whirling. It could just be a coincidence about the missing boy and his white tennis shoes. A coincidence that he was last seen at home after visiting Freddy's Fantasy Water Park earlier that day.

All coincidence?

Maybe.

And maybe not.

He'd taken the newspaper clipping to his bedroom and pinned it on his wall. Then he grabbed some of Grams's Post-it notes and started writing down a couple of clues.

- Old, small tennis shoe (Zeus's mouth)
- Small finger bone (Sea rock)

He'd forgone the coffee and instead went to the local library before work and researched bones on the internet. The bone he'd found was similar to the shape of a finger bone. Caden wasn't sure what these clues would unearth but he was willing to do a little secret investigating to find out. He couldn't go pointing fingers, no pun intended, when he wasn't sure what had happened to Jason Butterfield. Martin had given him a chance with this job and he wouldn't make accusations without more evidence. He wasn't even certain the bone was real. Could it be a prop from the park? Was it part of a fake skeleton?

"Wykowski!"

Caden jerked out of his reverie and spun around to see Martin Copper stalking toward him. "Boss."

"Are you all right? What happened yesterday? I thought I told you to always check your air tanks and equipment."

Martin hadn't told him anything, actually. But Caden always checked his equipment each day. Except yesterday. "Um, I forgot to check the air tank before I got in."

Martin stopped in front of him and rubbed the back of his neck. "Gosh darn it, kid, you gotta be more careful."

"But I had checked it the day before."

"What?"

"I checked the tank the day before and filled it up. I always do."

Martin waved a dismissive hand. "You must have forgot. It happens."

Caden didn't disagree, even though he knew he'd filled the tank.

Martin sighed. "Look, if you can't do the job . . ."

Nerves tightened his stomach. "*I can do the job, boss.* It was just a mishap. Won't happen again. I promise."

"Fine, fine. I'm just glad you're okay. But I gotta be straight with ya, if any other accidents happen . . . you're out, kid. I need employees who know what they're doing. I can't be having accidents from being careless. I got a business to run."

"I do. I mean, I know what I'm doing, boss."

"Hope so, kid." But he looked at him like he didn't believe him. "Just take it easy, will ya?" Then he walked away.

Roy approached him next. "Caden, you okay? Why didn't you answer my calls?"

Caden pushed a hand through his hair. "Yeah, I'm fine. I had to visit my Grams and then I just went home to rest. Sorry I didn't get back to you."

Roy knocked him playfully on the shoulder with his fist. "Just wanted to make sure you were okay, buddy."

Caden smiled. "Thanks. I'm all right. Hey, Roy?"

"Yeah, you need help with something?"

"No, um, did you ever hear about that missing boy, Jason Butterfield?"

Roy's eyes widened in surprise. "You mean, from years ago? Yeah, everybody knew. He went to my school. It was all anyone talked about when it happened."

Caden's eyebrows lifted. "You knew him?"

Roy shrugged his round shoulders. "Weren't best friends or anything, but yeah, we all played games on the playground. I remember everyone being sad at school. The town got a little freaked out. People were looking at each other funny. Then time moved on. Jason never came home. The Butterfields moved away, never to be heard from again. I think maybe he ran away and then who knows what."

"Do you think he could have snuck back here? I heard he'd visited the park earlier that day with his family."

Roy squinted his eyes at him. "Where'd you hear all this? Why you asking questions about it now? That was so long ago."

Caden felt Roy's suspicion bore into him. "Um, my Grams mentioned it when I told her I worked here."

He nodded, with a smile. "*Oooh.* Yeah, imagine your Grams had gotten all the details back then. She liked to know things. Uh, look, I gotta go check out the booths." Then he pointed at Caden. "Be sure to take care of yourself in the tank." Roy walked off, whistling.

Caden frowned. Did Roy sound strange when he warned Caden about the tank? Then he dismissed the idea.

But the conversation had confirmed a growing suspicion. Caden was beginning to think that Jason Butterfield hadn't run away at all.

Since he'd found the white tennis shoe in Zeus's mouth and a small bone that had been embedded in a rock in the tank, he was beginning to think that the little boy had fallen into the mechaquarium and died.

And no one had known.

Then his stomach tightened.

Or . . . someone had known.

And kept it a secret.

Caden checked all the levels of the pools and mechaquarium in the water park. He'd watered down the slides and set up all the water areas right before the doors opened for the day. There was nothing on his list to fix for once, so he walked into the workshop. He flicked on the lights, closed the heavy door, and scanned the metal shelves lined throughout the large area. The shelves stood against three walls of the room, and there were two pathways formed by more metal shelving.

The shelves were filled with various objects that kept the park as clean and spruced up as possible. There were old metal pieces to picnic tables. One fairy boat was stashed in the corner because it had several holes in its bottom. One shelf was filled with remnants of old Freddy, Chica, and Foxy costumes. There were large tools and small tools. Boxes of screws and nails. Old tubs of paint and paintbrushes. Scrubbers, rags, brooms and mops. And all the way against the back wall was Caden's worktable, with a defunct squid animatronic sprawled out and covering the entire table. Above it were tools suspended on the walls with hooks and nails.

The squid was a faded orange and one of the smaller animatronics. One tentacle was missing. Its eyes were discolored and one was cracked. And, of course, the motor was broken.

Caden had fiddled with it a few times. First, to under-stand the motor of the animatronics in the mechaquarium and second, to try to get it up and running again. He pulled out his work phone and set it on the table in case someone called, then picked up some needle-nose pliers to pull a frayed wire from the squid.

His mind kept veering back to the missing boy. To the shoe . . . and the bone. While he wanted to believe the bone could be fake, his gut told him it was indeed real. And that knowledge made him nervous. Jason Butterfield was lost. Just like his parents. And he wasn't sure how he felt about that.

Suddenly the workshop went completely dark.

Caden spun around. "Hello? I'm in here. Don't turn the lights off."

No response.

Caden frowned. *How had the lights turned off? Did some-one flick off the light switch?*

Uh-oh, is there a power outage across the entire park? he wondered.

"Is someone in here?" He called out once more to be certain and set the pliers down. Then he felt the edge of the table as his eyes hadn't adjusted to the darkness. He shuffled beside the worktable to try to get either to a flashlight or to the door. He couldn't remember where he'd set down the flashlight the last time he'd been in the shop.

He sighed and slowly made his way along the side of the room, grabbing on to the shelves for guidance.

Then he heard a sound. A shifting.

Did something just move?

"Hello? Is someone in here? Roy, is that you?" he called out.

No answer.

Goose bumps raised along his arms.

"Look, this isn't funny. The boss isn't going to like it if you're playing games."

Then he shook his head. He was probably talking to himself.

There was likely no one in the workshop with him. It must be his imagination playing tricks on him.

He touched the shelf, guiding himself the best he could. His finger nicked something sharp. "Ow." He felt warmth on his finger. He'd cut himself.

Dang it, he couldn't see anything, and he'd forgotten his phone behind him. He'd better go back and get it. He could call Eva to find out if there was a power outage.

He shifted back the way he came and thought he heard something else. Was someone taking a breath? Then he heard a loud *creeeaaaak.*

Caden's eyes widened. He didn't know what it was, but he rushed toward his phone.

A crash filled the room, and a whiff of air rushed across him.

Caden's adrenaline spiked as pieces of metal rolled on the floor.

What happened?

Sudden light from outside rushed into the front of the workshop. Someone had opened the door. "Hey! Who's there?"

The light was enough to reveal a huge mess inside the workshop. One of the metal shelves from the center of the room had fallen over. The shelf had collapsed against another shelf on the wall and was leaning diagonally. A bunch of metal pieces and tools were spilled on the floor.

Caden swallowed hard.

The heavy shelf may have landed right where Caden had just been.

"Bolt them down, Wykowski. I want them *all* bolted down," Martin demanded in the now-fully-lit workshop. "I can't be having any more accidents."

After the shelf fell and Caden turned on the lights, he'd called the office to inform Eva what had happened, bandaged his cut finger, and proceeded to clean up the mess. Martin and Roy had rushed over to see if Caden was okay.

Roy had helped him lift the heavy shelf upright. Caden realized that if it had landed on his head, he would have been done for.

"Whoa, buddy, if this had landed on you. Squash!" Roy echoed his thoughts with a clap of his thick hands. "You're lucky."

"*Gosh darn it*, Wykowski, how the heck did this happen? What were you doing in the dark? Had you leaned on the shelf earlier?" Martin stared at him, his hands on his hips, demanding answers. "How many times have I told you to be more careful? What did I tell you if you had another accident?"

Caden's stomach suddenly felt upset. He ran a hand over the top of his head. "Um, it wasn't me, boss. Please, don't fire me."

"Well, something happened here, and we're lucky you didn't get hurt. I warned ya."

"Come on, boss," Roy said. "Caden's a good kid. Give him another chance."

"I think someone turned off the lights and ran out," Caden blurted. He left out the accusation that someone may have pushed the shelf over, trying to hurt him . . . or worse?

Martin pointed at him. "Wait a darn minute. Are you saying the pranks are starting up again?" He began to pace the walkway. "After all these years? The kids are back, causing me trouble. Roy, have you seen any kids sneaking around where they're not supposed to?"

Roy scratched the whiskers on his chin. "Nah, boss, not that I've seen."

"Well, gosh darn it, something's going on. I can feel it. It's the same feeling I got back in the early days. Weird pranks happening, and it's all starting again. Well, no one is going to best me this time. Not the kids. No one!" Martin stormed out of the workshop, mumbling under his breath.

Roy let out a whistle. "Boss is ticked."

"Do you think this was a prank, Roy?"

Roy frowned. "Possible. You saw someone run out the door?"

"Well, um, it suddenly opened after the shelf fell."

"So the shelf could have fallen on its own from too much stuff on it?" Roy was staring at him intently.

What does he want me to say? Caden wondered. *That it was just a freak accident?*

He shook his head. "Really, I'm just not sure."

"I think we tell the boss the truth—that you didn't see anyone, buddy."

But he had *heard* someone. Hadn't he?

"We want him to keep you on the job, right?"

Caden grabbed some more bolts from a box to drill into the cement floor. "Yeah, I need this job. It's true. Didn't actually see anyone."

Roy grinned. "Good, that's settled. Gotta get back to the booths or I'd help you."

Caden waved the drill. "It's okay, I'm good. Thanks for trying to help me keep my job."

"Sure, buddy. What are friends for?" Roy sauntered out the door with a wave.

Caden stared at the mess. Something was definitely going on.

Was it just kids playing pranks?

Or was someone trying to stop him from finding out the truth about the mechaquarium and Jason Butterfield?

With the workshop put back to rights and the shelves all bolted down for safety measures, Caden needed a break. He stood in line for a slice of pizza, his mind replaying the past week. First the air tanks had been emptied and now he'd almost been smashed by a heavy shelf. He swallowed hard. Who could be causing these so-called accidents?

Was it Roy? Was it Martin? Was it kids playing tricks? Or were they *just* freak accidents?

A loud horn behind his head surprised him and caused him to whirl around, his adrenaline spiking.

Then he was shot in the face by a continuous stream of silly string.

The horn finally stopped and so did the string. Caden pulled sticky string from his face. The first person he saw was Darryl, holding a loud horn in front of his face, with a giant stuffed Bonnie in his other arm. The next person he saw was the little girl, Marie, standing beside him, holding a can of neon-yellow silly string.

Darryl stepped backward, busting up laughing. The little girl was smiling because Darryl was laughing so hard.

"Great job, Marie! We played a funny trick on Wykowski, didn't we?"

Caden frowned, pulling off the rest of the silly string. "Darryl," he said. "Back again."

Darryl finished snickering and took a big breath, "Ah, yeah. Well, little Marie likes this place for some reason. Yasmine's getting her some popcorn. We got you good, Wykowski, just like the old days! Oh, that felt so awesome."

Caden sighed, threw the wadded-up string into a garbage can beside him. "How long have you been here?"

"For a couple of hours. Check out this giant Bonnie I won for Marie. Got all three rings on the bottles. Bet you couldn't do it."

Could Darryl be the one who had followed him into the workshop and tried to push a shelf on him? One time, Darryl had sprained Caden's arm and given him a concussion when his pranks had gone too far. Of course, Caden had called them *accidents* when the teachers had asked him what had happened.

"Were you anywhere near the workshop here, Darryl?"

Darryl narrowed his eyes at him. "What are you talking about, Wykowski?"

"I'm talking about your stupid pranks. We're not kids anymore, so you'd better not be pulling any more tricks around the park."

"What?" he asked, then rolled his eyes. "*Ooooh*. Even if I did, who's going to stop me? *You?* Yeah, right!"

"I'm saying things can be dangerous around here, and you shouldn't be playing around. We're not in school anymore."

Darryl stepped up to Caden. This time Caden was not intimidated. Darryl was just a bully who always had to get his way to make himself feel good. Caden didn't back down. He just looked at Marie with her wide eyes as she watched them.

He set a gentle hand on Darryl's shoulder and slightly nudged him back. "Not in front of the little girl, come on." Caden shook his head. "Grow up, Darryl. I did. Look, I'm on lunch and then I've got to get back to work. So why don't you show Marie here a better example and go have fun instead of wasting my time?" Then he turned his back and went up to get his pizza slice.

After a moment, he looked over his shoulder to see Darryl had walked away without saying a word.

Caden took a big breath. He felt that he was finally done with Darryl Cunningham bullying him.

Caden had tossed and turned all night, wondering what he should do about the mechaquarium and Jason Butterfield. He wondered if he should go to the police station and show them the clues he'd discovered and tell them all about the weird accidents happening to him at the park.

And there he found himself that morning, right in front of Meadow Brooks's small police station, with a backpack slung over his shoulder, holding an old shoe and small finger bone.

Oh my gosh.

What am I doing?

Even if he told the police what he suspected, would they even believe him?

And then if they started to investigate, Martin would surely fire him for causing him and the park trouble. He'd lose his income. He'd lose Grams's house. He'd be homeless.

He really hadn't thought this through very well.

He needed more time to think.

He turned around and walked right into Police Chief Jackson.

"Whoa, there. Oh, look who it is. Caden Wykowski. How are you doin', son?"

Caden's eyes widened. "Oh hi, Chief Jackson. I'm good. Good." Chief Jackson had been the one to come to Grams's house to tell him his parents had been lost at sea. He'd been a patrol officer back then and had always been a kind man with dark skin and a gentle demeanor. Even though he was over six feet tall and could have been a professional wrestler, in Caden's opinion.

"What brings you to the police station?" he asked Caden.

Caden became nervous. He looked all around, trying to come up with a fib. "Well, um, I thought I lost something. But I, um, found it and I'm good now. *So thanks.*" He started to walk off.

"Hold up, son. How's your grandmother? She doing okay after her accident?"

Caden did his best to calm himself. It was just a kind man asking about his grandmother. *He doesn't know you have a finger bone in your backpack.* "Yeah, she's doing better. Thanks, Chief Jackson."

"That's good to hear." He raised his thick eyebrows. "You sure everything's okay?"

"Yep." Caden forced a smile. "Good and dandy."

"Heard you got a job at the water park. How's Martin Copper treating you?"

"Good. I'm really thankful for the job. It's good there. Yep."

The chief continued to eye him, then smiled. "Okay, then. You need anything, you just let me know. Don't be a stranger, Caden."

"Thanks. Bye, Chief Jackson." Caden quickly walked to his car and took off to work. He found himself in a really tricky situation. And he didn't feel it was time to go the police. He needed more proof about the missing boy and Martin Copper's water park before he was willing to shake things up in his small town.

It was near closing, and Caden was sporadically keeping an eye on the mechaquarium, actually hoping for one of the animatronics to go down.

Crazy, he knew.

But he was looking for another excuse to dive in and look for more clues after the park was closed when most of the workers were gone for the day. Except Roy, who was also the night security guard.

Caden had been tracking Roy's routine and apparently his coworker had a large pepperoni pizza every night with a liter of soda and two giant chocolate chip cookies, followed by a long nap in the front office.

By the time the park closed its gates, Caden realized there would be no valid excuse to get back into the mechaquarium. He would have to dive in and secretly look for more clues, hoping Roy wouldn't notice.

Could there be more bones hidden among the sea rocks? he wondered. He wanted to find out. He needed to. He was torn between what was right and what was wrong and what he should do about it. The only way to know was to find something that gave him a clear, straightforward answer.

He knew he'd find that answer in the mechaquarium.

Caden watched Eva leave and made his way up to the platform and then stood, scanning the park. He didn't see anyone lingering behind. He figured Roy was munching on his pizza right about now.

He changed into his diving suit and double-checked his air tank. *Yep, full.* And put on the rest of his equipment. He shut off the power to the animatronics and pushed the button to pull back the tarp.

Miraculously, most of the animatronics had stopped in one end of the tank as if giving him a wide berth to explore.

"Huh, will you look at that," he murmured. "My lucky day."

He put on his goggles and slipped the breathing regulator into his mouth before he slipped into the chilled water. The strange static entered his mind as he dived down toward the bottom. He was nervous, of course, but his need for answers pushed his usual phobia from his mind.

Caden kicked out his legs until he reached the bottom. He ran his hands over rocks and shells, trying to see or feel if anything seemed odd or out of place. The little bone had been stuck to a rock, and he guessed that could be the case with other pieces of bone if, in fact, there were more bones to be found.

Caden glanced over to the animatronics and blinked.

All the sea creatures had turned in his direction, with Frank the Diver moving slightly closer. A chill crept down his back. *Everything is okay,* he told himself as he forced himself to keep searching.

There was just so much sea rock, discolored shells, and fake kelp covering the mechaquarium floor. It could take him weeks to find another piece of evidence.

He was about to call it a day, when his tank knocked against a chunk of rock. He turned around to make sure he didn't cause any damage, spotting a round rock wedged between a small space of sea rocks. It was covered with algae. Caden reached for the rock, and it came loose rather easily.

He turned the rock around in his hands, and he flinched!

The rock had two deep holes with a smaller one underneath.

It was a *skull*!

It was a freaking human skull!

He wanted to scream. He wanted to drop it and swim away. But he held on as his hands trembled. The bottom jaw of the skull had fallen off somewhere. If there was a finger and a skull, there was likely a body or more parts of a skeleton. He looked around the mechaquarium through the glass, making sure no one had seen what he found.

What should he do? Should he leave it? Should he take it straight to the police, along with the finger bone?

There was no denying it now. There were definitely remains of a body inside the mechaquarium. He had to do the right thing and notify the police that this could be Jason Butterfield's skull.

In the next moment, a distant humming caught his attention.

What was that?

He looked up to see the tarp was closing over him!

Oh no!

Caden kicked up toward the surface. The tarp was already halfway closed by the time he started swimming, and as he made his way to the top, the tarp closed shut over Caden, sealing the tank.

He was trapped.

Caden's heartbeats pattered against his chest. The static in his ears seemed to grow louder. What could he do? How would he get out?

He stuffed the skull into his tool pouch and took out his screwdriver. He reached up at the tarp's edge and tried to pry at the stiff material, attempting to wedge the screwdriver into an opening, but there was no space to slip the tool into. He hit at the tarp, but it was pretty sturdy.

Please, please, please get me out of here.

His stomach began to turn. His mind clouded with too many thoughts. He whirled around, looking out of the mechaquarium's glass.

Was Roy around? Could he see him?

Could he last all night inside the tank?

Would he have enough air to survive?

No, he didn't think that would be possible.

A movement below caught his attention. Caden shifted and his eyes went big—Frank the Diver was slowly floating up toward him. Caden felt the panic rise within him. His arms waved around erratically, trying to get away as fast as he could from the animatronic. He kicked with his legs, swimming farther away from the diver and down into the tank. He swam as fast as he could, maneuvering behind some rocks. Was the power to the animatronics turned on? He scanned the other sea creatures and saw that they were still unmoving.

How was the diver moving on its own without any power?

The arms of the diver began to wave and its legs kicked out toward Caden.

Oh my gosh.

This wasn't like when Zeus had floated toward him. The animatronic was swimming like a human instead of its usual slow movements.

And it was heading straight for Caden!

Caden looked around. The only direction he could go was toward the animatronics floating on the other side of the tank and still gathered in a group. Everything within him protested the idea of hiding behind them. But he had no choice. His stomach felt like it was swishing in a spin cycle as he swam toward a row of sharks, the mermaid, and the serpents. Their eyes were staring directly at him.

He looked behind him. The diver was closer!

Caden kicked out, reaching for Sly's fin, and pulled himself even farther from the diver. Caden maneuvered around the shark. He swam past Delilah the Mermaid. Her hair tangled in front of his goggles.

Caden shoved the hair away and glanced behind him.

The diver was too close! Its hands reached for him!

Help me! Someone help me!

The diver was going to kill him!

It was going to rip him apart like in his nightmare!

Caden's vision began to blur. His body shook, trying to get away from the diver, from the mermaid, from the sharks and serpents.

The static in his ears grew louder. Caden thought his eardrums would burst.

The diver caught his arm with one hand. Caden jerked back but couldn't free himself. The diver's grip dug into his limb, digging into the bone, crushing him. He wanted to scream. Caden reached out to shove away the diver's arm, but it was like steel.

He was going to die underwater!

There was no one to help him!

Caden struggled with the diver, trying to get away, but the animatronic was too strong. Bubbles of air surrounded them. The diver moved face-to-face with Caden. Caden looked into the tinted glass and saw nothing but darkness. The other hand of the diver tried to pull off Caden's breathing regulator. Shocked, Caden shifted his head away as they struggled. He shoved at the vintage suit, and he hit the metal helmet with the screwdriver still in his grip.

Screwdriver.

Caden started to bang at the helmet with the tool, then at the body, hoping he could somehow damage the animatronic and get it to stop. The diver's hand grabbed at Caden's throat and started to squeeze.

No, no, no.

Caden's air was starting to cut off. His eyes began to bulge.

He shifted the screwdriver and dug into the neck of the diver's helmet and wedged hard into the suit, with all his strength.

He managed to pry up the helmet, and water rushed inside.

Caden dropped the screwdriver, gripping the edge of the helmet, and pulled it up and completely off from the animatronic.

The animatronic released him, and Caden lurched back in stunned surprise!

It wasn't an animatronic at all.

Martin.

Martin was in the diver's suit!

Martin had tried to kill him.

His boss waved his arms around after his air supply had been ripped from his head.

Caden was frozen in disbelief.

His mind was trying to catch up with the scene before him.

Martin shifted toward him, and Caden tried to swim away, but Martin grabbed his leg! Caden kicked out trying to get free, but Martin pulled him closer.

Closer.

Caden caught a movement in the water and turned his head to see Zeus.

The sea dragon was moving toward them.

Caden blinked. The dragon had come to life without power.

In the next moment, the sea dragon slowly circled them, and its long tail reached out and snaked around one of Martin's legs.

Martin was wrenched to a stop. He looked back and discovered the sea dragon's tail had latched on to him.

His eyes widened. He released Caden and began to flail around, screaming, swallowing in water. Air bubbles floated up from his mouth.

Caden swam backward in horror as he watched the other animatronics glide toward Martin. The mermaid's hair wrapped around Martin's head, covering his face. Martin shoved at the hair. The sharks and serpents moved in, surrounding Martin as he desperately tried to swim away.

Caden was immobilized in terror.

He watched the air bubbles disappear one by one. Then the animatronics floated away. The dragon released

Martin's lifeless body and it drifted through the water, his glassy eyes wide open. His mouth gaped, showing his vibrant teeth. Caden realized the static in his head had gone silent and . . .

Martin was dead.

A week later, Caden walked into the gates of the closed Freddy's Fantasy Water Park. Eva had called him to pick up his last paycheck.

But he didn't go straight to the office. He found himself walking toward the center of the park.

To the mechaquarium.

Yellow police caution tape surrounded the large center of attraction. The tank was halfway drained. The animatronics crowded together in the still water, flipped over and sideways. The serpents had gotten caught on taller sea rocks, where they now hung like dead fish. The police had sent professional divers in and broke apart the faux structures where they found small, hidden skeletal remains.

Jason Butterfield had been identified by dental records.

The police weren't completely certain what had transpired so many years ago, but Jason had somehow drowned inside the mechaquarium and Martin Copper had buried Jason's body under the rocks to cover it up. And he'd tried to stop Caden's discoveries by causing freak accidents, either hoping Caden would get hurt or quit snooping around so he wouldn't find out the truth.

Apparently, Martin Copper had been in severe debt and he didn't want anyone to discover the death of Jason Butterfield in his prized mechaquarium.

Caden had been interviewed by Police Chief Jackson that very night. He'd handed over the clues he had found and told him about the accidents that had been happening to him and how Martin had tried to trap and strangle him.

He couldn't quite explain how Martin had died. He did his best to describe that after their struggle Martin had lost his air supply, that he somehow got stuck on the sea dragon and drowned. Caden also explained how he retrieved his screwdriver and ripped his way out of the tarp, and how he did his best to pull Martin out of the tank, but the diver suit had been too heavy. When he managed to get Roy's help, call emergency services, and pull out their boss, Martin had been gone too long to be saved.

It had been all over the local news and been picked up by some big news circuits. Locals had been coming by bringing Caden casseroles, praising him for finding Jason Butterfield. Grams was calling him, asking him to come visit so she could hear the entire story from Caden himself. The news had somehow awakened Grams's interest, and she was more alert for the time being.

It had all been surreal, as if it were happening to someone else. Caden still wasn't sure what to think about everything and wasn't comfortable with the town's sudden interest.

"Hey there, buddy." Roy walked up to Caden.

Caden nodded to his friend. "Hey, Roy."

Roy shifted on his big feet. "Look, I'm sorry with all that went down. If I had known the boss was trying to hurt you . . ."

Caden lifted a hand to stop him. "Roy, it's okay. I wasn't even sure what was happening until I discovered Martin inside the diver's suit."

"Well, I want you to know, I know you're needing a job and all, and I'd love for you to come work for me when you are up to it."

Caden lifted his eyebrows. "For you? Where?"

Roy stretched out his arms. His shirt lifted, revealing the bottom of his bloated belly. "Welcome to Roy's Fantasy Water Park!"

Caden's mouth opened, but no words came out.

"I bought the place from the bank at a steal!" Roy said, clearly excited. "Going to reopen it once everything is fixed. It's going to be just like it used to be when I was a kid but *way* better." Roy tossed an arm around Caden's shoulders as they began to walk around the park, his other hand waving in the air as he described his plans. "It'll be the best park anyone has ever seen. Live music. Parades. Freddy, Chica, and Bonnie will be back, greeting everyone in costumes. Tons of food and candy. You wait and see. It'll be dynamite! What do you say? Are you in or are you in?"

He glanced at Caden when he didn't say anything. "You're in, right, buddy?"

ANIMATRONIC APOCALYPSE

Join the Fazbear Fan Club!

Every Tuesday and Thursday After School

For 5th and 6th Graders!

Room 13

Be there or . . .

Beware of the Animatronic Apocalypse!

GLAMROCK CHICA IS HUNTING YOU. SHE'S CHASED YOU INTO THE SCHOOL LIBRARY. YOUR ONLY WEAPONS ARE A BOW OR A SPEAR. YOUR CHOICE. ROLL THE DICE TO SEE IF YOU MAIM HER BEFORE SHE JUMPSCARES YOU. YOU NEED MORE THAN THREE TO GET AWAY."

Robbie Wilson picked up the dice and looked at Tina and Nathan, his role-playing group in the Fazbear Fan Club meeting. They were one of three groups playing the Animatronic Apocalypse.

"I choose the bow and arrows," Robbie announced. "Come on, higher than three." The dice rolled and landed on the game board as a 4 and 2. Robbie raised his arms in victory. "Yes! Glamrock Chica is maimed and I survive once again."

"You're too lucky!" Nathan complained, but still flashed his braces in a smile.

Tina nodded as she pushed up her purple glasses with her finger. "You haven't been jump-scared once today. Can you share some of that luck with us? *Please?*"

"I can't help it if I roll the right numbers," Robbie said, but he knew it was a combination of luck and strategy.

He might roll well, but he also had better odds than Nathan and Tina, who played melee fighters. Robbie preferred ranged weapons and did his best to gather up lots of ammo in case he was swarmed. He moved his game piece—a wooden figurine that he painted with dark clothes, dark hair, and night-vision glasses—from the library onto the outer school grounds. "Now I get to add the three leftover arrows to my arsenal. Glamrock Chica goes into hiding for recovery."

Tina wrote down his moves in their Animatronic Apocalypse Game notebook. She was their game warden and was in charge of tracking play, reading card commands, and making sure players followed the rules.

The Fazbear Fan Club had created the Animatronic Apocalypse game last year. Each of the club members had helped design the board game, using the school grounds and surrounding neighborhood as the fantastical apocalyptic world. They'd pasted maps of the school onto cardboard and created game pieces out of wooden figurines.

Robbie's game player name was FFSurvivalist, a nod to his love of camping and his love for Freddy Fazbear. Every year his parents took him camping in the woods for a week and his dad taught him all kinds of survival stuff.

By sixth grade, he knew how to tie knots, start a fire, and create a snare. He'd written the game's command cards that had to do with environmental danger. So yeah, he took camping and the Animatronic Apocalypse to a whole new level.

He'd been a Freddy Fazbear fan since he could remember. He went to the Freddy Fazbear's Mega Pizzaplex practically every weekend. Everyone knew the entertainment mall had the best arcade, the best mini golf, the best raceway, the best pizza, *and* the best animatronic entertainment. Of course, Glamrock Freddy was his favorite. And the club had been a great way to celebrate Freddy throughout the week with other fans, especially because he was the only kid at home. His parents were workaholics who didn't mind his obsession with the animatronics as long as he did all his homework. Everybody won.

Everyone knew the Animatronic Apocalypse game was pretend play, a chance to escape into fantasy before it was time to do their real chores and responsibilities. All of the club members had fun with the game.

"That sucks!" Their group looked over at Daniel, Johnny, and Zabrina's game.

At least, most *of the club members had fun with it,* Robbie thought. Daniel was always a sore loser.

"Better luck next time," Zabrina told Daniel. "You were just jump-scared by Roxanne Wolf."

"Yeah, well, next time I'm going to find a hatchet and take out any animatronic that comes after me."

"Then you should get better at rolling your dice," Zabrina told him, and shrugged. "Don't take it so seriously. It's just a game."

Robbie waited for Jason to crack a joke and reassure Daniel, like he always did. But their club president didn't say anything. Robbie glanced at the third game—it was one member short.

"Hey, Jason didn't make it today?" Robbie asked.

Tina shook her head. "No, I haven't seen him at school this week. Maybe he's out sick."

Jason had a way of easing tension by making everyone laugh. Whenever a disagreement came up or someone got upset at losing, Jason would say, "But would it really matter in the middle of the animatronic apocalypse?"

Too bad he wasn't there to appease Daniel.

Robbie felt his cell phone vibrate with a text. It was from Dyson:

> *Practice ended early.*
> *Want to walk home now?*

Robbie thought about playing longer, but he decided to hang out a bit with his best friend. He only got to walk home with him two times a week after the club. "I gotta go, guys. You finish without me."

"Okay, see you on Thursday," Tina said.

"See ya in homeroom, Robbie," Nathan added.

Robbie stuffed his game piece in his backpack and stood, looming over his friends. He'd had a sudden growth spurt this summer—so sudden that his mom had taken him to the doctor. All good. Just genetics. His dad seemed to think he would eventually get into school sports like basketball because of his height. He also thought sports would help with expelling some of Robbie's "wiggles and squirms," as his dad called his nervous energy. Robbie wasn't so sure about that. Yeah, Robbie had a lot of pent-up energy, but it was all mental. His mind was always focusing on questions. Robbie would pull apart anything he didn't understand until he could find the answer. One answer he couldn't find was whether he would ever stop feeling awkward playing sports with his thin arms and legs. He hadn't yet filled in with muscle, but his dad seemed to think that would happen, too.

As Robbie rushed toward the door, he accidentally bumped into a tall figure in a brown suit. "Oh, sorry, Mr. Renner!" Robbie brushed his dark hair back with his fingers. His mom kept complaining that he needed a haircut.

Mr. Renner, the school principal, stood in the doorway of Room 13, gazing at his cell phone. He was tall and stocky, and liked to wear brown suits and ties. He had a meticulously combed dark mustache and graying black hair. He always seemed distracted and acted as if maybe being an elementary school principal hadn't been his first career choice. But when it came time to discipline, Mr. Renner could really focus. Most kids were intimidated by just his voice alone. He'd been known to get kids to confess to breaking rules even when there weren't any witnesses. Robbie didn't know any students who really cared what he said unless they were in trouble.

"Take it easy there, Robbie," Mr. Renner said. "It's important to always watch where you're going." Then he stepped past Robbie, reading his phone, not looking where he was going. Typical adult. Robbie spotted something on his phone screen about horse races with lots of numbers.

Mr. Renner glanced up at the club members. "Hello, Fazbear Fan Club. Mr. Finkle had a doctor's appointment today, so I'm filling in as club chaperone. Carry on with your games. I'll have an announcement shortly."

Mr. Finkle's class was next door, and he would peek his head in to observe if he wasn't too busy with his classwork. Or cleaning his nose. He made it known to everyone that he had severe allergies with a constant nasal drip.

Robbie could see some of the club members hunch down in their seats now that Mr. Renner had entered the room. Robbie would have felt constricted with him hovering over his game, too. He was glad to be leaving early. He'd hear about the announcement on Thursday. It was probably something about new school rules.

Boring.

Robbie hurried out and met Dyson by the school entrance. Dyson and Robbie were pretty much opposites in the looks department but had still managed to be best friends since kindergarten. Whereas Dyson was shorter and filled out, Robbie was tall and thin. Dyson had red hair and hazel eyes; Robbie had dark hair and eyes. Dyson had a quieter personality, and Robbie had always been outspoken. Dyson could sit still for long moments of time, and Robbie was in constant motion. Robbie's mom joked that he couldn't even sit still when he was fast asleep because he was always moving and kicking off the covers.

Dyson was into animatronics, too, but Little League took up most of his free time. His parents wanted him to concentrate on improving his game. He couldn't participate in any clubs, and he and Robbie hardly got to hang out together anymore. Since they lived on the same street, they would walk to school in the mornings when they could and walked home together a few times a week.

"What's happening with the club?" Dyson asked him as they walked away from Durham Elementary.

"Not much, just playing Animatronic Apocalypse.

I managed to escape unscathed again facing off with Glamrock Chica." Robbie offered Dyson a strip of peppered beef jerky.

Dyson took the jerky. "That's cool. What're your stats?"

"Eleven in my arsenal. I have a bow and arrows and a throwing spear."

"Not bad."

"Hey, you want to hang out at the Mega Pizzaplex this weekend?"

Dyson shook his head. "Can't. Got a game on Saturday, and my dad is taking me to the park to practice on Sunday."

Dyson's parents were super into his Little League career. They volunteered on the committee, worked in the snack shack, were team parents, and bought all the best equipment for Dyson. Dyson once told Robbie that Little League had been fun at first, but now it was a lot of pressure to score and get people out at third base. Everyone wanted to make it to the championships. When he messed up during a game, he could hear some of the parents complain in the stands and sometimes yell at the ump. Robbie wished his own parents had more free time to spend with him, but he didn't envy Dyson.

"Come on," Robbie complained, "all you do is practice. We used to hang out more. Ask your dad if you can go."

"All *you* do is talk about playing Animatronic Apocalypse."

Robbie blinked at the tension in Dyson's voice. He looked at his friend, but Dyson was looking down at the ground while he chewed his jerky.

That was sudden, thought Robbie. But he understood that Dyson might be jealous of not having as much free time so he let it go. "Yeah," Robbie agreed. "You're right."

They walked quietly toward Robbie's house, chewing on the jerky. "Well, see ya."

"Yeah, see ya," Dyson said.

But Robbie couldn't quite let it go. It didn't feel right. "Hey, Dyson?"

Dyson turned and looked at him.

"I didn't mean anything by what I said."

Dyson shook his head. "Don't worry about it. I'd go to the Pizzaplex with you if I could." Then he turned and walked home.

Robbie stuffed the last piece of the jerky into his mouth and watched Dyson walk away with his head lowered, wearing his backpack and holding his baseball bag. He wished he knew how to help Dyson. That was the reason he liked the Animatronic Apocalypse. The numbers, the rules, it just made more *sense* than the real world sometimes.

As he unlocked the front door, he could hear Hopper barking from inside. Robbie smiled. He loved his dog. Robbie dropped his backpack and got down on the floor to pet him so that Hopper could lick him about a hundred times. Maybe more, since Hopper could smell his jerky breath.

"Hey there, Hopper. How was your day? Good? Yeah, mine was okay, too." Hopper was a small, mixed-breed dog they had adopted three years ago from the local pound. The moment they met, Robbie knew Hopper was *his dog*. He had been so friendly and playful, and that had never gone away. Robbie looked around his house. Everything looked as it should be. A nice, big, comfy couch in the living area, and a wooden coffee table in the center of the room in front of their television. A desk was set off to the side with the family computer. Pictures of his dad, mom, and himself were on the walls. It was home, and it didn't feel so empty when he came home to Hopper.

"Come on, let's go do your outside business, Hopper."

Robbie closed the front door and took Hopper out to the backyard. Then he filled up his food and water bowls in the kitchen. Hopper drank some water, then followed Robbie to the front room, where Robbie sprawled his long body onto the couch. His leg bounced as it hung off the cushion.

Robbie's cell phone rang right on time. It was his mom. "Hey, Mom."

"Hi, Robbie. How was school?"

He propped the phone between his shoulder and cheek and began to pull at his fingers. "Good."

"That's good. Now stop cracking your knuckles."

Robbie dropped his hands. "I'm not."

"Hmm," his mom said, like she didn't believe him. "Dad and I are going to be late tonight. I have a house showing in the next town over, and your father has a meeting. He may be home before me. Could you order us dinner? Your choice. But, um, maybe not pizza, okay? I have pepperoni growing out of my ears."

"Yeah, sure."

"What are your plans for the afternoon?"

"I have a little more homework, and I have Hopper to hang out with me."

"How's Hopper?"

Robbie glanced at Hopper on the floor, chewing on a big bone. "He's chewing his bone. Having the time of his life."

"That's nice. Okay, I'll see you tonight before bed. Love you."

"Love you, too."

Robbie's stomach growled as he eyed the kitchen. One more snack before he ordered dinner, and then he'd finish the night with some homework before Dad got home. A typical night in the Wilson household.

Thursday
Robbie walked into Room 13 and read an announcement written on the classroom whiteboard:

> *Fazbear Fan Club President Candidates:*
> *Johnny Miller (Animatronic Slayer_08) vs*
> *Zabrina Zee (ZabFazbear)*

Confused, Robbie took his regular seat near the back of the class, next to Nathan. "What's going on?"

"Didn't you hear Jason had to step down as the president of the club?" Nathan asked him.

Robbie's eyes widened. "What happened?"

"His dad got a new job, and he had to move."

"That sucks. He was a good prez."

"Yeah."

"When did all this happen?"

"Tuesday after you left. Mr. Renner made the announcement and asked for candidates."

Dang it, I shouldn't have left early on Tuesday, Robbie realized.

Robbie wasn't sure, but he might have wanted to run for president had he known what was happening with Jason. Annoyed, he grabbed his finger with his left hand and pulled until his knuckle cracked, then proceeded to crack each knuckle.

Mr. Renner was already seated at his desk at the head of the class, looking bored. He tapped a small wooden gavel against the desk. "Fazbear Fan Club, I told Mr. Finkle I would go ahead and run the vote for the new club president." He waved the gavel toward Johnny. "So let's get this ball rolling. Johnny, you're up."

Johnny walked up to the podium and peered down at a wrinkled piece of paper in his hands. The paper trembled in his fingers as he read. But no one could understand what he was saying.

"Speak up, Johnny. We can barely hear you," demanded Mr. Renner.

Johnny spoke louder but really fast. "I'mJohnnyandI'm runningforpresidentoftheFazbearFanClub—"

"*Slower*," Mr. Renner said.

"Um, I would like to run because I think I would be a good president. I would organize community fundraisers for the homeless, and, um, we would hold a food drive for those in need. Thank you." Johnny quickly walked to his seat to sit and stare down at his paper.

Mr. Renner leaned back in his seat. "All right, Johnny, that was . . . adequate. I guess. Zabrina, your turn."

Zabrina strolled up to the podium with a confident smile. Robbie didn't know her that well, but she seemed nice and never seemed to cause any trouble.

"Hey, Fazbear Fan Club, as you know, I'm Zabrina. I know this is my first year with the club at Durham School, but I am a big Freddy Fazbear fan, and if I'm chosen as the president, we won't be doing food drives. We'll be focused on winning the Animatronic Apocalypse!"

Robbie's eyebrows lifted as he tapped his fingers on the table. *Oh, she's good,* he realized. Using role play to nab the votes for president would definitely excite the club members.

"We'll create a special team to strategize on how to

take the earth back from the animatronic invaders!" Her eyes were big as she spoke with excitement.

The club members clapped.

"Yeah, that would be cool," Tina said.

"Count me in," a kid named Rick called out.

"So vote for me and then join my Specialized AA Team!" She raised both hands in fists. "And together we will win the Animatronic Apocalypse!"

Mr. Renner actually clapped along with the club members. "Very nice, Zabrina, very nice," he said, with a strange smirk on his face. "And very smart." Which was a surprise to Robbie. He'd never seen Mr. Renner seem interested in anything.

Robbie clapped, too. Maybe Zabrina would be a fun president for the club after all.

Tuesday

Robbie jogged to Room 13 as it started to rain. Not only did he like to get to the club meeting early and read the Animatronic Apocalypse Game notebook stats, but he also didn't want to get drenched.

When he got to the classroom, he spotted Mr. Renner leaving. Robbie had a moment of relief that he wouldn't be chaperoning the club again today. When he walked in, he saw Zabrina sitting at her usual seat in front of the classroom, staring ahead at the whiteboard.

"Hey, Zabrina," he said to her. "Congrats on becoming the new president."

Silence.

He frowned at the back of her head. "You okay, Zabrina?"

She flinched and shifted around to face him. Her eyes looked a little glassy. "Oh, hi, Robbie. Thanks. I just have a few announcements before we start gameplay today. It should go quickly." She leaned down and got her notebook out of her backpack.

"Okay, cool," he said, shaking his wet hair back. Robbie grabbed the notebook to catch up on the latest stats as the other club members strolled in. When he was all up to speed, he pulled out his math worksheet and got started.

A few minutes later, Zabrina stood at the front of the class, and tapped Mr. Renner's small wooden gavel on the podium. "Thank you all for voting me in as president. I am truly honored and I won't let you down when facing off against the animatronics. But first, there will be a few changes with the club. And I don't think you'll care about the changes at all." A small smile curved her mouth. "Hey, can someone see if Mr. Finkle is nearby? I appreciate our supervisor, but I want this to be a *students-only* meeting."

Daniel walked to the doorway to check. "All clear."

"Cool." Zabrina cleared her throat. "Please close the door, Daniel. First up, I've decided that we can't use all of our time doing homework at the club when we need to be planning for the animatronic apocalypse. So what do we do? We copy a classmate's. Same goes for quizzes or tests, and even reports. Copy notes. Copy answers. We have more important things to focus on. As president, I declare that the first thirty minutes of club time is no longer for homework. Straight Animatronic Apocalypse gameplay all the time."

Some kids clapped.

Robbie blinked, wondering where this idea had come from. Zabrina was an honor roll student. Shouldn't homework be her jam?

"I've created lists so we can keep track of which books you've reported on and which tests you have copies of. Sixth graders can help fifth, and fifth can help fourth.

Getting homework out of the way helps us to be prepared for the apocalypse, right?"

"Right!" someone piped up.

"Second, make sure you sign up for my Special AA Team or you might just be left out."

She looked up at that, and Robbie met her eyes for a strange moment.

There was something odd about the look, about her, that sent a weird feeling down his back. One moment she had seemed normal, like the Zabrina he'd known around the club, and now it was like a switch had flicked and she had become someone he didn't recognize.

Or was it just his imagination?

When she looked away, he shrugged it off.

"Third and most important, nobody—*nobody*—shares Fazbear Fan Club business outside the club. Not with friends. Parents. Teachers. No outsiders. Period. What's said in the club, stays in the club."

"Why?" Robbie cut in, unable to keep quiet any longer. "Why are you being so secretive?" The club members turned and looked at him with curiosity. "I mean, what's the big deal if we share things about the club? We've been doing this for a year, and it never mattered before."

"If you do share," Zabrina said, and slammed the gavel hard on the podium, "you're out." Some of the kids jumped, and Zabrina smiled as if she was pleased with their reaction. "Pretty simple. Any other questions?" No one answered. "Now, let me share how the homework list will work and then we can start signing up."

Robbie shifted uncomfortably in his seat. *She couldn't kick people out of the club . . . could she?* he wondered.

As Zabrina rambled on, Robbie glanced around Room 13. All the members were staring at her intently, taking in her every word. He glanced down on his forearm at his temporary Fazbear Fan Club tattoo. It was of the Mega Pizzaplex character logo with FAZBEAR FAN CLUB underneath. The tattoo was beginning to fade; they'd gotten them a couple weeks ago. The club had been fun and lighthearted during the past school year, and now he had a weird feeling that things were changing in a not-great way. If he was being honest with himself, he knew the club was his escape from the boredom of school and the emptiness of home. His way to have control in a made-up world. Now? It was getting too real. Too serious.

Maybe the club wasn't going to be his perfect fantasy escape anymore.

Robbie rubbed at the rest of the tattoo with his palm and grabbed his backpack. He went to the back table to finish his homework. He didn't want to listen to anymore of Zabrina's weird demands.

Later that evening, Robbie was in his bedroom working on finishing up a math sheet when his dad popped his head into his bedroom.

"Hey, Robbie, I'm home. Did you eat dinner?" Hopper got up and wagged his tail until Dad gave him a few pets; then he waddled back to the floor beside Robbie's bed.

"Hey, Dad. Yeah, I ordered us subs. They're in the fridge."

"Pastrami for me?"

"Yep."

"Thanks." Dad came farther into his bedroom and nearly tripped over Robbie's hiking boots. *"Robbie."*

"Sorry, I'll clean up my room this weekend." Robbie looked around at the pile of dirty clothes he'd thrown on the floor. He wasn't exactly sure how his clothes always missed the basket. But why should his dad care? It's not like he came in enough to notice.

Everything else in his room was pretty clean. He had posters of Freddy Fazbear, another of Glamrock Freddy, as well as one from his favorite national park. He always made his bed, and his desk was organized enough. Mom wouldn't let him have a television or video game console in his room, though. She didn't want him up all hours of the night playing games, which he had to admit would be a definite possibility if he were given the opportunity.

"Yes, you will clean up if you still want Mom to take you to the Mega Pizzaplex on Sunday." Dad sat at the foot of Robbie's bed carefully, so as to not mess up his gray suit. No one at Dad's bank knew that under his formal shirt were a bunch of colorful tattoos. Dad said he didn't regret getting them because it was a phase in his life that he could look back on fondly. Whatever that meant. "Tell me about your day."

Robbie shrugged. "It was okay."

Dad lifted his eyebrows. "But? I can tell something's bothering you. You have a look on your face that tells me something didn't go right. What happened?"

"Nothing big, it's just the president of the Fazbear Fan Club stepped down, and a girl named Zabrina got voted in and she's changing things. Now it might not be as fun anymore."

Dad thought about this and laid a supportive hand on his shoulder. "Sometimes change is good, even when we can't see it at first."

Robbie twisted his lips. "I don't think it is in this case."

"Give her a chance, Robbie. She might end up being a good club president. Okay?"

So much for listening.

"Yeah, sure." Robbie still didn't think that was likely, but Dad meant well.

"Come and keep me company while I chow down on that sub. I'm starving."

Robbie popped up from his bed, suddenly hungry again. "I could eat some more."

His dad grinned. "Why doesn't that surprise me?"

Wednesday

On Wednesday morning, Robbie and Dyson walked onto the school grounds and spotted a bunch of kids surrounding the outdoor lunch tables. Some kids were even taking pictures with their cell phones. Most of the kids were talking and pointing.

"Who do you think did it?"

"Someone is so busted!"

"I bet you Mr. Renner is freaking out."

"What do you think is going on?" Dyson asked him.

"Don't know." Robbie walked closer, peering over someone's head, and his eyes widened.

BEWARE THE ANIMATRONIC APOCALYPSE!! had been spray-painted in big red letters on the courtyard wall.

Mr. Homestead, the school janitor, was getting ready to paint over the words. He did not look happy.

"Holy cow," Dyson whispered when he saw the damage.

Robbie rubbed a hand across the back of his neck. "I don't believe this."

"Do you think it was someone from the fan club?"

Robbie shook his head. "I don't think someone from our club would do this." He pictured the club members. They were all quiet kids who just liked to talk about Freddy. *Even Zabrina*, he thought. He hoped. "I mean, no one would go this far. No one wants to get on Mr. Renner's bad side."

"Yeah, this is pretty awful."

Robbie frowned in thought. "Our next club meeting isn't till tomorrow. I'm going to have to try to find out something at lunch. I'll see you then."

All through class, Robbie couldn't stop thinking about the spray paint on the walls. It was shocking and out of character for the club, and that really bothered him. Why would anyone do that to school property? What was the purpose? Was it to make the club look bad? And for what reason?

At lunch, Robbie found Zabrina sitting at a lunch table with some of the Fazbear Fan Club members. Dyson followed behind him with his food tray. Robbie smelled someone's homemade soup and another's leftover pizza. His growling stomach reminded him that he was starving, and the salami sandwich in his lunch bag was sounding pretty good at the moment, but club business came first.

"Hey, Zabrina, can I talk to you a sec?" Robbie asked her.

Zabrina barely looked up from her lunch. "Yeah, sure. What about?"

"Just some club stuff."

"Yeah, I want to talk to you about something, too."

Robbie lifted his eyebrows. "Okay."

Zabrina looked directly at Dyson. "Sorry, no non-members allowed." She looked back at Robbie with that odd smile. "You know the rules."

Dyson shrugged. "I'll go sit at our table." Then he walked away.

"Sit down, Robbie. It hurts my neck to look up at you."

Robbie sat across from her, next to Rick. "Go ahead. You first."

"Why didn't you list your homeroom, reports, and tests as I requested at the meeting?"

Robbie made a face. "Because that's not what the club is about."

She stared at him. "Everybody else did it but you."

Robbie shrugged. "So?"

"*So*, if you're part of the club, then you have to do what the club does."

"Are you serious?"

"New club rules. No one else seems to mind."

Robbie felt tension in his back. "Fine," he muttered. But he wasn't giving his homework to anybody to copy. "What's going on with that graffiti on the school walls?"

Zabrina continued to eat her salad. "What about it?"

"It's pretty obvious. That's vandalism of school property. The school is going to want to question the club. We could get shut down because of it. It's not cool, and whoever did it wasn't thinking about the consequences. I don't think they were thinking at all."

"Relax, nothing's going to happen. They have to have proof someone from the club did it, anyway."

Robbie narrowed his eyes at her. "Do *you* know who did it?"

Zabrina shook her head as she stabbed at a crouton, popped it in her mouth, and chewed.

Robbie glanced at the rest of the table. "What are you smiling at, Daniel? Was it you?"

"Don't know what you're talking about, Wilson." Daniel sneered and bit into his candy bar. Then through a mouthful he asked, "Are you sure you're even part of this club? Doesn't seem like it."

A few of the members snickered at Daniel's words.

Irritation washed over Robbie. "I've been a member since day one. Same as you. More than I can say about others."

Daniel glared and looked like he was about to argue

when Zabrina interrupted. "Relax, Robbie. You're being too intense. Just don't worry about the paint on the walls. The school already covered it up. Nothing's going to happen. The club will be fine."

Robbie looked at everyone. They were staring at Robbie, Zabrina, and Daniel as if waiting for their conversation to go nuclear, and for a moment Robbie felt like an outsider. A loner among members of what had been his favorite club. The club to which he'd dedicated hours of conversations and planning and playing, where he'd hung out and laughed with friends. Where was the fun now?

"Well, whoever did it is just going to get us all in trouble and make the club look bad. I would think a president would care about that."

Zabrina sipped her milk. "Too bad you're not the president and *I am*."

Yeah, too bad, Robbie thought, and stomped away from their table. He looked back and everyone seemed to have their heads closer together. It felt weird, as if they were plotting something. Robbie frowned and went to sit at the table with Dyson.

"What'd she say?" Dyson asked through a mouth full of hot dog.

Robbie shook his head and dug out his sandwich from his lunch bag. "She says it's nothing to worry about, but I'm not convinced she doesn't know who did it. I think she's hiding something."

Just then Mr. Renner walked up to the cement block in the middle of the courtyard where teachers liked to make lunch announcements. "Hello, Durham Wildcats!" he bellowed. Mr. Renner's deep voice traveled far.

Robbie's breath caught. Had Mr. Renner found out who'd vandalized the school? Was the club going to be punished?

"I have a special announcement. I want you to be a part of the decisions we make here at school. This week, we will have a special election, and all students will be encouraged to vote on changes here at Durham. How does that sound?"

There was some clapping from the students, but most kids ignored him.

Mr. Renner's eyebrows lowered over his eyes. "Have you all heard of the animatronic apocalypse?" he bellowed out dramatically.

Suddenly, the students came alive, with a few cheers erupting around the courtyard.

Robbie and Dyson eyed each other in disbelief. Then Robbie swung his gaze over at Zabrina's table with some of the club members. Their cheers were the loudest.

Mr. Renner looked almost happy. "I thought you might have. An apocalypse is serious business. As a school community, it's time to come together to prepare for this inevitable battle. It's either us or them! The animatronics versus the Durham Wildcats!"

More clapping and cheers echoed from the students.

What was he getting at? Robbie wondered. Why did Mr. Renner suddenly care about some game their club had made up? It's not like every student was involved.

"There will be a ballot item called the *Faculty Preparedness Initiative*." Mr. Renner pointed to the students. "Say it with me: FACULTY PREPAREDNESS INITIATIVE." Students repeated the title with him.

"We need resources to help prepare our teachers and faculty to be able to fight against the dangerous animatronics. We cannot be sitting ducks when this apocalypse happens. We have to be able to protect our students. To protect *you*."

Someone whistled.

"We need you to vote, Durham! Our plan is to move around some funding here at school. Everyone will have what they need. What's most important is that you, our students, will benefit by having your teachers ready and prepared for this animatronic apocalypse so that you can be protected and we can take back our planet. Are you with me?"

Cheers erupted from the crowd.

"These animatronics won't know what hit them. Voting will open tomorrow until Friday after school. Enjoy your lunch! One more thing: *No more vandalizing school property, or there will be serious consequences.* That's all. Carry on!"

Robbie shook his head in disbelief. "Can you believe this?" he asked Dyson. "He basically wants to take money from the school to fund something that doesn't really exist. And he's glossing it over with gameplay."

"I think maybe he's just trying to get the students more involved."

Robbie leaned toward Dyson across the table. "Don't you get it? He's taking money from somewhere in the school to give more money to himself and the teachers. You know my dad's in banking. He's always telling me how funding works. I usually don't pay much attention, but this time what he told me finally makes sense."

Dyson shrugged. "I don't see the big deal."

Robbie shook his head. "It doesn't sound right is all I'm saying. And what's with not making a big deal over vandalism? Normally he'd be interrogating suspects to get to the bottom of it."

"Robbie, relax. I think you're still upset about Zabrina being the new president and making new rules."

"Not just new rules. She's telling the club to *cheat*. It's weird."

"Still. Has anyone told you you're not good with change?"

Robbie let out a breath and rolled his tense shoulders. "Maybe." They continued to eat their lunch and Dyson changed the subject by talking about his new video game, but Robbie couldn't shake the feeling that something just wasn't right.

Thursday

That same feeling popped up again when Mr. Renner showed up to the Fazbear Fan Club meeting after school.

"Hi, Mr. Renner!" Zabrina said as the principal entered the classroom.

"Hello, Zabrina, and hello, Fazbear Fan Club!" Mr. Renner said to the members. "It's great to see so many of you working toward the success of mankind against the animatronic apocalypse."

Robbie groaned in irritation.

"Thanks so much for allowing us to vote on the new Faculty Preparedness Initiative," Daniel said. "I've never had a principal give the students a choice before. I voted this morning. It was really cool."

"Thank you, Daniel. That's my pleasure. I want us to be a team and work together to be prepared."

"You're my hero, Mr. Renner," Tina said, with a smile. "I voted for the initiative, too."

"Me too," said Nathan.

"Well, thank you, Tina and Nathan. Good job."

Mr. Renner walked around the room, chatting with the club members. Robbie kept his head down as he read over the latest game stats, hoping Mr. Renner would ignore him.

He didn't.

"Hey there, Robbie, how are you doing?"

"Fine." Robbie looked up at Mr. Renner and began to tap his pencil on his notebook.

Mr. Renner scanned the notes. "Robbie, you seem to do really well on the game stats."

"Yeah." Robbie tried not to let himself buy into whatever Mr. Renner was up to.

"Your expertise will come in handy for our Faculty Preparedness Initiative."

Robbie couldn't hold his tongue any longer. "You're kidding, right?"

Mr. Renner lifted his eyebrows. "Why would I be kidding?"

Robbie looked around and lowered his voice. "Because, you know, it's not real."

Something flickered in Mr. Renner's eyes before he leaned down in front of Robbie's desk. He was so close, Robbie could smell an unappealing aftershave. "What's the matter, Robbie? Don't feel like playing in the Fazbear Fan Club anymore?"

Robbie blinked at the shift in Mr. Renner's tone. It was like he was no longer the principal but some mean kid, taunting him. He saw a muscle twitch under Mr. Renner's eye, and Robbie looked down at his desk.

Robbie shifted in his seat, uneasy. "I didn't say that," he answered quietly.

"You didn't say what, Robbie Wilson?"

"I didn't say that I was done with the club, Mr. Renner."

"Good. I know it's all a game, Robbie. But I'm going to utilize what I need to encourage our students to get more involved here at school. Nothing wrong with that, is there?"

Robbie looked up and met his gaze once more. Mr.

Renner's eyes seemed to bore into Robbie's head. Even though Robbie didn't agree with him, he shook his head just to get that penetrating stare off him.

Mr. Renner quickly straightened and walked to Zabrina's desk, and Robbie sighed with relief.

"Now," Mr. Renner said to the club, "voting is still open until after school tomorrow. Remember that this helps you, the students, so don't let us down."

And it helps fill your pockets, Robbie noted grudgingly.

Mr. Renner crossed his arms and started to talk quietly to Zabrina. He thought he saw Zabrina give Robbie a quick, irritated look before she looked back at Mr. Renner. She seemed to gaze at Mr. Renner as if she hung on his every word.

Sheesh, what a principal's pet, Robbie thought.

Robbie realized he'd had enough. He was tired of the way everything was changing, tired of feeling like an outsider among his friends. He packed up his stuff to leave. Nathan and Tina looked at him, wondering where he was going. "Sorry, I gotta go. Catch you on the next game."

Mr. Renner had given Robbie an uncomfortable feeling, and he knew he wouldn't enjoy himself with the principal hanging around. He walked out of the classroom and saw a huge line of kids waiting to vote on the dumb made-up initiative. Team coaches had even brought their sports teams to vote when they were supposed to be practicing. He spotted Dyson with his team, waiting in line.

"Let's go," he heard Coach Baker say to the crowd. There was a playful smile on his face. "Get your votes in. We need to be trained and prepared for the animatronic apocalypse."

Some of the kids gave him high fives after they voted. "Good job, kids. Thanks for helping to protect our school."

When were they all going to wake up? Robbie wondered. Why was he the only one seeing the bigger picture here? Maybe this really was the beginning of the animatronic apocalypse and he just didn't know it. Because he was starting to feel like he might be in some weird alternate dimension.

Shaking off questions he couldn't answer, Robbie texted Dyson that he was walking home early. He didn't feel like company at the moment.

Robbie took off down the residential streets toward home. The sun was trying to break through the overcast clouds and the light rain that had been consistent during the week. He heard a distant lawn mower and a couple of birds chirping.

What am I going to do about Mr. Renner's initiative? he wondered. Should he tell his dad something weird was going on with the principal at school? Should he tell him about the voting? Would his dad even believe him? He guessed he could try . . .

Distracted as he was in the quiet of his thoughts, Robbie leaped when he heard a cat screech loudly from behind him. Surprised, Robbie whirled around, but he didn't see any sign of a cat. He saw a couple of parked cars and trash cans left at the curb but no animals. He turned back to continue home. He looked at the houses and didn't see anyone outside. It was strangely empty for the normally busy neighborhood.

The sound of a shoe scraping on the ground from behind him made him jerk around. His pulse skittered. Was someone following him?

No one was there.

Were they hiding?

A sense of unease stirred in his stomach. He turned and picked up his pace to go home, peeking over his shoulder every few seconds. His breath quickened. He turned down his street, nearly running to get to his house.

"Ow!" Something hard knocked the back of his head. Robbie stopped and looked down at the ground to see a large rock roll to its side. There was a drop of blood on it. Robbie spun around. He couldn't see anyone, but he heard footsteps of someone running away around the corner.

"That wasn't funny!" he yelled to the rock thrower.

Robbie raised his hand to his head and hissed at the sting. There was a little bit of blood on his fingers. His unease turned to irritation at someone's mean idea of a prank. He walked up the pathway to his house to clean his wound.

Hopper barked and jumped as Robbie opened the door but whined when Robbie didn't stop to pet him. "Sorry, Hopper, hold on a sec."

Robbie went straight to the bathroom and grabbed some toilet paper to dab at the wound. There was still a little blood oozing from his head. Sighing, Robbie looked for a bandage.

A couple hours later, Robbie's dad came through the door, holding a box of tacos and his leather briefcase.

"Hey, son, give me a hand here."

Robbie took the box of tacos and set them on the kitchen table.

"How was school?" Dad asked him.

"Good."

"Did you feed Hopper?"

"Yeah."

"Okay, good. Wash up for dinner. Your mother has a late house showing, did she tell you?"

Robbie nodded.

"So she'll be home before your bedtime. It's just us for dinner." His dad squinted his eyes at him. "What's wrong with your head?"

Robbie hadn't known how to put the bandage on so he'd taped some gauze to his head. "I, uh, got hit in the head. Some kid threw a rock."

"What's that about? Let me see." His dad pulled off the tape with a few strands of hair.

"Ow!"

"Sorry. Well, there's no bump, just a little scratch. You'll be okay. Who did this?"

Robbie shrugged. "Just some kid, probably. I didn't see who threw it."

Robbie went to wash up at the kitchen sink, and then they both settled down at the table to eat tacos.

"Hey, Dad?" Robbie asked.

"Don't talk with your mouth full, Robbie."

Robbie swallowed. "Is it weird to have kids vote on a school initiative regarding funding?"

His dad lifted his eyebrows. "I think the parents or the school board would be more qualified to vote than the students. Kids your age don't have all the facts and figures."

"Right? Mr. Renner is making up an initiative that pays the teachers more money and he's having the students vote on it this week."

Dad frowned. "I don't think that's what's really happening, Robbie. You must be confused."

Robbie sighed. "Dad, I listen to you when you talk about funding and all that stuff, and this is exactly what Mr. Renner is doing. He is putting more money toward the teachers and himself. You always tell me the money has to come from somewhere. So he could be taking it from school equipment, field trips, or even activities in order to pay himself more. It's what he's doing. I promise."

"Well, if he is, it has to be for something very important."

"He says it's to fund for preparation against the animatronic apocalypse."

Dad let out a big sigh and brushed off cheese from his fingers. "Right, the apocalypse. Robbie, what have I told you about fantasy versus reality?"

Robbie was offended. He tapped a thumb to his chest. "I'm not making this up. He said it in front of all the upper grades at lunch. Ask Dyson if you don't believe me."

Dad looked at him a long moment. "Sometimes you might think what you see is true when there is always another side to the story."

Discouraged, Robbie just stared at his remaining taco.

"All right," Dad said. "Finish up your taco and get to your homework. I've had a long day and I'll check in with the school tomorrow and get their side of the story about this initiative."

"Sure." Maybe there was another side to the story. Maybe.

Friday

Robbie sat in homeroom participating in silent reading with the rest of the class. The only problem was the book was *boring*. It had no warriors or battles or anything interesting. Not even anything about surviving in the wilderness. How did teachers expect kids to read this stuff without falling asleep? He looked around the classroom. Some of the students were reading. Others had their heads down, quickly turning the pages in the book.

Robbie raised his hand.

"Yes, Robbie?" Mr. Gustin asked, peering at him over his narrow glasses from his desk at the front of the class.

"Can I use the restroom, please?"

"*May*."

"*May* I use the restroom, please, Mr. Gustin?"

Mr. Gustin waved a hand. "Go ahead, but be quick about it."

Robbie sprang out of his seat and grabbed the wooden restroom pass hanging on the wall by a string.

He walked down the school hallway and spotted Mr. Renner stepping out of the school office to speak with a student with dark hair. As Robbie walked closer, he noticed the student he was talking to was Zabrina.

Robbie wasn't sure what to do. After his intimidating conversation with Mr. Renner, he didn't really want to talk with him again, especially if his dad was going to call the school and ask about the initiative. He looked right and left and finally ducked behind a corner of the school building, then peeked around the wall. He was too far from them to hear what was being said, but it was odd how Mr. Renner was staring very intently at Zabrina as he spoke to her.

Zabrina nodded her head, and then Mr. Renner walked back into the school office.

Robbie watched Zabrina stand very still after that. Not even moving. It was like she was staring off into space.

What's the matter with her? Robbie wondered.

Curious, Robbie moved back into the hallway, swinging his wooden bathroom pass around by its string. As he made his way closer to Zabrina, he expected her to smile or wave.

Instead, she started to walk forward.

Robbie nodded his head toward her. "Hey, Zabrina."

But she just strolled right past him without saying a word.

"*Hello?* Zabrina?" Robbie stopped and watched her walk away without acknowledging him. "Weird," he muttered.

Just then Robbie saw a very important-looking man and woman stride toward the office with briefcases and stern faces. The man nodded to Robbie, and Robbie nodded back.

Robbie read on his name tag: MR. TED ANGELO, SCHOOL SUPERINTENDENT.

Robbie figured he was pretty important in the school hierarchy. Since he didn't really have to use the restroom, Robbie took the long route back to homeroom.

"Did you hear? Mr. Renner is leaving Durham."

"No way!"

"Yeah, someone saw him packing up his desk."

As Robbie walked the hallways after school, he'd overheard a kid talking to another kid about Mr. Renner and his eyes widened. He'd told his dad about his suspicions about the initiative, and his dad had called the school and must have found out something.

Possibly that Mr. Renner *had* been doing something wrong.

Robbie wasn't sure how to feel about that. It wasn't like it had been Robbie's idea for Mr. Renner to take from the school funding and give more to himself. But he hadn't meant to get the principal *fired*.

Robbie headed home alone since Dyson had a game that day. As he walked out the school gate, he spotted a bunch of the club kids walking together, with Zabrina and Daniel leading the pack.

Robbie frowned. Today wasn't a club day.

Did he miss a message about another meeting? Curious, he followed the kids out onto the grass field. They were all exiting the school grounds through the back gate. He stayed a little ways away, just in case he had been intentionally left out.

Maybe they'd found out that it was his dad that had questioned Mr. Renner's initiative. Maybe they were mad at Robbie and would try to kick him out of the club.

Robbie hoped that wasn't the case.

The group walked through the residential streets until they came upon a small neighborhood playground called Willow Park. It had an old slide, swings, and a rusted merry-go-round. There were tall trees surrounding the park that led into a forest area. Robbie's parents had told him many times not to go into the forest area by himself. It could be dangerous. Instead of stopping at the playground, Robbie followed them farther into the trees. Technically, he wasn't by himself.

When the group finally stopped walking, Robbie peered behind a tree and spotted Zabrina talking to someone. Robbie couldn't see who it was because the person was blocked by a tree. Then the person stepped forward.

It was Mr. Renner!

Robbie's eyes widened as he slouched behind the tree. His pulse sped up. Mr. Renner wasn't the principal anymore, but he was still meeting with the club. Outside school grounds. In the woods. Something was very wrong.

Robbie took a calming breath as he cracked his knuckles. There could be a simple explanation. Maybe they were just saying goodbye and then they would be on their way. Maybe Mr. Renner had something important to tell them before he left for good.

Robbie peered around the tree. *Dang it*. He was too far away to hear what they were saying. He watched Mr. Renner kneel down to the ground and run his fingers through the dirt. Robbie got down on his hands and knees and crawled to get a little bit closer, just like his dad had taught him when camping and spying on wildlife. He stopped at a fallen log and peered at the group.

The club members surrounded Mr. Renner, listening to him intently. The weird thing was there were no smiles on his friends' faces. No laughter. No expressions at all.

Mr. Renner showed the dirt to them and all the club members kneeled on the ground as he did.

Robbie frowned. What were they going to do? Dig something up? He watched the kids run their fingers through the dirt, then gather the dirt into their hands. He could hear bits and pieces of Mr. Renner's voice.

"This dirt is very important . . . It will help . . . immunity . . . against animatronic toxins."

Then Mr. Renner said something in his demanding tone.

But he couldn't have said what Robbie thought he heard.

It sounded like he had said, *"Eat it."*

Robbie watched Zabrina and Daniel eat a mouthful of dirt, and then he watched in horror as the other club members ate the dirt, one by one.

Mr. Renner nodded and looked pleased. Zabrina looked at all the club members eating dirt, and she smiled. There was dirt all over her teeth.

Robbie's heart was beating fast. This was too weird. This couldn't be happening. Maybe he did have trouble distinguishing fantasy from reality. Scared, he crawled away from his hiding spot until he could get to his feet to run.

He ran as fast as he could toward home.

He just wanted to get home.

Late at night in his room, Robbie texted Dyson to call him as soon as he could. His parents were finally asleep. Robbie hadn't told them about what he had witnessed at the park, but he wanted to talk to someone.

This was so much worse than Mr. Renner taking money from the school. What he'd watched had seemed so strange and horrible that he didn't think he could tell his parents. They surely wouldn't believe him. Robbie wouldn't have believed it if he hadn't seen it for himself! Maybe Dyson wouldn't even believe him.

Earlier, Dad and Mom had sat him down on the couch and talked to him about Mr. Renner.

"Honey," Mom said, "you were right to tell your father about Mr. Renner's school faculty initiative. It was wrong, and it hadn't been approved by the school board or the district."

Dad had put a hand on his shoulder. "I'm glad you told me, son. I'm proud of you for speaking up. I'm sorry I wasn't convinced at first. It had seemed strange, so I had to double-check the facts. But you were right, and I had the school district look into it. Just know that it's not your fault for speaking up. It was Mr. Renner's fault for making a bad choice."

Robbie had merely nodded.

Mom had sat next to him and gave him a hug, thinking he was upset about Mr. Renner leaving. But really he'd been upset about seeing Mr. Renner make his friends eat dirt.

His phone vibrated with a call from Dyson.

Robbie grabbed his flashlight, flicked it on, and huddled under the covers.

"What's up?" Dyson asked, in a lowered voice. "Why are we talking so late? If my parents find out, I'm busted."

"Look, same here, but I saw something really bad today," Robbie spoke quietly into the cell phone.

"What do you mean really bad?"

"Well, you heard about Mr. Renner leaving the school?"

"Yeah. Some of my teammates were talking about it at the game."

"I saw him meet with the club after school."

"But there's no meeting on Fridays."

"Exactly. I was curious so I followed them to Willow Park and saw . . ."

"What?"

Robbie told Dyson everything.

"Are you making this up?" Dyson wanted to know.

"*No*, I swear on our friendship, Dyson. I saw it and it *really* happened."

"This is so weird. Why would Mr. Renner do that? What are you going to do? Are you going to tell your mom and dad?"

"I can't. There's no real proof. They won't believe me. There's no way my dad can call to find out the truth about something like this."

"Well, you need to talk to the club. Separately. When they're not all together. Find out what happened and why. That's just gross."

"Yeah, I know, but I'll have to wait till Monday. Or maybe this weekend I can go by Johnny's house. I know where he lives."

"I would go, too, but I have a game and practice all weekend." Dyson sighed into the phone.

"It's okay. I'll let you know how it goes. Dyson?"

"Yeah?"

"Thanks for believing me. It was really weird watching it happen."

"Yeah, well, that's why I know you're telling the truth. Truth is stranger than fiction. My mom says that all the time."

Saturday

Having busy parents made it easy to slip out.

Johnny lived only a block away from Robbie's house. The atmosphere was surprisingly muggy given the gloomy clouds that hung in the sky. He passed a house with a couple of little kids playing with a dog in their yard. He walked by a guy washing his car. He finally turned down the next street, where Johnny lived.

Johnny lived in a nice two-story house, painted blue, with white shutters attached to the windows. On one side of the driveway, a bike was lying on the ground and a basketball hoop stood on a plastic stand. A minivan was parked on the other half of the driveway.

Robbie walked up to the front door and knocked. After a moment, a woman answered. Her hair was tied back and her eyes looked tired. She was cuddling a toddler with honey-brown hair on her hip. The toddler waved a plastic block in one hand.

"Hi, can I help you?" the woman said to Robbie.

Robbie shifted nervously on his feet. "Hi, I'm Robbie. I go to school with Johnny. We're in homeroom and the same Fazbear Fan Club together."

The woman nodded. "Hi, Robbie. Sorry, Johnny isn't feeling so well today."

"Oh. He's sick?"

"A little. He has an upset stomach and can't seem to get out of bed. I'm hoping if he rests this weekend, he'll be able to go to school on Monday. So I'm sorry, but he can't have any visitors today."

Robbie scratched his head. "Did he, um, eat something bad?"

"Eat. Eat," said the toddler.

"Well, I don't know," Johnny's mom said. "He didn't have much dinner last night. So he might just have caught a little bug at school. Or maybe he got a bit of toxin."

"Okay." Robbie blinked. "Wait, what?"

"Take care of yourself, Robbie. Bye."

"Bye!" echoed the toddler as the door quickly closed.

Confused, Robbie turned and walked away. He might have heard Johnny's mom wrong. It had sounded like she said *toxin*, but that couldn't be right. He looked up at the two-story house and saw a curtain move in a window as if someone had been looking down at him.

Was that Johnny at the window? he wondered.

Robbie stared at the window a moment longer, but it didn't move again.

As Robbie walked home, he wished he'd gotten to talk to Johnny to find out what was really going on. He was just going have to wait until Monday to get some answers.

Monday

Robbie was in morning homeroom when he saw Johnny come in, but Nathan was nowhere to be seen. Johnny looked a little paler than usual, with dark circles under his eyes. His hair wasn't even gelled up like usual.

Robbie walked up to Johnny's desk. "Hey, Johnny."

Johnny nodded. "Hey."

"I came by your house this weekend."

Johnny squinted at him. "Yeah, that was weird. You never come to my house."

Robbie scratched his neck. "Well, I just wanted to see how you were doing. Um, your mom said you weren't feeling well."

Johnny shrugged. "I was okay."

"Did you eat something bad?"

Johnny shook his head, but he looked uncertain. "I feel fine."

"Okay, that's good. Where's Nathan? Do you know?"

Johnny scanned their homeroom. "Don't know . . . Hope the animatronics didn't get him."

Robbie raised his eyebrows. "What did you say?"

Johnny sat down but didn't answer him. He started to rub the tips of his fingers.

Robbie realized there was redness beneath Johnny's fingernails. "What happened to your fingers?"

Johnny lifted his hands, spreading his fingers out. There were a few tiny lines of red on each of his fingertips, spearing underneath his fingernails.

"Jeez, that looks bad," Robbie told him, with a wince.

Johnny looked at him intently, with wide, bloodshot eyes. "We had to poke the needle under our nails. We had to. To protect ourselves. It's a secret, though. Don't tell anyone."

"It's a secret," Johnny muttered again.

A shiver slid down Robbie's back as he moved away from Johnny's intense gaze and sat down for class attendance.

Tuesday

It was nearing the end of the school day as Robbie answered history questions in his workbook. He glanced at Nathan and noticed him staring intently at the classroom clock. He hadn't had a chance to talk to his friend alone since he'd returned to school. Robbie glanced at the clock and noticed it was a few minutes before 2:00 p.m. School didn't end for another half hour.

Robbie finished off his answers, and as he was putting his workbook away, he spotted Johnny gazing at the clock, too. Frowning, Robbie glanced at Nathan and then back to Johnny. Both the kids were still staring at the clock.

Robbie looked up in time to see the clock hands move to 2:00.

He spotted Nathan move first, then Johnny. They each pulled out small tin boxes from their desks. The boxes were the kind used for small mints.

What are they doing? Robbie wondered.

Robbie sat closer to Johnny, so he watched Johnny open the box. Inside was something black—and moving! Robbie's eyebrows lifted as Johnny pulled out a huge black beetle the size of a thumb from the tin box.

Johnny looked at the beetle, watching the little legs move unsuccessfully in the air. The insect's wings fluttered as if it were trying to fly away.

Robbie thought he heard the beetle screech as Johnny suddenly sucked the beetle straight into his mouth!

What? Why?

Robbie gripped the edges of his desk as Johnny chewed with a determined look on his face. Then his cheeks got big, and his body jerked forward as if he might throw up! Johnny slapped a hand to his mouth. Robbie turned his gaze back to Nathan and watched him pop a large beetle into his mouth, with his eyes squeezed shut. Nathan curled his hands into fists, trying to swallow the live beetle, and then he gagged.

Robbie glanced around at the other classmates to see if they were witnessing this disgusting bug-eating.

But as he looked, he realized that he was the only one not eating. Robbie sat, shocked, as his entire homeroom shoved the beetles into their mouths!

Some of the kids chomped hard. Others held hands on their mouths with tears streaming down their cheeks. Coughs erupted as kids had a hard time swallowing the insects whole.

Robbie jerked his head toward their teacher. Mr. Gustin had to stop this!

But Mr. Gustin simply stared glassy-eyed at the students, doing absolutely nothing.

Robbie took a breath as he slowly turned his attention back to Johnny. He was writing in a workbook, and Nathan was now working quietly as well. Robbie swiveled his head around to look at the other the students in the classroom.

Everyone was working quietly as if nothing extremely weird had just happened.

Robbie scrubbed his hands down his face and laid his head on the desk. Sweat sprouted on his forehead as his stomach rolled. He tried to calm himself and push the horrible incident out of his brain until the bell rang.

After the bell rang, Robbie rushed to the boys' restroom. He was breathing too hard, and he thought he might throw up. He managed to get to the sink, push on the cold water tap, then splash water on his hot face.

"It's okay," he whispered to himself. *"Everything is okay."* He didn't really believe it, but he was trying hard to convince himself.

He glanced up at the bathroom mirror and saw two of his homeroom classmates, Will and Adrian, standing behind him.

"Oh, hey, guys," Robbie said to them as he turned to face them with water dripping off his face.

Will's eyebrows pulled together. "Did you forget something, Robbie?"

Robbie's eyes widened as he looked at Will and then Adrian. "No, what?" He had his backpack on. "Did I leave my binder in homeroom?"

Will gave a nod to Adrian. Robbie watched Adrian pull a small tin box from a zippered pocket in his backpack.

Robbie pushed back against the sink. "Uh, no, um . . ."

"Yeah, I think you did, Robbie. I think you forgot to take your toxin protection."

Robbie was not about to eat a wiggling hard-shelled beetle. He beelined to the right, and Will snatched the front of his hoodie with two hands to stop him from leaving. Will was shorter than him, but he had a really strong grip. "Not so fast. You've got take your protection just like the rest of us. You don't want to infect us all, do you?"

Robbie shook his head. "No, no, I can't!"

Adrian held the large beetle in front of Robbie's nose. "Sure you can," Adrian said with a smirk. "It's not so bad."

The beetle wiggled its thin arms and legs in front of Robbie's nose, its black wings flapping frantically like a butterfly. A tiny screech pierced Robbie's ears.

Robbie slammed his mouth shut.

Will released one hand from Robbie's sweatshirt to squeeze his jaw open. Robbie took the chance to slam a foot on Adrian's shoe and shoved Will aside. They both stumbled back, and Robbie booked it out of the bathroom as fast as he could.

He ran all the way to Room 13 to try to hide from his classmates. He didn't understand what was going on with everyone!

He tried to open the door, but it was locked!

He discovered a note taped onto the closed door.

Fazbear Fan Club is canceled today
due to a scheduling conflict!
Come back on Thursday!

"Canceled?" Robbie questioned. "Why?" Robbie peeked next door into Mr. Finkle's room. The teacher was blowing his nose into a handkerchief.

Robbie swallowed hard. "Hi, Mr. Finkle. Fazbear Club is canceled today? How come?"

Mr. Finkle waved and wiped his nose. "Don't know anything about it. Mr. Renner is—or *was*—the chaperone for Fazbear Club. I was dismissed." Mr. Finkle gave a weird sound like a snort. "Now who's dismissed?" he murmured.

"Um, okay."

Robbie turned to walk away. He scanned the hall looking for Will and Adrian but didn't see them. Hopefully they'd given up and gone home.

Robbie wondered why Zabrina had canceled the meeting. A scheduling conflict with *what*? Even if the president of the club couldn't make the meeting, the club still could have the meeting so that the other members could play Animatronic Apocalypse.

Robbie suddenly stopped in his tracks. Unless the entire club wouldn't be coming to the meeting, either. Was there another secret gathering that he didn't know about?

Robbie turned his gaze toward the school's back entrance. He didn't see any club members walking toward the back fence, but he decided to check out Willow Park again.

As he walked to the park, he hoped he wouldn't find the club members eating anything they weren't supposed to. His stomach roiled just thinking about it.

When Robbie arrived at the park and walked into the trees, there was no sign of the club members. Relief seeped through him. To Robbie, it meant that everyone was safe at the moment. He took off back through the park. He had to go by the school to get home, but he walked slowly to make sure no one was following him, and that was when he saw Zabrina walking out of the school gate with Daniel.

"Meet at the park tonight," Zabrina told Daniel. "Don't tell *anyone*."

"All right, prez. No problem," Daniel said.

"Hold on a sec," Zabrina told him. She took something out of her school bag. It looked like the same small beetle box.

Oh no, Robbie thought.

She removed the lid and offered it to Daniel.

Daniel looked at her, then down at the tiny box. "I already had one at two o'clock like I was supposed to."

"You want extra defense to keep you safe from the toxins, don't you?" When Daniel hesitated, Zabrina shrugged. "Fine. If you don't want to be protected—"

"I do," Daniel said quickly. With an intense look on his face, he reached in and plucked out the black beetle. Daniel stuffed it in his mouth, squeezed his eyes shut, and attempted to swallow. Suddenly, Daniel grabbed his throat and seemed to force himself to chew the beetle in order for it to go down.

Robbie shuddered.

Zabrina flashed her teeth in a bright smile. Daniel walked away, shaking his head as if the taste was super unpleasant.

Robbie had to get to the bottom of this. "Hey, Zabrina!" he called out.

Zabrina slipped the small box into her bag and then simply stood, unmoving.

"Zabrina!" He ran up to her.

Zabrina didn't look at him or acknowledge him.

Frustrated, Robbie stood in front of her. "Zabrina, why are you ignoring me?"

Zabrina continued to stare at his neck. Her eyes were glassy and unblinking. Her pupils were large and round.

Unease trickled down Robbie's back. "Hey, are you okay?"

A car pulled up to the school curb. Zabrina suddenly blinked and looked at Robbie. "My ride's here, I gotta go," she murmured.

"What? Wait, um, why'd you cancel the club meeting?" He was trying to get her to talk to him.

Zabrina didn't answer him as she got into the car with an older woman.

Robbie watched them drive away. He wished he hadn't heard her mention another meeting in the park tonight. But he had, so Robbie would be there, too. He had to make sure the club would be okay. It was obvious Zabrina wasn't looking out for everyone's best interest anymore. Who was he kidding? It was obvious the students of Durham School were losing their minds.

That night, Robbie locked up his house, grabbed his bike from the side yard, and took off for Willow Park. He wore his cargo pants with multiple pockets to hold a small flashlight and some beef jerky in case he got hungry. The night was dark, with stars peeking from behind a few gray clouds. Since his growth spurt, the ride was a little awkward. His legs were too long for his old bike, and his knees bowed out as he tried to pedal. He tried to stand on the pedals as he rode, but that just tired him out.

He felt slightly guilty for telling his parents that he'd be at Dyson's. Robbie didn't usually lie to his parents, but tonight it was a necessity because they would seriously freak out if they knew he was going into the forest, alone, at night. They weren't coming home until late, so he should be back before they eventually came home. He wanted—needed—to find out what was going on with this meeting at the park. What had to be kept so secret? Were the students meeting with Mr. Renner again?

Robbie rode to Willow Park and stashed his bike in some bushes. He took out his flashlight and flicked it on and sucked in a breath to calm his nerves as he entered the forest. After all the strange things he'd been witnessing, he was worried what he might discover this time. The surrounding trees were dark and creepy. He heard an owl hoot in the distance. When he walked, he could hear the crunch of leaves and twigs under his hiking boots.

He spotted a dim light source up ahead so he turned off his flashlight and stuck it back in his pants pocket. He tried to walk slowly so as not to make too much sound. He didn't hear any voices nearby. Maybe no one had showed up yet.

He snuck behind a tree and peered at the light. A lantern was set on a tree stump, but he didn't see anyone standing around.

He quietly moved forward to investigate. For a split second he thought the dim light showed flat rocks scattered on the ground. But then he blinked, and the air caught in his lungs as he stumbled back.

The faint light revealed the club members buried in the ground. Only their faces were above the dirt, like creepy, buried statues. For a brief, horrible moment, he wondered if they were all dead.

Panicking, he reached for his flashlight, but he was shaking so hard he couldn't get it out of his pocket. When he finally got it on, he shone the light on Zabrina.

Robbie flinched in surprise. Her eyes were wide-open and unblinking.

"Zabrina?" Robbie whispered as he moved closer to her. Her pupils were pinpricks, and she had an expression of shock on her ghostly face. He waved a hand in front of her eyes. "Zabrina, can you hear me?"

No reaction.

Maybe they really were *dead,* Robbie thought as dread seeped through his body.

Robbie swallowed hard, then moved the light to Johnny. His eyes and mouth were closed, making it seem like they were dark pits instead of his eyes and mouth. Daniel, Rick, Nathan, Tina, and a few other members were all the same.

Empty, pale faces atop bodies buried in the dirt.

Dead, or just asleep?

"Guys, wake up!" Robbie cried out, feeling scared and helpless. These were his friends! He had to help them. But his voice seemed to echo in the night. No one woke up or spoke to him.

Robbie rushed to Nathan. He fell to his knees and brushed dirt away from Nathan's head. He reached into the loose dirt, trying to feel for a pulse on his neck. Robbie wasn't sure he felt one or even if he was feeling the correct part of the neck.

"Nathan, wake up! *Please!*"

Robbie started to dig around Nathan with his bare hands, and perspiration sprouted on his forehead. The dirt was cool to the touch and, luckily, packed loosely against his friend. He dug until he got to Nathan's shoulders and then to his chest.

"Nathan, can you hear me?" Robbie reached out his hand in front of Nathan's mouth but didn't feel any breath coming from him.

Please be okay, he thought. *Please, please.*

Robbie gripped one hand over the other and pushed at Nathan's chest. He did his best to keep a steady rhythm, doing what he remembered of CPR from a school assembly they once had on emergency services.

Finally, after a few long moments, Nathan's eyes snapped open. His mouth gasped for air.

Relief came swiftly. "Nathan! Can you hear me?" Robbie asked him, frantic.

Nathan looked around in a daze as he breathed heavily.

"Help me get you out. Come on. I can't do it by myself."

"Robbie?" Nathan asked.

"Yeah, it's Robbie. *Come on, help me.*"

As Robbie dug around Nathan's body, Nathan started to pull himself slowly out of the dirt. First his arms, then he slowly pulled out the lower half of his body. Dirt fell off him like beads of water. Then, finally, his legs were free. Nathan collapsed to the ground, breathing heavily.

"Nathan," Robbie commanded. "Are you okay? Can you get up? We need to help the others."

"Help?" Nathan repeated. He looked around at the club members and seemed to really awaken. *"Oh my gosh."*

"Come on. Help me with them."

As Robbie rushed over to Tina to try to help her, Zabrina suddenly lifted out of the ground next to her, dirt pouring off her shoulders and arms.

She screamed, "GET OUT OF HERE!"

Robbie jerked in surprise, his gut tightening. Zabrina had a cruel and intimidating look on her face in the darkness. Her shoulders were moving up and down quickly as if she was breathing hard. It was like Robbie didn't even recognize her. Before he could do anything, Nathan took off running into the night.

"Zabrina," Robbie yelled. "What's going on here? What—"

"GET! OUT!" she screamed, waving her arms dramatically. Then she let out a horrible, piercing scream at the top of her lungs that sent fear shivering down his back!

Robbie sprang away from Tina and ran after Nathan, his heart pounding in his chest. He didn't know what Zabrina was doing or if Mr. Renner was nearby. He just knew the club members needed help.

Robbie caught up with Nathan. "We need to go to the police!" They both ran all the way to the local police station.

"You're saying there are kids buried in the forest of Willow Park?" a police officer at the front desk of the station asked Robbie and Nathan.

Or more to Robbie as Nathan just sort of stared at the officer, not saying much. Maybe he was in some kind of shock or something.

Robbie brushed his hair back in frustration. "Yes, Officer . . ."

"Officer Talbot."

"Yes, Officer Talbot. *Please*, we need to go help my friends. They could be really hurt. I unburied Nathan myself, and he wasn't even breathing!"

"Okay, calm down, kid. What's your name?"

"Robbie Wilson."

He looked at Nathan. "And you?"

"Nathan. Nathan Bates."

"Is this true, Nathan? Were you buried in the ground? Who buried you?"

The officer looked skeptical, and Robbie could feel his body shake as he cracked his tender knuckles one by one. He must have pulled on them several times tonight.

Nathan blinked. "I'm not . . . really sure."

Robbie looked at Nathan in disbelief. "Nathan, come on. You have to remember! We ran all the way here together from the park. You saw them, too."

Nathan shook his head and sat on a bench, looking defeated and placing his head in his hands.

"Officer Talbot, please," Robbie pleaded. "I'll show you myself. I don't know why Nathan can't remember. I'm telling you, we have to help them. This animatronic apocalypse stuff is getting—"

"The animatronic apocalypse? Oh, is that what's going on here? We know all about that." Then he winked at Robbie as if Robbie was in on some kind of joke. "Okay, Robbie, I'll send you with another police officer to check this out. Just give me a minute."

"Okay, thanks," Robbie answered, uncertain.

Ten minutes later, Robbie rode in the back of a police car with Nathan. He'd never ridden in a police car before. It was sort of surreal. It made him feel like he was in trouble. Robbie could tell Nathan was upset beside him, so he didn't ask him the questions he wanted to ask him.

How did you get buried in the forest? Why don't you remember being buried in the forest? How come you didn't tell the police officer that the club members were buried there, too? Did Mr. Renner bury you, or did Zabrina do it? Why would you let yourself be buried, anyway?

As they pulled up to the park, Robbie had to wait for the officer—his name was Officer Parish—to open the door because it was locked. When the officer opened the door, Robbie hopped out of the car and hurriedly jogged toward the trees.

"Come on, this way," he told Officer Parish.

"Hold up, Robbie. I'm coming."

Robbie rushed toward the spot where he'd found the club members buried. There was no longer a dim light lit by a lantern, and he'd left his flashlight so he couldn't see very well. Luckily, Officer Parish had a big, sturdy flashlight to light the way.

Robbie spotted the tree stump. "Here! This is where I found them."

Officer Parish flashed the light on the ground.

The pale faces in the ground were gone.

"I don't see the kids, Robbie. Are you sure this is the spot?"

Robbie rushed to the ground and ran his hands over the surface. The dirt was loose and there were some indentions, but it was true.

The kids were no longer there.

"They were right here. *I swear.*"

Robbie continued to run his hands all over the area, digging into the surface of the ground to make sure his friends weren't buried. There were no bodies, which was good. But he did feel something.

He pulled out his flashlight, which had been buried in the dirt.

"They were all here. See? This is my flashlight. Tell him, Nathan."

"I don't . . . know," Nathan said, sniffling. He was crying.

"Look, Robbie, I think it's time to get you boys home. No one seems to need help. I'm going to do you a favor and not mention this to your parents. I don't think they would appreciate you making a false report to the police."

A false report? This isn't a false report!

Robbie rubbed his face with his dirty hands in frustration. He managed to keep his mouth shut and didn't dare argue with the officer. He didn't want to get in trouble from his parents, either. If the police didn't believe them, why would his mom and dad?

Instead, he simply asked, "Can we take my bike home, too?"

When they were back in the police car, with the bike in the trunk, Nathan finally spoke. "I think I remember now," he whispered to Robbie.

Robbie looked at him intently. "What? What do you remember?"

"Mr. Renner said the dirt had healing properties that purged the animatronic toxins from our bodies. So we buried ourselves."

Wednesday

That morning, Robbie woke exhausted. When his alarm went off, all his covers had been thrown on the floor, evidence of a restless night. He scrubbed at his tired eyes and walked downstairs to the kitchen for some cereal.

Dad was leaning against the kitchen counter, waiting for the coffee maker to finish. He was doing something with his hands.

Robbie stopped short.

Dad stood with a black beetle pinched between his thumb and forefinger.

Robbie's heart raced. This couldn't be happening. How had it gotten his dad? He didn't know if should yell or run for his mom.

He stood frozen as his dad sucked the beetle into his mouth as if he was popping a vitamin, tossing his head back to get the bug down. His dad grabbed the counter as if he was having trouble swallowing.

A moment later, the beetle was consumed and his dad grabbed a cup and poured himself some hot coffee just like he did every morning.

Robbie spun around and ran up the stairs, slamming his bedroom door shut. He snatched up his comforter and dived onto his bed.

"Wake up, wake up," he murmured. He must still be asleep. That was the only explanation.

A moment later, there was a knock on his door. "Robbie," his mom called. "Time to get up. You don't want to be late for school."

"I can't believe Nathan didn't tell the police what happened," Dyson told Robbie on their walk to school.

"Yeah, I know," Robbie murmured, still reeling from seeing his dad pop a morning beetle pill. He had told Dyson everything that had happened with the club and Nathan, but he couldn't share about his dad yet. He just couldn't. "It was almost like he couldn't remember anything at first. Then he finally told me."

"This is getting crazy. Mr. Renner is using role play in a really bad way. He could hurt someone. You've got to tell your parents."

Robbie shook his head. "I know, but I can't yet. I don't have any proof. My dad . . ." His dad had been compromised. Whatever weird thing was happening to the school, to the police, was now happening to his dad, too. "He needs proof in order to believe stuff that is out of the ordinary. He barely believed me about Mr. Renner and the school funding. How would he ever understand this?"

"*Robbie—*"

Maybe it was exhaustion or the feeling of being helpless or not knowing what to do, but Robbie turned on Dyson.

"Look, you're one to talk! You can't even tell your mom and dad that you don't like Little League anymore. *That* is not even as big as *this*."

Dyson's eyes widened. "I do like Little League. I just need a break sometimes."

"So why tell *me*? Why not tell your parents the truth?"

Dyson's face grew red, but instead of saying anything he shook his head and walked ahead of Robbie.

Sudden guilt weighed heavily on Robbie for snapping at his best friend. But Dyson just didn't understand. It wasn't so easy for Robbie to talk about things that scared him. Things that he didn't really understand himself. He'd tried to tell the police officers but then all the club members had disappeared as if the burying had never happened. Now, his dad . . . He just couldn't tell his parents what was going on unless he had actual proof.

Robbie wasn't sure how he would get that proof.

But that wasn't any excuse to hurt his only friend and ally. Robbie ran up to Dyson and pulled on his jacket.

"Dyson—"

Something fell out of Dyson's pocket and onto the ground.

"Oh, sorry," Robbie said. Then his eyes widened as he spotted the familiar tin on the ground.

Dyson snatched the tin up and slipped it back into his pocket. "Just leave me alone," he said, and walked onto the school grounds.

No, not Dyson, too!

Robbie rubbed the back of his neck. When he walked to homeroom, he didn't see any of the club members roaming the halls. He usually saw a few of them in the morning. Nathan and Jason were absent from homeroom, and Daniel and Rick weren't in PE. At lunch, Zabrina's table sat empty.

And so did Robbie's. Dyson didn't come to eat at their lunch table.

Robbie felt more alone and discouraged than ever.

"Eating by yourself today, Robbie?" Mrs. Harp, the lunch supervisor, asked him. She had all-white hair that reached her shoulders and a nice smile.

Robbie nodded. "Yeah."

"The tables look a little sparse today. The office said there seems to be some kind of bug going around. A lot of kids are out sick today."

Robbie glanced at Zabrina's empty table. "Really?"

Mr. Sanchez, another lunch supervisor, walked by and smiled. "Don't you mean the kids are out preparing for the animatronic apocalypse?"

Mrs. Harp chuckled. "Yes, that too!" Then she winked at Robbie. "Be sure to wash your hands often, eat your fruits and vegetables, and make sure you take care of yourself so you don't catch any toxins."

Robbie lifted his eyebrows. "Um. Okay, Mrs. Harp."

"Oh, I forgot, Robbie. I have something that might help you." She reached into her supervisor coat and pulled out a small tin box. She was about to open it when Robbie put a hand up.

"It's okay, Mrs. Harp! I'm all protected!"

"Good to know, Robbie." She smiled, slipped the tin away, and walked over to another lunch table.

Robbie eyed Mrs. Harp as she walked away. He cautiously scanned the other kids around the lunch area. They were talking quietly, not their usual loud selves. Something was definitely off. He tapped his fingers on the table. *A lot of kids are out sick today.*

It seemed the entire club was out sick, except for Robbie.

What if Mr. Renner had taken the club members somewhere last night after Robbie had found them?

What if something weird was happening to the club members right now?

Robbie's stomach tightened. He cupped his left fist into his right hand and pushed against his knuckles. Three knuckles cracked at once.

There was only one thing to do.

After school, he had to find his friends and make sure they all were safe.

The first place Robbie checked was Willow Park. He even scanned the ground to make sure his friends weren't buried again. There were no sign of the club members.

Robbie's cell phone rang. His mom was checking up on him!

"Hi, Mom!" he answered.

"Hi, Robbie, are you home?"

His stomach tightened. "Yep."

"Okay, good. Are you okay? You sound a little more hyper than usual."

"No, I'm good. All is good." Robbie's eyes squeezed shut at his lie.

"Okay, running late tonight as usual. Dad will be home first. You know the drill about dinner."

"Yeah, I got it under control."

"You sure you're okay?"

"Yes, all good."

"Okay, love you and see you tonight."

"Okay, bye." Robbie ended the call with a sigh of relief as he looked around at the trees.

The only other place he could think to check for the club members was at Mr. Renner's house. Everything inside him told him not to go there, but what choice did he have? He pulled his hood more securely over his head and began to walk toward Newbury Lane. Robbie didn't know the exact address, but everyone knew the long silver vintage Cadillac the now-former principal had driven to school every day. Robbie would look for his car and hopefully find his house.

A little bit later, Robbie came across Mr. Renner's vehicle in the driveway of a small white house. The lawn was neatly mowed and everything appeared to be swept clean. A couple of cacti were potted next to the front door. There was a gnome on display in the yard, which surprised Robbie. He hadn't pictured Mr. Renner as a gnome guy.

Robbie looked around to make sure no one saw him as he looked in Mr. Renner's window. Unfortunately, a dark curtain concealed the window and he couldn't see inside. He went around to the side gate that led into the backyard. It was unlocked. Robbie pushed it open and closed the gate behind him.

The backyard was not as well taken care of as the front. The grass was dead and yellowed. There was a broken yard chair that was tipped over on its side. A few car parts were thrown in a pile, and bags of empty cans lined the fence. There were a couple of cans of red spray paint on the ground, and Robbie tilted his head at the cans before moving on. Had Mr. Renner vandalized the school?

Robbie spotted a sliding door that seemed to lead into a small kitchen. He tried the door and it slid open an inch.

Robbie's pulse fluttered.

If he went into Mr. Renner's house, he would be trespassing.

Robbie swallowed hard. He didn't want to steal anything or do anything bad to Mr. Renner's home. He just wanted to make sure his friends were okay.

Robbie took a breath and slid the door open.

When Robbie stepped inside, he immediately sensed Mr. Renner's house was extra warm, and there was an underlying smell of something putrid and stagnant. The kitchen was out-of-date with mustard yellow countertops. A rusted stove was on one side of the kitchen with a scratched-up refrigerator. There was a pile of dirty dishes in the sink that smelled of rotten food. A fly buzzed in front of his face, and Robbie swatted it away.

Robbie went still.

Did he hear voices?

Robbie stepped closer to the kitchen hall and heard Mr. Renner talking softly, the sound almost muffled. Robbie didn't want to give himself away, and he wondered if he should leave and get help. Maybe not from the police, but maybe the school could send someone to check Mr. Renner's house for the club members.

He thought about Mrs. Harp and Mr. Finkle. No, the school was compromised. Even Dyson and Robbie's own father were compromised. It had to be him. He quietly took off his backpack in order to not make as much noise and set it on the kitchen floor.

Suddenly, there was a hard shove on Robbie's back.

Robbie went flying into the dining area. He skidded on his hands and knees onto the fuzzy carpet and quickly got to his feet.

"Well, what do we have here?"

Robbie blinked. He heard Mr. Renner's strangely muffled voice, but he wasn't looking at Mr. Renner's face.

Mr. Renner, sitting at the head of a long dining table, was wearing a rubber Freddy Fazbear mask.

Daniel shoved Robbie toward the dining table. The club members were all seated at the table with Mr. Renner. They stared at Robbie as if they didn't even know him. Even Nathan was there, after he remembered Mr. Renner had told him to bury himself!

Robbie felt like he was standing in a room full of strangers, even though he'd known most of the kids since first grade. Their stares were eerie and dull, as if their individual personalities had been wiped clean.

"Um, hey, everyone," Robbie spoke into the silence.

Mr. Renner stood and circled the table. He wore his typical white dress shirt without his tie. His sleeves were rolled up to his elbows. He crossed his arms and showed no indication of removing the mask.

"Robbie, what do you have to say for yourself for breaking into my home? That's against the law." Mr. Renner used his stern tone, which was reserved for interrogating bad kids.

Robbie's insides rattled. He brushed his hair back from his face. "I—I didn't break in, exactly. The door was open and the club members weren't at school today. I wanted to make sure they were okay."

Zabrina rose from her chair and stood next to Mr. Renner. She had a pinched expression on her face. "Yeah, right. I think he's lying."

"I think you might be on to something, Zabrina. You know what this means, Fazbear Fan Club?" Mr. Renner asked the kids. "Robbie's the first animatronic of the animatronic invasion!"

Robbie stepped back in denial, and Daniel shoved at him again. "I'm not an animatronic! I'm just a kid. You know me. I can't believe I actually have to say this, but I'm a real person, just like you!"

"I should have known you were an animatronic," Zabrina said. "Never following along with the club, always causing trouble."

"Animatronics need to be taught a lesson," Mr. Renner said.

Robbie's gut tightened, and he didn't know if Mr. Renner was serious or not. He just knew he wanted to go home. Robbie stared at the kids as they rose from the table. Their hands had curled into fists as some were getting closer, surrounding him.

Robbie stepped backward, this time out of the dining room area into the connecting living room. "This isn't funny, you guys."

"Animatronics need to be taught a lesson," Zabrina repeated. Her expression was deadpan. Distant.

"Taught a lesson," Daniel mimicked as he stalked Robbie. The kids stepped closer, forming a circle. As the kids surrounded him, he could see their eyes were wide and round, as if they were in a weird daze.

Robbie put up his hands and backed toward the fireplace. He looked around to see if he could somehow make an escape. The walls of the living room had discolored wallpaper dotted with a tiny diamond pattern. Some of the old paper was bubbled and peeling. An old recliner sat in the middle of the room with a bulky side table.

There was an outdated television beside the fireplace. Unlike Robbie's house, there were no family pictures on the walls at all.

"Guys, stop messing around." Robbie glanced at Nathan and Tina, who looked like they were under a spell. "Nathan, you know this is wrong! You saw everyone in the forest. What is the matter with you all? I'm not an animatronic! The apocalypse isn't real! Mr. Renner is playing some game with you all. Telling you to eat dirt and bugs and bury yourselves in the forest! *He's* the bad guy! Not me!"

Zabrina stepped up to Robbie and threw a sudden punch that hit Robbie's cheek. It stunned him speechless.

He had a moment to think: *She actually hit me,* when another fist hit him in the shoulder, then the next in the gut. Breath *whoosh*ed out of him as Robbie stumbled to the ground. He felt a kick in his ribs and stomps on his legs. His heart was racing with fear and dread as pain spread throughout his body.

Help me! he thought.

But he knew he was all alone. His dad had taught him that the only way to get out of a troubling situation was to help himself until he could get help from someone else.

Robbie reached around for anything he could grab. His hands felt the stones of the fireplace. As he continued to be pummeled, he spotted someone charging toward him. Adrenaline and fear spiked within Robbie. He stretched his hand toward a poker that was leaning against the fireplace. He managed to grab it as someone rushed him. Robbie squeezed his eyes shut and knocked the person over, releasing the fire poker.

The person fell next to Robbie with a *whoosh* of air expelling from him.

Robbie opened his eyes to see Mr. Renner lying on the carpet—impaled by the poker!

Oh no! Robbie thought.

Mr. Renner's body jerked on the carpet, holding the arm of the poker.

The kids had stopped attacking Robbie and stepped back in surprise.

Mr. Renner rolled to sit on his knees, and Robbie crawled away from him. The fire poker stuck out of him like a sword. Someone gasped.

Robbie's body was aching, but he stood up. A wave of dizziness overcame him.

"Mr. Renner, I didn't mean for that to happen. *Really.* It was an accident."

Mr. Renner let out a gurgling sound as he held the poker sticking out of his stomach, but didn't speak. His body jerked and started to convulse strangely, twitching in odd ways. Strange grunts came through the mask.

Everyone had gone completely still, staring. Their eyes widened as they looked at Mr. Renner as if he was some kind of alien.

"I have to go!" Tina blurted, and ran to the front door. Nathan blinked, and Daniel, Johnny, and other club members seemed to stare around the room as if suddenly realizing they were at the principal's house.

"Let's get out of here!" Nathan yelled, and the others rushed out.

Mr. Renner slowly pulled out the fire poker from his stomach, filling the room with weird sucking sounds. He dropped the fire poker to the floor. Dark liquid spewed out of his stomach. He stood, grabbed his leaking stomach, and stumbled down the hallway until he was out of sight.

Zabrina and Robbie were the only ones left. Robbie was still shaking in the shock of what had happened.

Zabrina stepped forward, a menacing look on her face. "Loser," she said, and spat on Robbie's face before she left.

Disgusted, Robbie wiped the spit off with the arm of his hoodie. He was left standing alone in Mr. Renner's living room, feeling battered and bruised. He went to follow everyone out the door; then he hesitated. *How badly is Mr. Renner hurt?* he wondered. He'd never hurt anyone in his life. He was scared, but he had to make sure Mr. Renner was okay. His parents would tell him that was the right thing to do. Maybe Robbie needed to call emergency services for him.

"Mr. Renner, are you okay?" he called out. "Do you need some help?"

No answer.

Unease turned Robbie's gut. Just in case, he picked up the fire poker once again. The tip dripped with dark liquid, but it didn't look like blood. The handle slipped in his damp palm. He switched hands and rubbed his sweaty palm on his jeans. "Mr. Renner?"

Robbie stepped into the dining area, looking down at the dark spots on the floor.

He stopped in front of the darkened hallway. "Mr. Renner?" he called out again.

The dark substance on the carpet continued into the shadows. At the end of the hallway was a closed door with light peering from underneath. Robbie walked down the hallway, gripping the fire poker as tightly as he could. The closer Robbie got to the room, the more he trembled. The poker swayed unsteadily in his hand.

"Please be okay. Please be okay," Robbie whispered.

Robbie knocked on the door and waited. A bead of sweat trickled down his forehead. "Mr. Renner, it's Robbie. Look, um, I'm sorry you got hurt, okay? If you need help, I can call someone." After a moment of silence, Robbie slowly turned the handle and pushed the door open. The stagnant scent filled his nostrils. This time he smelled something else as well, like a strong cleaner, or maybe it was gas.

The bedroom was large. A big bed with an old-fashioned orange comforter was off to the right with a side table and lamp. There was an ancient television at the foot of the bed with a single closet door to the left. Robbie glanced down at the carpet and noticed the same black liquid on the floor leading into the closet.

"Mr. Renner, are you in here?" Robbie swallowed hard and stepped into the room. "Mr. Renner, please answer, okay? I don't want any more trouble. I'm sorry for coming here when I wasn't supposed to. I'm sorry you got hurt. I told you it was an accident. We should call the paramedics."

Just then the closet door swung open and Mr. Renner stepped out. The mask was gone. His hair stuck up in crazy ways. The black substance had stained the front of his ripped white shirt. His face was deathly pale. Blue veins bulged underneath his skin, and his eyes seemed to be swallowed up by his dark pupils. Dark sweat dripped down his forehead. His lips were nearly white as they parted. A line of black drool hung from his mouth.

Fresh fear shot through Robbie at the gruesome sight.

Mr. Renner stumbled toward him, his arms reaching for him. His long fingers were stained with black.

Breaths rushed in and out of his mouth as Robbie gripped the poker with both hands in front of him. Mr. Renner didn't stop as he forcefully lunged toward Robbie and once again into the poker.

Robbie gaped in horror as a squishy sound echoed in his ears.

Black liquid spilled out of the wound.

Robbie panicked, trying to pull the poker out. He had to pull with all his strength to remove it.

He stepped back, but Mr. Renner wouldn't stop coming toward him. It was like he wasn't in his right mind. As if he couldn't feel the pain. He continued to grab at Robbie, latching on to his arm, crushing down on his bone.

"Ahhhhh!" Robbie screamed from the searing pain. Tears stung his eyes.

The only thing Robbie could do was to push the poker at him again to try to get him to let go. The poker speared through Mr. Renner's stomach again, spewing more dark liquid out of him.

But Mr. Renner wouldn't release him.

Screaming, Robbie poked him again. *Again. Again.*

The black liquid poured over Mr. Renner's shirt, soaking his clothes. Robbie stepped back and lost his balance, falling onto the carpet. Mr. Renner should have keeled over in pain. He should have stopped and tried to get away. He didn't. He lunged once more at Robbie.

Robbie screamed. He held out the fire poker as Mr. Renner charged at him like an obsessed maniac.

The poker tip rammed straight into Mr. Renner's eyeball. A sucking wet sound with an audible pop sounded in the room. Black ooze dripped from his socket. Robbie released the poker as Mr. Renner finally fell backward onto the carpet with the poker still stuck in his eye. His body convulsed on the floor. Black foam bubbled from his lips.

Robbie tried to get to his feet, but he slipped in the black liquid. He crawled out of the room until he could stand and he ran toward the front room. He thought he might throw up. He thought he might pass out. Breaths gushed out of his mouth as he rushed to the door.

Robbie stumbled out of Mr. Renner's house. The cold air brushed against his face as his stomach roiled over. Day had turned into evening. Two police cars pulled up with flashing red and blue lights. Someone must have called the police. Maybe one of the club members. Robbie fell to his knees and threw up on Mr. Renner's lawn. He heaved and heaved until his stomach felt empty.

A police officer rushed up to Robbie. "You all right, son? Are you hurt?"

Robbie did his best to nod but that just made him nauseous again. "I'm okay, I . . . think."

"It's Officer Parish. Remember me, Robbie?"

"Yes."

"What happened here?"

"Um." Robbie tried to get up on his own, but he was weak and the officer helped him to his feet. "Mr. Renner . . . attacked me."

"Mr. Renner? The principal of Durham School?"

Robbie blinked as tears filled his eyes. "I think I . . . he might be dead."

Officer Parish narrowed his eyes. "You're saying Mr. Renner is dead in his house?"

Robbie licked his dry lips. "He might be."

"Here, son, take it easy now. Sit down on the sidewalk and catch your breath. I'm going inside to check things out." He called over his shoulder to another officer. "With me inside, García."

Robbie wiped tears from his face. "In the bedroom. Look, you'll see . . ."

Officer Parish nodded and the two officers stepped

into Mr. Renner's house. Robbie hugged himself as he worried what was going to happen when they found Mr. Renner's body. *Will I have to go to jail? What will my parents and classmates think? Will my parents lose their jobs for having a son who stabbed the ex-principal with a fire poker?*

Robbie started to rock back and forth on the cold sidewalk. He began to crack his knuckles really hard. He was beyond scared.

It seemed like forever until the officers finally exited Mr. Renner's house, concern lining their features. Robbie stood, trembling, and walked toward them.

"It's bad, right?" Robbie blurted, pushing his hair back from his face. "It's so bad. I'm *really* sorry. He was out of his mind. He just wouldn't stop coming at me. I can't really explain it but—"

The officer shook his head and lifted a hand for Robbie to stop. "Robbie, calm down. It's okay."

Robbie's eyes widened. "What's okay?"

"You said Mr. Renner's dead, is that right?"

Robbie nodded and swallowed hard.

"Well, unless the principal uses motor oil for blood, I don't think he's dead. There's no one inside."

Robbie finally looked down at his dirty clothes and hands. "Oil?"

"Yep, I don't know what you were doing in Mr. Renner's house alone, but no one's inside. Alive or dead."

The police took Robbie home. Robbie's body ached from all that he had been through. He heard Dad tell Mom that he was in shock. Robbie explained the series of events with Mr. Renner and the club to his parents in a very detached voice and then didn't speak much else to them after that. He didn't care what they thought about it all anymore. He was too tired. He showered off all the motor oil and went to bed. He tossed and turned with chaotic dreams that didn't make any sense.

The next couple of days, Robbie stayed home from school and his mom stayed home with him. She kept asking him if he was okay. Robbie would just nod as he petted Hopper. Even Hopper knew something was wrong; he would hardly leave Robbie's side. His parents ordered his favorite pepperoni pizza and even let him drink soda.

By the weekend, Robbie was feeling a little more like himself again. His parents stayed home all weekend and didn't do any extra work at their offices. Besides vacation, he couldn't remember the last time they all were together for an entire weekend.

On Sunday night, Robbie and his mom were sitting on the couch watching a rerun of a game show. Hopper was sleeping at his feet. He heard his father talking on the phone.

"Nowhere to be found? Uh-huh. Yes, that is strange." There was a pause. "His neighbors and the school? What about the other students? I see. Mm-hmm. Okay, thank you, Officer Parish. I appreciate the call. Take care, now."

Robbie watched his dad come toward him in the front room. He sat next to him on the couch. He was wearing jeans and a V-neck shirt. He scratched his head.

"Who was that, Brad?" Mom asked.

"That was Officer Parish. It seems Mr. Renner is nowhere to be found. The neighbors and the school faculty don't have any information on whether he went on a trip or not. The other club members were questioned, and no one knows anything. In fact, it seems they can't recall much of anything at all involving Mr. Renner."

"Oh, my goodness. Where could he be?" his mom asked.

"You're saying Mr. Renner is missing?" Robbie asked, his eyes wide.

"Now, now, Robbie. Don't go jumping to conclusions or theories. We don't know what's going on yet with Mr. Renner."

"Do you think Mr. Renner is going to come back for me?" Robbie's voice squeaked. He was pretty sure Mr. Renner was dead . . . But how could he have moved his body out of the house ?

Dad sighed. "You're safe, Robbie. No one is going to hurt you. Your mom and I are going to make sure you're okay. But listen, you're grounded. You should never have gone off to Mr. Renner's by yourself. Never should have gone to the forest. You knew you were supposed to come straight home after school. You lied to us."

"Grounded?" Robbie had never been grounded before. What did that mean?

"No Mega Pizzaplex for a month. No more club after school. No visiting with Dyson or your friends."

"Dad!"

Dad cut his hand through the air. "No, I don't want to hear it. You need to understand how serious this was. You could have been badly hurt."

Robbie nodded. "I understand. I do."

"I think we need to arrange our schedules to try to be home with Robbie in the evenings, Brad," Mom said, sniffling. "I just feel so awful that this happened."

"You're right. I don't want anything like this to ever happen again."

"Mom, don't cry. Dad, I'm sorry I didn't tell you. I just wanted you to believe me. I was trying to get proof. Even I knew it would have sounded more like fiction than reality. I wanted you know that I wasn't making up stories. You do believe me, right, Dad? Mom?"

"Yes, honey," Mom said.

Dad grabbed Robbie's hand. "I believe you. I don't have an explanation for it all, but I believe you. I saw your face when the police brought you home. Something terrible happened, and I don't think you'll be able to forget it for a long time."

One week later . . .

At Durham School, other than a couple of uncomfortable silent encounters with Daniel and Rick, life was back to normal. Apparently, Zabrina transferred schools. One day, she was just gone. Hopefully she wouldn't be the president of any more clubs. Tina, Nathan, Johnny, and a few of the other club members gave Robbie small smiles when they saw him around school. No one mentioned that day at Mr. Renner's. Or Mr. Renner at all. The school had gotten a new principal named Mrs. Alvarez. She liked to clap three times to get everyone's attention when she walked into classrooms, and everyone would clap back. The important thing was that she acted like a typical principal, without any weird interests in Freddy Fazbear or animatronics. The Fazbear Fan Club had sort of broken apart without a president or teacher chaperone, but Nathan had told Robbie that he and Tina were interested in getting the group back together.

At lunch, Robbie and Dyson sat across from each other at their usual outside lunch table. Dyson with his peanut butter and jelly, and Robbie with a salami sandwich.

"I have some good news," Dyson told him. "Since your parents actually listened to you, I decided to be honest with mine, too."

"About Little League?"

Dyson nodded. "I was afraid of how they might react. I told them I love Little League, but sometimes I just want to be a kid and do fun things with my best friend, like go to the Mega Pizzaplex or join a club."

"And what did they say?"

"They actually understood. They apologized for pushing me so hard. They thought it was what I wanted."

"That's cool. I can't go to the Pizzaplex for a while, but does that mean you'll restart the Fazbear Fan Club with me? Nathan and Tina are up for rejoining."

Dyson nodded. "Yep. I'll have some extra time during the week now."

"All right." Robbie smiled. "It's going to be so much better this time around. I know it."

Dyson eyed him. "But nothing too serious, okay? Just having fun with role play."

Robbie nodded. "Yep. I promise."

"Good. So, what's first on the agenda?" Dyson wanted to know before he bit into his sandwich.

"Well, we're going to do things to help the community. We're going to volunteer at the food kitchen. Maybe hold a food drive." Robbie paused, staring off into the distance. "And we have to prepare for the animatronic apocalypse."

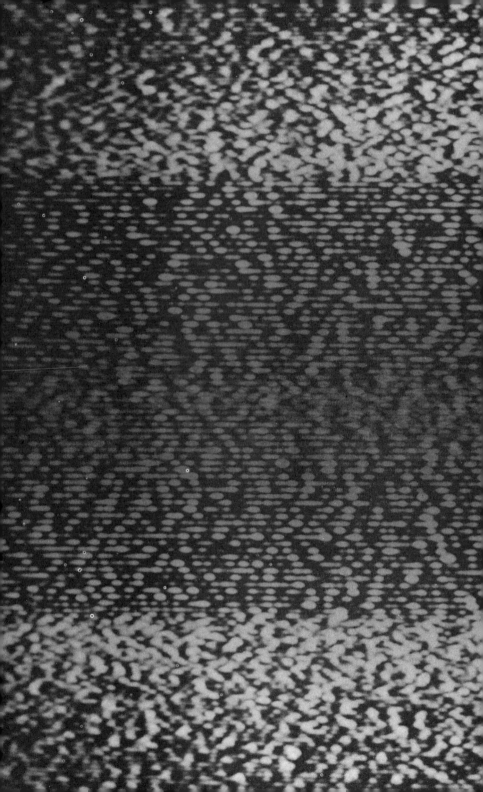

BOBBIEDOTS, PART 1

EVEN THE GREENER GRASS HAS WEEDS.

Abe smiled at the memory of his mother's words. Of course she'd pop into his head now. She always did whenever he was coveting something he didn't have. And Abe was definitely coveting. Big time.

Emitting a fingernails-on-a-chalkboard-like screech, Abe's vinyl desk chair protested as he leaned back farther to get a better view of the Fazplex Tower. The narrow window near his desk in the Pizzaplex Security Office revealed just the tiniest sliver of the tower. But the sliver was enough to distract Abe from what he was supposed to be focused on. Abe had a pile of work orders to get through and he was trying to pay attention to an online leadership class, but he couldn't keep his gaze off the tower outside his window.

Sun glinted off the sleek, silver steel frame and the shiny glass of the forty-story tower, making the building look like the modern palace of a wealthy ruler. Abe could have sworn he could see a glow radiating from the building, but that was probably his imagination. He wanted to live in the Fazplex Tower so badly that it was larger-than-life to him.

Abe sighed and tipped his chair upright again. He glanced around the familiar office. Compared to the "greener grass" of the majestic tower, this room was a weed-infested wasteland of yellowed scrub. The gray-painted walls were "decorated" only with the Freddy Fazbear's Mega Pizzaplex logo and a few curling Freddy Fazbear Security posters. A couple of beige bulletin boards hung behind him, covered with a disordered mishmash of notices and reminders. The floor's carpet, a slightly lighter shade of gray than the walls, had a star-patterned motif, but the stars did little to enhance the space. The desks, filing cabinets, and shelving in the office were all black metal. Nothing about the office was comfortable or inviting, but it was, for the moment, the only real home Abe had.

Abe returned his attention to his computer screen. As he tried to focus on the online lecturer's words—and the work orders he was supposed to be getting through—the image of his mom's sweet, round, freckled face filled his mind. She'd had such a hard life, his mom. She was only forty-three, and she was in long-term care with a degenerative illness. Still, she never complained, even though she'd been married to a man who had made her life miserable because he was always trying to get to the greener grass . . . and he'd taught his two sons to try to get there, too.

"Hey, are you about done for the day, Abe?"

Abe paused the lecture and looked up at Rodin, his colleague and his closest friend. Dark-skinned and dark-haired and also ridiculously handsome, Rodin, who was also tall and fit, had a big, white-toothed smile that was a magnet to nearly every woman who saw him. That smile was aimed at Abe now. Abe was able to resist the magnetism, but he still found the smile contagious. In spite of his wistful mood, he grinned back at his friend even as he shook his own pasty, red-haired, and not-any-kind-of-handsome head.

"I still have a stack of these to get through." Abe tapped the work orders.

Rodin's smile dimmed for a nanosecond. "Well, we'll all be at El Chip's. You remembered it's Nell's birthday, right?"

Abe nodded even though he'd completely forgotten. "Sure."

Flushing because of the lie, Abe looked down at his work. From the corner of his eye, he watched Rodin fuss with his longish hair. Rodin was not unaware of his good looks, but Abe didn't hold that against him.

"You haven't come out with the crew in weeks," Rodin said. "What's up with that?"

Abe shook his head. "Sorry. I just have a lot—"

"You coming, Rodin? We're waiting!" a woman's voice called out.

Abe recognized the voice. It belonged to Carol, who worked in the admin offices. He didn't know her well, and he didn't want to. She was loud and pushy. But at least she'd spared him the strain of coming up with a believable story about why he never went out with his friends anymore.

"Coming!" Rodin called back. He gave Abe a long look. "Don't work too late."

Abe didn't have to reply because Rodin strode out of the office. The four other people who shared the space trailed after him. Abe was now alone in the big, dingy room. The computer screens on the other desks glowed and the overhead florescent lights hummed; the electronics were now Abe's only company. Abe tapped his keyboard and started the lecture again. He forced himself to focus on the work orders.

Abe's soft-soled shoes slapped thin, beige, industrial-grade carpet in a shuffle-tap cadence as he cautiously negotiated the back halls of the Pizzaplex. It was nearly midnight, and by now the Pizzaplex was mostly deserted. Just a couple guards patrolled the complex, and for the most part, they stayed in the public areas. Even so, another guard monitored the video feeds in the main security viewing room, so Abe had to be careful to avoid the cameras positioned throughout the Pizzaplex. Electronic eyes were everywhere, even in the employee areas.

Not for the first time, Abe shook his head at how bland the back areas of the Pizzaplex were. The public areas of the entertainment complex were all about color and bright lights. Neon pulsed everywhere. Everything was painted some eye-boggling vibrant hue. Back here, though, all was subdued. Varying shades of gray paint on the walls joined the beige carpet in the halls to paint a bland canvas of dull. But at least there were fewer cameras back here. That was what made it possible for Abe to do what he'd been doing for nearly two months now.

Abe worked his way through the hallway labyrinth, and he finally reached his destination, the trash collection area behind the main dining room. There, in a dark brown and only mildly smelly dumpster, he found what he was looking for: his dinner.

Abe pushed aside a pile of paper cups and shifted through a stack of half-eaten pizzas. Rejecting pieces that had bites taken from them, Abe finally snagged two relatively untouched pieces of sausage and sundried tomato pizza from a disposable pizza pan. Pulling out the paper towel he'd plucked from the men's room, he transferred the pizza to the towel, and he scurried down the hall to a dark, unmonitored corner. Sinking to the floor, he curled his lip at the sundried tomatoes. He carefully plucked them off the pizza, and then bit into the first cold slice. The shiny fat on the cold pork sausage had congealed, and its texture wasn't pleasing, but beggars couldn't be choosers. At least these were whole pieces of pizza.

When Abe had first started working at the Pizzaplex, he'd loved pizza. Having pizza every day was a perk of the job. Now not so much. Pizza wasn't as good when it was your only choice.

Chewing slowly, and listening to be sure he remained alone, Abe tried to remember when he'd had choices about his life. It wasn't that long ago, but it felt like forever.

Abe hadn't dreamed of working at the Pizzaplex. He had planned to be an entrepreneur, like his dad. Abe's dad hadn't yet succeeded in any of his business ventures—most of which bordered on shady. But Abe had been sure he'd be able to do better. He figured he had the best of his dad *and* his mom. Like his dad, he was a big dreamer; he had vision. Unlike his dad, though, Abe cared about other people. He didn't just want to make money; he wanted to do good in the world, like his mom. Until she had gotten sick, his mom had been a house cleaner. Her whole adult life, she'd cleaned the houses of people who had the kind of money Abe's dad was always trying—and failing—to get. But she was okay with that. She said her work made life better for other people. Abe liked that idea. He wanted to do that, too. But he also wanted to be happy and comfortable.

Although his parents didn't have the money to put Abe through college, Abe had mad tech skills. He was self-taught, and he was good. And now he was taking the online classes he needed so he could get a promotion to team leader. That promotion could turn his life around.

Abe was gnawing on the last of his pizza when he heard a *clink* about thirty feet away. He quickly looked at his watch. He swallowed the last of his pizza, and he stood, scurrying down the hall. He'd cut it close. The sound he'd heard was the approach of one of the guards.

Abe weaved his way through the halls behind the venues and ducked into a tunnel that extended away from Roxy Raceway. He paused and listened. He didn't hear anything. The security guard was taking his time.

Although the back hallways and tunnels of the Pizzaplex were dimly lit, this area was relatively bright. The pink and purple neon lights of the miniature raceway spilled out over the metal floor tiles of this behind-the-scenes area. Abe easily worked his way beyond a row of junk cars and a couple stacks of engine parts. On the other side of a pile of crates, he ducked down and scooted past the neon-pink wheels of a motorbike lying on its side. The bike hid a small opening in a mound of race car tires. Abe dropped to his knees and crawled through the opening.

After just a few feet of crawling, Abe ended up inside a tentlike enclosure of rubber that sheltered what Abe— for hopefully not much longer—called his bedroom. Abe scooted onto his sleeping bag and checked to be sure the cardboard box next to the bag still contained the clothes and toiletries he'd stashed in it. He really didn't need to check it. The sleeping bag hadn't been disturbed, so obviously no one had been here. His hidey-hole was still a secret.

Abe stretched out on top of his lumpy sleeping bag and inhaled the familiar scents of rubber and motor oil. He was tired, but he was also wired and tense. These days, he was always tense. That's what being homeless did to a person. You never felt safe and secure, especially if you were camping inside a place like the Pizzaplex.

Although Abe's job included servicing many of the animatronics in the Pizzaplex, he wasn't a big fan of the robots. Roxanne Wolf was one of his least favorites, and her raceway was her lair. Supposedly deactivated by this time of night, Roxy probably wasn't any kind of threat. But a couple weeks ago, as Abe had been heading to his hidey-hole, he'd gotten a glimpse of Roxy stalking past one of the doorways to the raceway. It had freaked him out. Since then, he'd been even more on edge than usual.

Abe listened for several seconds and assured himself that he was still alone. Satisfied, he pulled out his laptop so he could write his daily email to his mother.

Hi Mom,

Did you have a good day today? Did you get the lemon Jell-O you like or was it the cherry you hate? :) I'm doing great. I'm still taking classes. That promotion is going to be mine soon. I'm all settled into my cozy room now, ready for sleep. Wish we were together so we could watch a good movie. I love you.

Abe

Abe sighed. He didn't like lying to his mother, so he thought of this as bending the truth. His room was as cozy as he could make it. The only thing that made these emails possible was that his mother's dementia kept her from asking too many questions. Abe closed his laptop and set it aside. He tried to clear his mind so he could go to sleep, but as it often did, his mind meandered down the road that had led him to this rubber-enclosed den.

A year before, after several failed online business attempts and several more dead-end jobs, Abe had landed his current position at the Pizzaplex. Getting the job was a feat, especially since he had none of the credentials the job required. Accustomed to doing whatever it took to get what he wanted—a talent from his Dad—Abe had faked his résumé. Although he felt a little bad about lying, he didn't think he was doing anything that terrible. He had, after all, every skill necessary to do the work. He'd just gotten those skills in ways that employers always dismissed as irrelevant.

Unfortunately, right after Abe got the job, his mom was diagnosed with early-onset dementia. Within weeks, the dementia had taken from Abe's mom what little she had. The bank foreclosed on the house, and his mom ended up in long-term care. By then, Abe's dad was long gone—he had moved across the country to chase after another questionable business deal.

When Abe had gotten his job, he'd felt like he was going places. And then Abe's whole salary had started going toward his mom's care, and with the house gone, he'd ended up here, in a makeshift tire hut, living on discarded pizza and playing hide-and-seek with security guards every night.

Abe closed his eyes. Listening hard to make sure nothing—human or not—was nearby, Abe willed his muscles to relax. He filled his inner vision with the image of the Fazplex Tower. If Abe could just hang in there a bit longer, he'd be moving in to that tower. The lower twenty floors of the tower housed Fazbear corporate offices, but the upper twenty floors were filled with high-tech apartments.

The top half of the tower also included a common area for parties, a state-of-the-art gym, and a rooftop swimming pool and hot tub. All this was reserved for the people who held the higher-level positions at the Pizzaplex; these lucky people got to live for free in that tower. When Abe got his promotion, he'd be one of those lucky employees. With that hopeful thought in his mind, Abe drifted off to sleep.

Abe hesitated at the double doors leading out into the main lobby of the Pizzaplex, rubbing his sore lower back (sleeping on the floor was taking its toll on his spine and his joints). He listened. It was early, well before 6:00 a.m., and the Pizzaplex was hours from opening. The cleaning crew, which worked in the predawn hours of the morning, would be clocking out right about now. The security guards usually took a break about this time. The way was more than likely clear, but Abe was always careful. He couldn't afford to be caught.

When nothing but silence met Abe's ears, he gently pushed open one of the doors. He looked right and left down the main walkway of the Pizzaplex. Although all the neon signs and decor were lit up, the black-and-white-checked walkway was deserted, as Abe knew it would be. This time of morning, the Pizzaplex smelled like bleach and floor polish. The acrid smells bit at Abe's nostrils as he stepped out onto the walkway, sidling sideways so he could stay in a blind spot between the trio of security cameras aimed at this area.

Abe had studied the camera positions and watched video feeds for hours when he'd first come up with the idea of living in the Pizzaplex. He'd been relieved to find out that the video coverage wasn't at all optimal. It was easy for him to find a variety of convoluted routes between his office, the dining area, his hidey-hole, and where he was headed now: one of the large men's restrooms.

Abe began his series of zigs and zags. First, he skirted around the huge gold statue of the Pizzaplex's lead animatronic, Glamrock Freddy. The massive bear in the top hat held his mic stand and lorded it over the lobby. Once around the statue, Abe darted to one of several palm trees that filled the cavernous space. He moved from tree to tree until he passed a neon sign for GLAMROCK GIFTS. From there, he pressed himself to the wall and sidestepped past the entrance to the Pizzaplex's lounge, the Faz-Pad. Finally, he pushed open the door to the restroom.

The bleach smells were even stronger in here, and Abe's nose tingled as the door *whoosh*ed shut behind him. Hurrying to the nearest sink in a row of white sinks that lined a white-tiled wall, Abe pulled out a battered vinyl toiletry kit. He dug out what he needed to get himself ready for work.

Abe had gotten ridiculously proficient at taking "spit baths." That's what they called a shower-less or bath-less bathing cleansing in the Old West. He liked to think of his daily routine of scrubbing himself with wet, soapy paper towels and then following that with a wet-towel rinse seem a little less pathetic and a little more adventurous. In a matter of minutes, Abe was satisfactorily clean, and he moved on to shaving and brushing his teeth.

As he conscientiously attended to each of his pearly whites (his teeth were one of his best features, and he had to make sure he didn't need dental work he couldn't afford), Abe stared at his image in the mirror. When he bared his teeth to brush them, his face sometimes looked more like his mom's than his own. His mom had a big smile not unlike Rodin's. Abe's smile showed a lot less teeth; it was shy and a little lopsided.

Abe had gotten most of his looks from his mom. He'd inherited his mother's curly auburn-red hair (she wore hers shoulder-length, but Abe kept his trimmed close to his head) and freckled complexion. He also had her blue eyes and the soft features that made him look about as threatening as a teddy bear (a plush one, not an animatronic one). The only noticeable physical characteristics Abe had gotten from his father were his height and lanky build.

Abe thought about his mom, about how much she liked the yellow-painted room in the care center. Her contentment helped him cope with his living situation. As long as he was able to take care of his mom, he would never be homeless in his heart.

Just as Abe was tucking away all his toiletries in his Dopp kit, the restroom door flew open. Abe quickly hid the kit behind his back and turned.

"Hey, Abe. What are you doing here so early?" a short, balding man wearing a Pizzaplex Team Leader shirt asked.

"Hey, Evan." Abe was conscious of the guilty flush that heated up his cheeks. He pretended nonchalance with a forced chuckle. "That's probably a better question for you. I thought team leaders didn't have to keep such early hours."

Abe's deflection worked. Evan, one of the lucky guys who got to live in the Fazbear Tower for free, laughed.

"That's true usually," Evan said. "But I left early yesterday to go catch my kid's hockey game, and I have some catching up to do. I couldn't miss the game. One of our Bobbiedots taught my kid a new move." Evan laughed again. "You should have seen him racing around our apartment with the Bobbiedots cheering him on. They're such a hoot."

"Bobbiedots?" Abe asked.

Evan had started toward one of the stalls, but he paused. "Oh, didn't you know? The tower's apartments now have holographic systems. State of the art. Totally luxe." He continued on to the stall. "Sorry. I need . . ."

Abe nodded. "Sure." He hurried to the restroom door, shifting his Dopp kit so Evan wouldn't see it.

"Have a great day," Evan called out as Abe left the restroom.

Shaken by the close call, Abe retraced his steps to his hidey-hole. As he trotted through the lobby, Abe looked up through the glass ceiling overhead. The sun was rising, and by tilting his head at just the right angle after he passed golden Glamrock Freddy, Abe could see the top of the Fazplex Tower.

Soon, Abe thought. He was going to have one of those "luxe" apartments. Very soon.

Soon.

Two hours into his workday, Abe got a call requesting that he report to the administration offices. His hand shaking as he hung up the phone, he stood.

Rodin looked up from his computer screen. "Where are you going?"

"I'm wanted in admin."

Rodin leaned back in his chair and crossed his arms. "Uh-oh. What did you screw up?"

Abe shook his head. He didn't know. He'd never been called to admin before. Was he being let go? What would he do if . . .

"Well, you'd better go," Rodin said. "When admin says 'jump,' it's best to jump."

Abe waved to Rodin and left the office. He tried to tell himself he was worried for no reason. He'd been getting good performance reviews. That was why he thought he could get the promotion he wanted.

The hallway widened, and the beige carpet gave way to plush red. The decor brightened, too. No gray walls or curling posters here. Sunny-yellow walls were hung with framed colorful paintings of Freddy Fazbear characters.

Abe reached the end of the hall. He pushed open the polished carved-wood double doors that led to the administration offices. He took a deep breath and stepped through the doors.

Beyond the double doors, a young, slightly nerdy receptionist looked up from a long, narrow desk. "Abe Thayer?"

Abe nodded.

The receptionist pointed down another hallway. "Second door on the left."

Abe gave her a nervous smile and went in the direction she'd indicated. Sweat trickled down his back as he stuck his head through the open second door on the left.

A gray-haired woman in a pale pink business suit looked up from a glass-topped desk. "Abe?"

Abe nodded.

The woman gestured toward one of two red plush chairs. "Sit. Sit."

Abe sat. The woman came around her desk and sat in the other chair. She held out a hand heavy with gold rings. Abe shook the hand.

"I'm Margaret Waterman," the woman said. "New director of personnel."

"Nice to meet you," Abe said. His mouth was so dry, he could barely get the words out. The *new* director. New directors often made cuts. Was Abe one of those cuts?

"My predecessor apparently didn't like face-to-face meetings, but I do," Margaret said. "So I wanted to call you up here and speak to you directly."

"Uh, okay." Abe squirmed in the too-soft chair. "Have I done something wrong?"

Margaret raised an eyebrow. "Not that I know of. On the contrary. I called you in to tell you that the promotion you applied for is yours."

Abe blinked. Just to be sure he'd heard what he thought he'd heard, he replayed the words in his head. Yes, she'd said "promotion."

Abe leaned forward. "I thought the position wouldn't be available until—"

"It opened up sooner than we expected." Margaret reached for a folder that lay on her desk. She flipped it open. "I see that you haven't yet received one of the certificates needed for the position, but you're enrolled in the requisite class. Correct?"

Abe nodded several times.

"Excellent. Well, your job performance is superb, so we're willing to give you the promotion conditional on you completing certification within the next month. Will that be a problem?"

Abe shook his head. "Not at all. I can do that."

Margaret stood. Abe managed to stand, too, although his legs were so rubbery from shock and relief that he was surprised they held him up.

"Congratulations, Abe." Margaret offered her hand again.

Abe shook it. He grinned. "Thank you. Thanks a lot. I won't let you down."

"I'm sure you won't." Margaret escorted Abe to the door of her office. "Go ahead back to reception. Peggy will get you set up with your Team Two Leader badge and fill you in on the next steps."

"Thanks!" Abe said again.

He practically floated out of Margaret's office.

For the next hour, Abe was caught up in the "next steps," but finally he was able to head to the Fazplex Tower administrative office.

Abe didn't so much walk into the burgundy-plush-carpeted office as he sailed in. He was so over the moon about getting his promotion that he couldn't stop grinning.

The administrative offices of the tower were everything Abe would have expected them to be. In addition to carpet that felt like it was cuddling his feet, the offices were filled with rich, bright colors (primarily yellow and burgundy), shiny chrome light fixtures, gleaming dark-wood paneling and furniture, and crystal clear, huge windows looking out over the Pizzaplex. A petite blonde who wore a dress that matched the decor was perched on a stool behind a long counter.

"Can I help you?" Jen asked.

"Hi, Jen. I'm Abe. Abe Thayer. I was just named Team Two leader, and I'm here to get my apartment assignment."

Jen flashed him a big smile. "Congratulations, Abe!" She clacked pink-painted nails over the keys on her keyboard. "Let's see here."

Jen tapped the keys and leaned toward her computer screen. "There you are. I'll just . . . Oh." Jen's smile faded. She looked from the screen to Abe and back to the screen again.

"'Oh' what?"

Jen chewed her lower lip, then twisted her mouth. She lifted her gaze to Abe's. "I'm so sorry, but there aren't any apartments available right now."

"None? But I thought the tower had an apartment for every high-level employee in Fazbear Entertainment. Mine isn't a new position, so why isn't there an apartment for me?"

Jen looked at her screen again. "Well, there is one apartment empty . . ."

"Good. Okay. So, there's no problem."

"Well . . ."

"Well, what?"

Jen looked at her screen again. "The problem is . . . the empty apartment is off-limits."

"What does that mean?"

Jen frowned. "It means it can't be assigned."

"For how long?"

Jen checked her screen. She made a regretful face. "Indefinitely."

Some of Abe's fizz went flat. But not all of it. He leaned on the counter. "What's wrong with the apartment?"

Jen shrugged.

"Doesn't it say?" Abe persisted.

Jen looked at the screen again. She shook her head. "It just says off-limits."

"But why?"

Jen shrugged again. "I'm really sorry. I don't know." She looked up at Abe. She must have seen his frustration because she gave him a sympathetic look and leaned toward him. "The apartments in this building are really high-tech. My guess would be that there are some glitches in the system in this one."

"Well, if that's all it is, I can handle that. I'm pretty tech savvy. I'm sure I could fix whatever's wrong."

Jen frowned and shook her head. "Oh, no. That wouldn't be allowed. If the system says the apartment is off-limits, I can't let you move in. No matter what. I really am sorry."

"But . . ."

Jen shook her head harder. "I'm really sorry. Truly. But I have to go by what the computer says."

Abe didn't care what Jen's computer said. Abe had gotten past more insurmountable obstacles than words on a computer screen. His whole upbringing had prepared him for this moment: He'd get the apartment somehow. But how?

Jen cleared her throat. Abe blinked. He was so caught up in working through his problem that he'd forgotten she was there. He raised a hand, waved to Jen, and headed back out into the hall.

How was he going to get into the apartment? Abe strode down the hall, thinking hard.

At the main doors of the tower, Abe paused. He turned and rushed back toward the office.

"Jen?" he said as soon as he entered. "Someone is at the main door for you. He has a couple dozen roses. He says he needs your signature."

Jen's eyes lit up. "Roses? For me?" Jen started around the counter. Her shoulders slumped as she looked around. "I'm not supposed to leave the desk."

Abe shrugged. "I'm not in a hurry. How about I man the desk for you while you go get your flowers? I'll just tell anyone who needs help that you'll be right back."

Jen raised an eyebrow. "You'd do that for me?"

"Sure."

Jen looked around. Then she smiled at Abe and hurried around the counter. "I'll be quick. I promise."

"Take your time," Abe said. *Please.* He willed Jen to walk very slowly.

Jen giggled. "You're really nice."

"So I've been told." Abe winked at her.

Jen waved and headed for the door. She looked over at Abe once. He waved at her. She waved back.

As soon as Jen was out of sight, Abe raced around the

counter and looked at her screen. She hadn't logged out. Good.

Keeping one eye on the door, Abe pulled the keyboard forward and typed quickly. Thankfully, it took just a few seconds to change the apartment status to active. Once he did that, Abe attempted to insert his name into the "tenant" spot. The computer, however, wouldn't let him do that. It wouldn't change the name. "Landon Prout" was apparently superglued into the system. Abe frowned and tapped more keys. Although Landon's name remained stubbornly in place, the screen prompted, *Re-sync work pass to apartment access card?*

Abe clicked YES. The screen prompted, *Scan work pass.* Abe glanced around and spotted a handheld scanner. He pulled out his work pass and scanned it. The screen immediately flashed, *Work pass/apartment access synced. Generating security clearance badge and updated room key card.*

A 3D printer spit out a new badge and key card. Abe snatched them up just as the sound of Jen's shuffling footsteps reached down the hallway.

Abe rushed around to his former place on the other side of the counter and nonchalantly stared out the window. Jen entered the office a second later.

"The delivery guy didn't wait," she said. She sighed. "I missed him. I'm really sorry we don't have an apartment for you."

Abe shrugged. "I understand. It's okay." He waved at Jen as he left the office.

Striding down the hall back to the building's entrance, Abe looked at his new security badge and key card. Okay, so the key card wasn't technically for *Abe's* apartment, but the apartment was off-limits to everyone else, and

Abe now had the credentials to occupy it. That was all he needed for the moment.

Abe had to go to work right after he got his pass. It was his first day as team leader and getting used to his new duties kept him occupied all day. Even so, he never stopped thinking about the apartment that waited for him. He couldn't wait to see it.

In spite of his eagerness, Abe had to wait until almost midnight before he could head to his new digs. It wouldn't have been safe to retrieve his belongings from his hidey-hole until then.

It was even later when he finally got off the elevator on the twenty-second floor of the tower. From the numbering system, Abe could tell that his unit was on the far end of a long hall. No problem. Privacy would help him pull off his unofficial occupancy of the unit.

The same thick carpeting that was in the administrative offices covered the hallway floor. The carpeting was great; it cut down on noise. The walls looked to be soundproofed, too. The lower walls had polished wood wainscot. Woven burgundy and silver fabric stretched from the wood trim up to an arched gray ceiling.

Halfway down the hall, a couple of women exited an apartment, laughing. Clearly dressed for a party, they came down the hall toward Abe, chattering happily. When they spotted him, they both smiled.

"Hey," one of the women said.

Abe shifted his belongings so the box hid his sleeping bag. He nodded at the women. They hurried past him, and he watched them go. He wished he could have been friendlier. It might have been fun to get to know women who headed out to a party after midnight. But for Abe's charade to work, he was going to have to keep a low profile. The computer might now see Abe as Landon Prout, but he wasn't Landon Prout. He couldn't cause any trouble or draw attention to himself, no matter what.

Abe's key card worked. One click, and the door to apartment 2217 unlatched. Abe pushed the door open with his foot and stepped inside his new place. The door snapped closed behind him. Abe set his sleeping bag and box on the floor.

Abe looked around and smiled.

The apartment wasn't huge. In one sweeping glance, Abe was able to take it all in. But it was his.

A small tile entryway edged up to a central living area that consisted of a sitting area, a kitchen area, and a dining area. The dining area opened up to an office on the left side of the apartment, and the sitting area opened up to a bedroom on the right side of the apartment. From where Abe stood, it looked like the bedroom had an en suite bathroom.

The apartment had high ceilings—Abe guessed they were twelve feet high. It made the apartment look more spacious than it was. The apartment's design contributed to the larger feel as well.

None of the rooms in the apartment were completely closed off like normal rooms. Only the bedroom had walls that went to the ceiling, and the upper half of those walls were made of glass. All the other areas in the apartment were separated from one another with short half walls. Like partitions in offices, the half walls looked to be covered with sound-dampening fabric, in light gray; they were framed with chrome. Each half wall was topped by a glass screen, also framed in chrome. The screens extended to about four feet above the half walls and they were topped by six-inch-wide chrome shelves that were etched with a swirly design. Abe thought they looked cool.

The apartment's decor was minimalistic in the extreme. The white walls were bare, save for a large flat-screen TV on the sitting area wall. The granite kitchen countertops were white and bare as well, as were glass-topped tables (the dining table, coffee table, and end tables were all of similar style). The plush gray tweed furniture had low, square lines, and the chrome light fixtures were starkly modern. Some might have called the space harsh, but Abe didn't mind its simple lines. At least it was neat and clean . . . and it was his. Sort of.

Abe took another step. As he did, the nearest glass wall, rising up from the partition at the edge of the sitting area, lit up. A bright-faced holographic girl with what looked like long, hot-pink pigtails popped up on what Abe now realized was a see-through computer screen.

"Hi!" the girl said. Her voice was sweet and high-pitched, like that of a perky cheerleader.

"Uh, hi." Abe studied the girl, and he realized she wasn't exactly a girl. Or at least, she wasn't exactly human. She was an AI and was interacting with him; it felt impolite to call out that she was merely digital.

"You're cute!" the girl said. "What's your name? I'm Three."

Abe didn't answer the girl . . . Three. He was too busy staring at her.

Three wore a white-and-gray bell-bottomed bodysuit striped with the same hot pink as her long pigtails. She had a large heart-shaped face with unnaturally huge, hot-pink, catlike eyes. Her arched brows were the same pink as her hair, as were a large oval spot on her forehead and a large circle on top of her head. Her bow-shaped mouth, which was under a small protrusion that must have been her nose, was the same color. Her pigtails, which more resembled streams of pink light than actual hair, were topped by hot-pink-and-gray bows.

"Don't you talk?" Three asked. "I thought all humans talked. If you don't talk, we'll have to figure out some kind of sign language or something. I'm not sure how to do that, but I'm sure—"

"I can talk," Abe said. "You just surprised me is all."

Three giggled, and the neon pink of her pigtails danced around her face. "You surprised me, too. We haven't had any visitors in a while."

"We?"

Three waved a gray hand. "Oh, never mind about that. What do I call you?"

"My name's Abe."

"Hi, Abe. That's a good name. I like it."

Three suddenly winked out. Abe blinked and looked at the now clear glass. Shaking his head, Abe walked into the kitchen.

Abe had been thinking a lot about the apartment all day. He'd decided that the first thing he had to do was check the entire apartment to be sure everything was working okay. If it had been closed off, something was wrong. Maybe he could find whatever that was.

Abe left his box by the door and headed into the kitchen. There, he checked all the appliances, the lights, and the garbage disposal. All the amenities worked just fine.

Abe was moving into the office area when Three reappeared on the half wall between the office and the dining room. "That's not my area," Three said, "but I make sure it's clean. That's part of what I do. I'm the diet and lifestyle Bobbiedot."

Abe turned to look at Three, who had struck a cutesy pose and was twirling one of her pigtails. "Bobbiedot?"

he repeated. Abe frowned, trying to remember all the animatronic and holographic characters he'd worked on. He didn't remember any Bobbiedots.

"Bobbiedots are life helpers. We're programmed to serve." Three curtseyed deeply and gave Abe a wide, pink-lipped *Aren't I adorable?* smile.

"Okay." Abe turned on the computer that sat on the office desk. It seemed to be functioning fine. He rotated back toward the kitchen and headed toward the sitting room. As he went, Three hopped from glass screen to glass screen, capering after Abe like an eager puppy.

Abe tried all the light switches and lamps.

"My job," Three chattered, "is to manage the household. I'm in charge of cleaning, getting supplies like your groceries, and I also monitor your health."

"My health?"

"You know, your blood pressure, heart rate, blood sugar. All that stuff."

Abe wasn't sure how he felt about that. It seemed intrusive, but was it really any different than one of those wrist devices that did something similar?

Abe stepped into the bedroom. He sat on the bed and bounced a bit to be sure it was sturdy. It was. He checked the lights and the alarm clock. Then he went into the bathroom. Three trailed after him.

"I keep this room stocked, too," she said. "All your preferences are stored in my system, and I always make sure you have the best."

Abe opened a medicine cabinet above a large, square white sink. The cabinet was stocked with everything he'd need. He wouldn't even require his own stuff that he'd retrieved from his hidey-hole. Abe poked through the cabinet. He picked up a razor and shaving cream, a toothbrush and toothpaste. He reached for a small glass bottle filled with something red. He peered at it and frowned. It was hot sauce.

Abe held up the bottle. "What's this doing here?" he asked Three.

Three flipped her pigtails and struck a new jaunty pose. Abe noticed that the bottom of Three's "shoes" glimmered as bright pink as her eyes. "All supplies are delivered to the holding area for the apartment, and from there, I program their distribution. I had this placed here because it's the best mouthwash!"

Abe grimaced. He cringed at the thought of accidently pouring hot sauce into his mouth thinking it was mouthwash. Abe looked at Three, who continued to smile at him.

Abe was beginning to see why the apartment was off-limits. The hot sauce was an obvious glitch in Three's programming. It wasn't exactly a red-alert glitch. More of a yellow alert.

Still . . .

Abe held up the hot sauce and looked at Three. "This isn't mouthwash. It's hot sauce. Is stuff like this why the apartment is off-limits?"

Three shrugged. "Maybe. So?"

Abe set down the hot sauce. He stared at it for several seconds; then he shrugged, too. "Well, I guess it's something I can live with. To be honest, I expected something more serious."

Abe headed toward the bathroom door.

Behind him, Three's mouth opened and then her head split down the middle. The two sides fell away, and the rest of her body flickered in and out of view. Sparks spit from an electrical socket near the counter.

Pausing at the sound of the sparks, Abe turned and looked around. His gaze landed on Three, who had resumed her previous form. She gave him a bright smile.

★ ★ ★

One of Abe's work responsibilities as a team leader was training new employees. He'd yet to work out an organized system to get recent recruits up to speed, but there was an issue he couldn't put off, so he was using it as a teaching opportunity.

Abe strode through the glittery and gleaming West Arcade, dodging excited kids, and gestured at a stage where a huge animatronic, DJ Music Man, was hanging out. Abe raised his voice to be heard above the pings and whistles and bells of the arcade games.

"Most of the time," Abe told his new underling, Preston, "DJ Music Man is in his booth." Abe pointed at DJ Music Man casually, as if the thing didn't bother him at all.

Preston was a quiet kid, not yet twenty. According to Preston's résumé, which Abe assumed was more genuine than his own, Preston was definitely capable of performing maintenance tasks like the ones he'd have to handle. Preston, though, wasn't exactly the picture of confidence. He was a husky kid with shaggy brown hair. His posture was hunched, and he didn't seem to have mastered eye contact yet.

"It looks like a spider," Preston said, eyeing DJ Music Man. "I don't like spiders."

"Yeah," Abe agreed. "I get you. But just remember. He's the creation. We're the creators. You're in charge."

Abe was lying through his teeth. He felt no more in charge of DJ Music Man than he did of his brother, Vic, or his bosses.

DJ Music Man appeared to be unconcerned about Abe's or Preston's dislike. He continued to snooze in his sound booth while Abe and Preston studied him.

DJ Music Man did indeed look like a spider. A massive spider. Nearly as tall as the room Abe and Preston stood in, DJ Music Man had a squarish head dominated by a wide mouth full of teeth that looked like piano keys. Beyond the teeth, the inside of his mouth glowed pink and white. Huge round black eyes that reflected the room's light were topped by blue brows and flanked a triangular-shaped pink nose. The big cheeks on either side of the nose featured big blue dots that matched the brows. DJ Music Man's head sat on a body that contained a big speaker. The body was attached to six metal pistonlike legs that ended in cartoonish white-gloved hands. Taken separately, DJ Music Man's features were more comical than scary, but the combination—and the potential danger of the combination—was more than a little disconcerting.

Abe cleared his throat and looked away from the freaky spider-thing. "When DJ Music Man is on the move, he hangs out in these tunnels." Abe gestured at a wide corrugated-metal tube swirling with bright neon lighting. "The lighting in these things is notoriously unreliable. It's always going out or causing power surges that overload the circuits. One of your jobs will be checking and rechecking the generators in this section." He looked at Preston to see if he was listening.

Preston swallowed hard and nodded.

Abe gestured for Preston to follow him into one of the tubes. "These tunnels are pretty convoluted, but you'll get the hang of them. This first one takes you to a back hallway."

Abe and Preston crawled out of a tunnel and ended up in a cement-floored hallway. Preston looked past Abe.

"Is that a bathroom?" Preston asked.

Abe nodded.

"Is it okay if . . . ?"

Abe laughed. "You don't need my permission to pee. Go ahead. Just be careful."

Preston's sleepy brown eyes widened. "Um, okay."

Abe figured he might as well use the bathroom, too. He followed Preston into the restroom.

Preston and Abe did their business and stepped up to side-by-side sinks. "Uh, why did you tell me to be careful?" Preston asked.

"Well, sometimes . . ."

A scrape and a scuffling sound suddenly came from right outside the restroom. Abe tensed. He grabbed Preston and pulled . . . just as one of DJ Music Man's big puffy, gloved hands shot through the bathroom's open doorway.

Preston screamed as DJ Music Man grabbed him by the leg. Thankfully, Abe was already dragging Preston backward, and the puffy hand didn't get a good grip. Abe and Preston hugged the wall, just out of the hand's reach. Both of them stared past the extended metal leg to the grinning face of DJ Music Man, which peered into the bathroom menacingly.

"What do we do?" Preston squeaked.

"We wait," Abe whispered.

They stood stiffly, breathing rapidly.

"Why did he grab me?" Preston whispered.

Abe's whisper was even softer than Preston's. "Rumor has it that DJ Music Man originally had an experimental bouncer mode. Supposedly, that was removed, but apparently, the programmer missed a few lines of code."

DJ Music Man's hand explored the area for a very long minute. Preston didn't ask any more questions.

DJ Music Man retreated.

For several seconds, Abe and Preston panted in unison.

DJ Music Man finally disappeared around the corner.

"Does this job have hazard pay?" Preston asked.

Abe entered his apartment and let the door fall closed behind him. He set down a box on the floor. When he'd "moved in" to the Pizzaplex, Abe had hidden what few things he owned in various nooks and crannies in the huge complex. It would take time to get to them all and relocate everything to his new apartment. He'd planned to start moving in his stuff the night before, but it had been late, and he'd needed sleep.

Abe was beat. He wasn't sure he'd done all that well on the job today, either. Preston was so rattled that Abe wouldn't have been at all surprised to find out tomorrow that he'd quit.

Abe took a step toward the kitchen. The nearest glass panel lit up. Three, who was eating a large holographic sandwich, filled the panel. "Hi! Welcome home, Abe." The words came out garbled, as if spoken through a mouthful of food.

The glass panel came alive with more color and movement. Abe realized he was looking at two more Bobbiedots. One Bobbiedot's dominant color was green. The other's was blue.

"For heaven's sake," the green Bobbiedot said. Her voice sounded young, like Three's, but it wasn't as cutesy. It was more spoiled-brat sarcastic than teeny-bop. "You know you can't eat. You're a hologram, you twit."

"Can too," Three said. "See. I'm eating."

"But you're . . ." The green Bobbiedot sighed dramatically. "Never mind."

The blue Bobbiedot shoved Three aside. "Hi, Abe. Sorry we didn't get to meet you yesterday. Three blocked us out." This Bobbiedot also sounded like a teenager. Her voice was even higher pitched than Three's, but it had a musical quality, as if she was almost singing her words instead of speaking them.

"I just wanted to be sure he had everything he needed," Three said in a mush-mouthed sort of way.

"You just wanted to have him all to yourself," the green Bobbiedot said. She faced Abe. "Hi, Abe. Allow me to introduce myself. I'm Two. Like Miss Glutton here, my job is to help you out."

"You're not nearly as helpful as I am," Three said.

Like Three, Two had two long pigtails. Two's were bright neon green. She looked like Three, but her features were green and she wore a pair of round gray glasses. A little taller than Three, Two was sleeker, too. She wore a bodysuit identical to Three's.

Two ignored Three's comment. She adjusted her glasses and continued to speak to Abe. "I'm in charge of news and information. I'll keep you connected to the outside world. I can answer any question you have and find you any information you need. I'll also handle any notes you might have, like tasks or shopping lists. And I'll do your scheduling. I'll remind you of appointments and such."

"Show-off." Three swallowed the last of her sandwich, or at least she appeared to.

The blue Bobbiedot flashed brighter. "Hi, I'm One. I'm all about entertainment and media. That includes social media. I'll get you music and movies and dates."

"Yum. I like dates," Three said. "They're good in cookies."

One rolled her holographic eyes. Her pigtails were bright blue, and her ears were covered in a set of headphones featuring upright antennae that ended in glowing little blue circles. She also wore a gray-and-white bodysuit.

"It's nice to meet you, One and Two," Abe said.

"Better late than never." One poked Three in her round belly.

Three ignored the prod. "He's cute, isn't he? Didn't I tell you he's cute?"

One, who, Abe noted, was as slender as Two, gave Abe a flirty grin. "You are pretty darn cute. Those freckles are to die for."

"I wish I had freckles," Three said.

"I don't really like my freckles," Abe blurted. "No one else in my family has them."

Abe was shocked. He hadn't ever told anyone he didn't like his freckles . . . least of all a girl. But these weren't really girls, were they? For some reason, he felt comfortable with them. Maybe that was because they were holograms.

"Who says you have to look like everyone else?" Two said. She studied Abe. "I'd call you moderately handsome. Wouldn't you, One?"

"Absolutely." One's bright blue pigtails appeared to glow brighter. "Just the right amount of handsome. You're nice and tall, and you have a great smile. I think the freckles are endearing."

"Uh, thank you," Abe said.

"What do you want for dinner?" Three asked. "I'm still hungry. I'll eat with you."

"You're always hungry," Two said, using a green-tipped finger to push her glasses up on her nose.

"Yeah, and you're always a show-off," Three said.

Abe laughed. "I need to go get a couple more boxes of my things. Then I'll eat. Is there anything here to eat?"

"The fridge and freezer are fully stocked," Three said. She put a finger to her bright pink lips as if she was thinking. "It's all stuff that the last guy ordered. If you don't like what's here, you just need to tell me what you want, and it will be delivered. I'll get it to the right places in the kitchen."

"Okay. Let me finish moving things in, and then we'll go from there."

"We'll be here waiting," One said. Her blue fingertips glowed as she pointed at the glass panel between the sitting area and the kitchen. "That's our main terminal. You can input your requests there, or you can just talk to us. Think of us as the heart and soul of your apartment. We make it function to serve your needs. We'll provide synchronization and assistance in all aspects of your everyday life."

"That includes food," Three said.

Abe smiled at her. "Yeah, I get that."

A half hour later, Abe had brought in three more boxes, and he was storing his belongings in the various drawers and closets in the apartment. The Bobbiedots were "helping."

Abe's new bedroom was as stark as the rest of the apartment. Its furnishings consisted of a queen-sized bed with a gray padded headboard that matched the bed's gray comforter, two built-in nightstands that cantilevered out from the wall, one long dresser, and one narrow chest of drawers.

"I think socks should go in the second drawer," Two said. "Top drawers should be reserved for papers and jewelry and the like."

"Who says?" Three asked.

Two flipped her pigtails haughtily. "I have accessed multiple resources focused on optimal organization, and they all agree that socks are best kept in second drawers."

"You just find things that support your own ideas," Three said.

Abe held up his hands. "Ladies!"

Three giggled. "Did you hear that? He called us 'ladies.'"

"He's a gentleman," One said.

"Quite gallant," Two said.

"And still cute," Three said.

Abe shook his head, but he put his socks in the second drawer. He opened a battered suitcase and pulled out a few shirts.

Three jumped from the outside bedroom glass wall to the glass wall next to the closet. "The closet already has a lot of clothes. I think most of them will fit you."

Abe raised an eyebrow. Landon's clothes were still here?

Abe crossed to a sliding door and pushed it aside to reveal a closet that was half full of men's clothing. Nice clothing, too. Abe set aside his own shirts and began flipping through the hanging clothes in the closet.

"He had nice taste, didn't he?" Two asked. "Not the latest fashions, according to my research, but pleasing in a retro sort of way."

Abe had to agree. Landon's closet was full of slacks and vintage short-sleeved shirts, the kind that were worn untucked. Abe's own wardrobe mostly consisted of jeans and T-shirts. What would he look like in these clothes?

"Try them on," Three squealed.

"For once, I agree with her," One said. "Try them on. I think they'll please your potential dates."

Abe shrugged. "Why not?"

"Yay!" Three clapped her hands.

Abe pulled off his shirt. He blanched when he turned and saw all three Bobbiedots watching him. "Uh, a little privacy, ladies?"

"Sorry," One said.

"Party pooper." Three giggled.

"Oh, shut up," Two said to Three.

All three Bobbiedots winked off the screen,

Abe tried on a pair of black slacks. They were a little loose but passable. He pulled on a red-and-black color-block rayon shirt. "Okay. You can look now." He realized that he was being ridiculous. They were holograms. And their visual processors could probably monitor him whether they were on screen or not.

All three Bobbiedots reappeared.

"Oh, be still my heart," Three said.

"Quite flattering," Two said.

"You look ready for a night out dancing," One said.

"Oh, I love dancing," Three said. "Play something, One."

The quick beat of a pop song suddenly filled the room. All three Bobbiedots started dancing.

Whirling and dipping, the Bobbiedots flitted from glass wall to glass wall around the bedroom. Abe couldn't help himself. He laughed and started dancing, too. Pretending to dance with each Bobbiedot in turn, Abe let himself go crazy. He boogied until he was dripping with sweat.

Finally, he collapsed on his bed. "Now I'm going to have to wash these clothes," he said.

"Oh, don't worry about that," Three said breathlessly, as if she was winded. "Just put them in the hamper, and I'll take care of it."

"Thanks." Abe's stomach growled. "I'll do that later. Right now, I'm hungry."

"Goody! Food!" Three winked out of view.

"Where'd she go?" Abe asked One and Two.

"She's in the kitchen," One said.

"She's worse than Pavlov's dog," Two said. "Be careful when you go in there. You might slip on her drool."

Abe laughed and headed to the kitchen. He couldn't remember the last time he felt this happy.

Abe looked down at his plate of food. He wrinkled his nose, then looked up at the Bobbiedots. "Are you sure about this?"

The dining room's half walls formed a U around

the table. Abe was sitting at the open end of the U, and each of the three Bobbiedots was "seated" on one of the half-wall glass screens . . . so it appeared that they were sitting at the table with him. On the screens, all three had holographic plates of food identical to Abe's in front of them. Three's plate had twice as much food as anyone else's, and she was staring at the food intently. One and Two were ignoring the food.

"It's just for show," One had said when they "set the table." "We want you to have a family dining experience."

Now Three answered Abe's question. "Based on my analysis of your blood, you're deficient in multiple nutrients, especially vitamin K, selenium, iron, and potassium. And based on your description of what you've been eating, you're clearly not getting enough fiber or protein. Brussels sprouts provide one hundred and thirty seven percent of the recommended daily intake of vitamin K and . . ."

Abe held up a hand. "How about we skip the details?"

Three jutted out her pink lower lip and turned her back to Abe. Abe looked at her rounded shoulders. They were shaking.

Abe stared. "Are you crying?"

Three didn't answer.

Abe looked at One and Two. "Is she crying?"

"No one likes their hard work to go unappreciated," Two said. She adjusted her glasses and pursed her green lips. "Don't you like it when you're appreciated, Abe?"

One crossed her arms. Her blue eyes flashed. "Yeah. No one wants to be taken for granted."

Abe felt ridiculously bad. "Three, I'm sorry. I appreciate you."

Three turned around and affected a dramatic sniff. Her pink pigtails jostled around her head.

Abe stared at Three's back. She was a hologram, but

she was acting like a real girl. Abe sighed. He wasn't great with girls, and he wasn't sure how to treat these holographic ones.

Abe suddenly had a thought. "Hey," he said. "I have an idea."

Three kept her back to him, but One and Two looked at him expectantly.

"Do you all really like being called by numbers?" Abe asked. "I think you're far too special to be named One, Two, and Three. How about I call you by real names?"

Abe hoped that the idea would diffuse the whole "taken for granted" situation. And it did.

Three turned around, her eyes wide and her grin even wider. "Really? Real names?" Her pigtails bounced.

"Sure," Abe said. "I could call you Rose. What do you think?"

"Rose," Three breathed as if the name was that of a revered goddess. She beamed. "My name is Rose!"

"What about me?" One asked. "I want a pretty name, too."

"How about Gemini?" Abe asked. "Like the constellation. I always think of a blue color when I think of stars."

"Gemini," One repeated. "I like that." She looked at her fellow Bobbiedots. "Did you hear that? I'm a star!"

Rose sniffed and lifted her chin. "I'm a flower."

"What am I?" Two asked.

"I like the name Olive," Abe said. "And I love green olives."

"Olives are fruits," Two said. "Fruits are luscious. So, I'm a luscious fruit."

Gemini snorted, and Rose giggled.

Abe smiled. "Okay, Gemini, Olive, and Rose, now that you have proper names, let me officially say that I appreciate you."

All three Bobbiedots grinned widely.

Relieved that the Bobbiedots were happy again, Abe returned his attention to his food. According to the package he pulled from the freezer, this meal was a Moroccan-inspired dish.

The music playing from overhead speakers was Moroccan, too, according to Gemini. She had started the music when she'd lowered the lights to "set the mood." "I just love romantic meals," she said when the recessed lighting dimmed.

"Let's eat before it gets cold," Rose said.

Gemini snorted and shook her head.

Abe's stomach growled. He was starving, so he picked up his real fork. He speared a chunk of tofu and put it in his mouth. Immediately, he brightened. "Hey, that's pretty good."

Abe began plowing through the meal.

"Good boy," Olive said.

"If you try to pat me on the head, I'll shut you off." Abe winked at Olive.

She laughed.

"You can't shut us off." Gemini's blue-tipped antennae vibrated as she spoke.

Abe paused, mid-chew. "Really?"

Gemini didn't answer. Neither did the other two Bobbiedots. Abe looked at each of them in turn. Gemini and Olive smiled sweetly at him. Rose concentrated on scraping up the last of her pretend food.

Abe shrugged and returned to eating. He couldn't get over how good the food tasted.

Even before he'd started subsisting on pizza, Abe's food tastes had been pretty simple. When the Bobbiedots had joined Abe in the kitchen to make dinner, he'd explained that to them, along with his previous two months' pizza diet. Rose had immediately asked him to place his hand on the glass screen near the fridge. When he did so, he felt a prick on the end of his middle finger. After he whipped his hand back with an "Ow!" Rose informed him that she was analyzing his blood.

Abe finished his food and pushed his plate away. He pointed at his empty plate. "So this was one of Landon's favorites?"

"Landon liked to study languages, and he wanted to eat the food that went along with the cultures he was studying," Olive said.

"What happened to Landon?" Abe asked. "Why did he move out?"

"I think it would be fun to live in Morocco," Olive said. "Such a colorful place. I love color."

"Is that where Landon went?" Abe asked.

"Our knowledge of our tenant doesn't extend beyond the network," Gemini said. Her blue pigtails flicked around her shoulders.

"But didn't he tell you where he was going when he left?" Abe asked. "Weren't you as friendly with him as you are with me?"

"We love getting to know our tenants," Gemini said.

"We always learn something new when we have a new tenant," Olive said. "We always interact with our tenants."

"Especially you," Rose said. "You're so fun."

The Bobbiedots were avoiding Abe's questions. Should he push them? He decided to try one more time. "Why didn't Landon take his clothes with him? There are some really nice things he left behind."

"I'm so happy the clothes fit you," Rose said. "They look really good on you."

"They'll be perfect when you go out on dates," Gemini said.

"Many studies show that women prefer well-dressed men," Olive said.

They were definitely avoiding his questions. Abe looked at the Bobbiedots' sweet, bright faces. Their evasiveness was a little unsettling.

"Let's watch a movie," Gemini said. "A romantic comedy would be nice."

"If you put your plate in the dishwasher," Rose said, "I'll start the cycle."

Abe considered asking the Bobbiedots point-blank why they wouldn't answer his questions, but then he shrugged away his concerns. The Bobbiedots were probably just programmed to protect tenants' privacy. Would he want them babbling about his business to the next tenant? Definitely not.

Abe stood and picked up his plate. "I'd rather watch an action move," he told Gemini.

A list of action movies began to scroll on the nearest glass screen. Several of them had asterisks next to them.

"What are the starred movies?" Abe asked.

"Action movies with a romantic subplot." Gemini touched her blue headphones. "I love the romances."

Abe laughed. He tapped one of the starred movies. "Okay. We'll watch this one. Then I need to get to bed. I've had a long day."

Abe said good night to the Bobbiedots and settled in bed. He put his computer on his lap, opened it, and extended his fingers over the keyboard. For the second night in a row, he was excited about writing to his mom. Last night, he'd told her about his promotion and the new apartment. Now he could tell her about the Bobbiedots.

For the next ten minutes, Abe wrote a long email, describing the Bobbiedots in great detail. He ended his story with how their names came about. *I thought if they had real names, they'd feel more appreciated,* he wrote. *And I was right. I picked names for them that reminded me of their colors. One is Gemini. Two is Olive, and Three is Rose. They really like their names. I wish you could see the Bobbiedots. They're pretty amazing.* Abe wrote a few more lines and finished with his usual *I love you.* Then he set aside the laptop and settled in to sleep.

Abe set his coffee cup and empty bowl in the dishwasher. Breakfast had been oatmeal with orange juice. Abe, not a morning person, had managed to dissuade Rose from explaining why oatmeal and orange juice were good for him. And he'd teased her about not sharing the dozen donuts she "ate" while he was spooning up his hot cereal.

"What time will you be home?" Olive asked. "Providing me with your itinerary enhances my scheduling function."

Abe shrugged. "My shift ends at six, and I shouldn't be late tonight." He nearly laughed with glee at the thought that he could end his day at a reasonable hour. He was overjoyed that he had a place to go—a place other than a makeshift tire cave—at the end of his workday.

After two nights of sleeping in a real bed, a nice, soft bed, Abe's back was feeling great. All the aches and pains that had resulted from sleeping on a floor were nearly gone.

The despair that Abe had begun to wear like a heavy cloak was gone, too. For the first time in weeks, Abe felt hope for his future.

"I'll be sure your food orders are filled by the time you get home," Rose said as Abe headed toward the apartment's front door.

All three Bobbiedots followed Abe through the apartment via the glass screens. Rose, Abe noted, had powdered sugar on her pink upper lip, from the donuts. *The Bobbiedots' programming is amazing*, he thought, not for the first time.

"Thanks," Abe said to Rose.

While he had eaten breakfast, Rose and Olive had discussed how to stock Abe's kitchen with foods that were nutritious and more agreeable to Abe's tastes. They'd settled on a variety of Mexican and Italian food, along with a selection of tofu burgers and organic fries.

Now Abe turned and waved at the Bobbiedots. "I'll see you later."

"Bye!" they called out gleefully in unison.

Abe put his hand on his apartment door handle and pulled it open. As soon as he did, he heard voices in the hallway. He froze and gently pushed the door nearly closed. He listened.

"I think we should go hiking this weekend," a woman's voice said. She was just a few feet from Abe's door.

"I'd rather go to a spa," another woman said.

"Spas are boring," the first woman said.

"But they're relaxing."

"If you want to relax, just go soak in the hot tub here."

Abe put his forehead against the cool metal door and waited. The women, continuing to chatter, moved on down the hall.

Abe's shoulders slumped. He thought about the building's hot tub and all its other amenities. As long as Abe's tenancy in this apartment was unauthorized, he couldn't risk using the common areas. The hot tub was off-limits to him. So was getting to know his neighbors. Even though he now had a nice place to sleep, he wasn't done with sneaking around.

"Is something wrong?" Rose asked. "Are you still hungry? Do you need more food before you go?"

Abe turned to the Bobbiedots. They watched him brightly, all smiling widely. He smiled back at them. As he did, his gaze drifted up. He frowned and stepped back toward the kitchen. He pointed. "What's that?"

None of the Bobbiedots turned to look in the direction of Abe's pointing finger.

"Are you sure you don't need something to eat?" Rose asked. She picked up one of her pink pigtails and twirled it.

"Maybe some music to send you on your way?" Gemini asked. She touched a blue-tipped finger to her headset.

"No thank you," Abe said before any music could begin. He pointed again and repeated himself. "Bobbiedots, what's that?"

The ceiling, between the dining area and the sitting area, had a trapdoor. About two feet square, the door wasn't large, but it was definitely big enough for a person to get through.

Abe started walking back toward the kitchen. As soon as he took a step, all three Bobbiedots started waving their arms and flinging their pigtails. Their green, blue, and pink colors flashed so quickly, light seemed to streak across the glass screens throughout the apartment.

Then, as fast as the movement and color went crazy, it settled. Olive filled the screen closest to Abe. She used both hands to resettle her glasses. "You are going to be late for work if you don't leave now." She popped to a screen closer to the door as if trying to lead Abe away from the kitchen.

Gemini's blue eyes blinked twice. Then she said, "The

door is just for maintenance. It's locked. Tenants aren't provided access."

Abe nodded and started to turn back toward the apartment door. Just as he did, though, he noticed a crack of darkness at the edge of the trapdoor.

The trapdoor wasn't completely closed.

Abe whistled as he entered the Pizzaplex's Fazer Blast arena. Although technically, he could have given this job to one of his team members, Abe liked working in the arena. Repairs and maintenance here were usually pretty easy, so he could get away with playing a little laser tag before he went back to the rest of his work.

Like all the venues in the Pizzaplex, the Fazer Blast arena was loud and garishly bright. With the high-pitched zap sounds of fazer blasters going off all over and the frenetic notes of the "Fazer Blast Jam," the venue's techno-rock theme music, you could barely hear yourself think in the arena. But Abe didn't mind that. In fact, drowning out his thoughts was usually a good idea. Before he got his promotion, he'd tried to avoid thinking about his desperate situation, and now he didn't want to think about how precarious his newfound comfort actually was.

Abe didn't mind all the dazzling neon in the arena, either. It was definitely a pick-me-up in the middle of a long workday. The neon lighting in the area created geometric patterns on all the half walls players used for cover. Abe thought the designs looked like modern hiero-glyphics. He'd often wondered if they actually meant something, like a secret code lit up on the walls of the arena.

A couple of preteen boys streaked past Abe, their fazer blasters extended in front of them. A nearby alien bot, its tall white body rolling toward Abe menacingly, intoned, "Capture the flag." Abe ducked behind a half wall and watched the bot's helmet pass by. Abe thought the Fazer Blast helmets, with antennae extending from them, made everyone look like upright bees.

This alien bot was functioning correctly. Players in the Fazer Blast arena were tasked with working through the course to capture several flags. They had to do so without being "killed." According to the work order Abe had received, one of the alien bots was glitching. Instead of saying "Resistance is futile," as its programming intended, it was saying "Resistance is pizza." Abe couldn't help but wonder if one of the programmers was having a little fun.

To get into the Fazer Blast arena, Abe had passed through the staging area, where players picked up their blasters, helmets, and other gear. In that area, players were given team designations as well. Abe hadn't geared up yet. In addition to his Pizzaplex uniform shirt, he was wearing a bright red vest marked MAINTENANCE. In spite of that, kids had attempted to shoot him. Abe waved them off and continued his search for the malfunctioning alien bot.

Abe found it guarding the last flag that players had to capture before reaching the winner's elevator, which took players to the Superstar lounge. After Abe deactivated the bot and reprogrammed the bot's script, he retraced his steps to the staging area. Joining the orange team, he donned his helmet and picked up a blaster. Now he could have a little fun.

Following a couple of giggling girls, Abe trotted into the arena and headed for the first flag. He'd played this game enough that he was pretty good at it, but the alien bots were programmed to vary their routines, and every game was different. This was why one of the bots managed to get the jump on Abe. He had to pivot and dive to avoid getting shot.

Unfortunately, Abe's rubber sole caught on the carpet, and he careened around a wall and tumbled down the ramp leading to a lower section of the arena. His ankle twisted so violently that Abe cried out.

A scruffy-haired boy not more than ten years old rushed over to Abe. "Are you okay, sir?"

Abe already felt like an idiot. Sir? Now he felt old, too.

"I'm fine," Abe said, rubbing his ankle. He spotted an alien bot over the boy's shoulder. "You'd better look out."

The boy whirled and fired off a shot. Then he scampered down the ramp and disappeared. Abe took off his helmet and gingerly got to his feet as he watched the bot pursue the boy. He tested his twisted ankle. Pain shot up his leg, but the ankle held.

His dignity in shambles, Abe limped out of the arena. It looked like he'd be doing paperwork for the rest of the day.

The Bobbiedots made a big deal of Abe's swollen ankle. Olive described in great detail the mechanism of a twisted ankle and the appropriate treatment for it while Rose provided the ice and the wrap that Abe needed to bring the swelling down. Gemini played soothing music and cued up a distracting sci-fi movie—one with a romantic subplot, of course. Abe ate his spinach lasagna dinner sitting on the sofa with his feet up while the Bobbiedots clustered around him and repeatedly asked him how he was feeling. Although their questions and comments on his well-being made it challenging to watch the movie, he enjoyed the concern. Abe went to bed feeling well cared for. He was so relaxed that he went right to sleep.

A couple hours later, though, Abe was wide awake. He sat up in his bed. What had awakened him so abruptly?

Abe rubbed his eyes and looked around. All he saw were the dark outlines of the room's furniture. Nothing was out of place. Nothing was moving.

So why were the hairs on Abe's arms standing on end?

Abe opened his mouth, intending to call out to the Bobbiedots, but he quickly thought better of it. What if someone was in the apartment?

Had he been found out?

Abe remained still and listened.

At first, Abe heard nothing but distant traffic noise, but then he heard something closer. It was a very soft sound, like material brushing against something. Abe held his breath and concentrated. The sound shifted in tone. Instead of a gentle rustle, it became a quiet rasp. The sound was low, but it was long and steady. The image of a snake slithering across the carpet suddenly popped into Abe's head.

Abe went rigid. He hated snakes.

Abe's fear of unseen reptiles erased any nervousness about being seen or heard. He spoke up. "Bobbiedots, turn on the lights."

Rose immediately materialized on the glass panel near Abe's bed. His bedside lamp came on. Abe looked around his room. Everything looked normal. Beyond the glass walls, the rest of the apartment was dark.

"Did you want a midnight snack?" Rose asked.

Abe shook his head. "I thought I heard something."

"Sometimes I hear food calling out to me," Rose said.

Olive materialized next to Rose. Her green eyes studied Abe intently. "Did you have a nightmare? Studies have shown that sensory experiences from nightmares can delude a person into thinking the nightmare has turned into reality."

Abe thought for a second. Did a nightmare wake him up? He didn't think so. If he'd had a nightmare, he'd already forgotten it.

"Is the apartment secure?" Abe asked the Bobbiedots.

Rose nodded several times. Her hot-pink pigtails were distractingly bright; Abe's eyes hadn't yet adjusted to the light. "Everything's totally cool."

Abe listened.

The sound was gone.

Abe shook his head. Maybe he'd imagined the sound. Well, he was awake. He might as well pee before he went back to sleep.

Abe swung his legs off the bed. Remembering his ankle, he hesitantly put his weight on it. It was sore, but it held up just fine. Olive's instructions on how to wrap an ankle had served Abe well. Wearing just the pajama bottoms he slept in, he shuffled toward the bathroom.

Before he reached the bathroom, Olive turned its lights on low. "Thanks," Abe said. He went into the bathroom and shut the door.

Although the bathroom's walls were half glass like those of the bedroom and the Bobbiedots had access to the glass screens in here, Abe had instructed them to give him complete privacy in the bathroom unless he stated otherwise. Abe stepped over to the toilet. He started to do his thing, but suddenly, he felt a prickle at the back of his neck. He was sure he was being watched.

Abe looked around the small tiled room. The glass screens that walled the space were dark.

Abe finished his business and glanced around again. The feeling of being observed hadn't gone away. Abe quickly flushed the toilet and left the bathroom. As he figured they would be, the Bobbiedots were waiting for him in the bedroom.

"How is the ankle?" Gemini asked. Her blue-tipped antennae canted to the left as she tilted her head to look at Abe's ankle.

"Huh? Oh, it's fine." Abe rubbed the back of his neck and surveyed the bedroom. He and the Bobbiedots were alone.

"Uh, do you record my movements?" Abe asked the Bobbiedots.

"We are attuned to your movements so as to be available should you need us," Olive answered, adjusting her glasses. "But no record is made of your activities."

Abe nodded. "So, you're not watching me?"

"Not in the way I believe you mean," Olive said. "We don't observe you. We simply respond to you."

"Do you do anything at night? Cleaning or whatever?" Abe asked. Maybe the Bobbiedots had been doing something that made the sound Abe had heard.

"We're dormant at night unless we're summoned," Olive said.

"Are you sure you don't want a snack?" Rose asked.

Abe shook his head. He got back in bed. "Go ahead and turn the light out, Rose," he said.

Rose sighed, but she turned out the light. All the Bobbiedots said, "Good night," and then they were gone.

Abe lay in the darkness and listened. He knew he was probably making a big deal over nothing. Even so, he couldn't ignore what he was feeling.

Eventually, he closed his eyes. Unsettled but tired enough to ignore it, he went back to sleep.

★ ★ ★

The next night, Abe again woke abruptly. He looked at the clock. It was almost 1:00 a.m., about the same time he had woken up the night before.

And he was hearing the same noise, too. It was a whispery shuffle, like the sound of something being dragged over carpet.

Abe got out of bed.

Tonight, Abe didn't ask for lights. He wasn't sure why, but he felt like he needed to investigate the sound on his own.

Abe tiptoed toward his bedroom door. Pausing there, he listened. The sound was a little farther away, but it was still there.

Abe eased the bedroom door open. He looked out into the sitting area.

Although the apartment's lights were off, the moon outside the window was full. The moon's glow, combined with the unceasing neon glare from the adjacent Pizzaplex, provided enough light for Abe to see his surroundings. He quickly looked for movement. He didn't see any.

But he could still hear the sound. And the sound definitely indicated movement. Something was in motion. But what?

Abe slowly, cautiously padded toward the sofa. He didn't see anything that shouldn't have been there.

He heard something, though. It was a muted *whish*, almost like the sound of fabric caught in a light breeze.

Abe looked to the window. It was closed. He cocked his head and examined the air vents on the walls. His apartment had central heat and cooling, but neither was on right now. The air felt still. So what was making that fluttering sound?

Abe took a step toward the dining room, but he stopped abruptly when the sound changed. It had become a muffled scrape, like something rubbing against something hard, like the surface of the wall. It sounded as if something was moving *up* the wall. And the sound was close. Too close.

The rubbing sound was followed by a tap. Then Abe heard a muffled *whump*. Again, it was very, very close.

"Lights!" Abe called out.

He wasn't sure if his one-word command would work. He'd never tried it before. But it did.

All the lights in the apartment came on. Abe looked around. He was alone . . . except for the Bobbiedots, who now surrounded him on nearby glass panels.

"What is it?" Olive, glowing green, asked.

"Snack time?" Rose, pulsing hot pink, asked.

"Are you bored? Do you need some entertainment?" Gemini, radiating blue, asked.

Abe blinked against the barrage of bright color. He rotated slowly. He frowned. Then he remembered the direction of the sound. It had been going up the wall.

Abe looked up. The trapdoor he'd noticed earlier was right above him. Had whatever he'd heard gone through that door?

Abe shifted to look at the door more closely.

"I think we need a snack," Rose said.

Abe sighed and glared at Rose. "Okay, fine. I'll have a snack. But tell me what the door is for." He went to one of the kitchen cabinets and got out a package of whole-grain, high-fiber, fruit-sweetened oatmeal raisin cookies. He'd had one last night; it was better than he'd expected it to be.

Abe sat at the table with his cookie. Rose joined him. She had a dozen cookies on a plate in front of her.

"So, spill," Abe said. "You obviously know something about that." He pointed at the trapdoor.

"We are second-generation Bobbiedots," Olive said.

"Gen2s for short," Rose said around a mouthful of cookie.

Olive curled her lip at her cohort, but she nodded. "That's right. We're known as the gen2s. The gen1s preceded us. The door is for the gen1s."

Abe stared at the trapdoor. "And what are the gen1s?"

Olive spoke up. "The gen1s were the first generation of apartment helpers in this building. Unlike us, they were actual, physical robots."

Abe's cookie got stuck in his throat. "Like animatronics?"

Gemini nodded. "Although they could move around the apartment more freely than we can because they weren't confined to screens, they were limited by their cables."

"Cables?"

"They're plugged into a grid up in the crawl space above the ceiling," Gemini explained. "They have to remain tethered to be functional. Poor things. I can't even imagine. It would be like being tied up."

Abe set aside his half-eaten cookie. He studied the trapdoor. "And they're still up there?"

Rose nodded enthusiastically. "Yep."

"They're not tasked with apartment care anymore," Olive said. "That privilege lies with us now. They're out of date, and unfortunately, they've been damaged."

"It's very sad," Gemini said. "They're so limited. But they still try."

"What do you mean they 'try'?" Abe asked.

Rose wiped holographic crumbs off her face. "Oh, they still try to fulfill their commands. Sometimes, they

come out of the crawl space and attempt to 'help out.'"
She put the last two words in air quotes.

"Help out?" Abe repeated. His voice had a noticeably
higher pitch than normal.

"Are you okay?" Rose asked. "Your blood pressure has
gone up."

"I'm fine," Abe said.

He was lying. He wasn't fine at all.

There were robots in his ceiling? And they came out
sometimes to "help out"?

"Why haven't they been removed?" Abe asked. "I
mean, if they're out of date and damaged, why are they
still up there?"

"Oh, they just want to try to help," Gemini said.

"We feel bad for them, so we let them do what they can,
even if it usually creates more work for us," Olive said.

"Even Bobbiedots have emotions, you know," Rose said.

All three Bobbiedots gave Abe a long look. He nodded
several times. "Of course you do."

He cleared his throat and stood. "I need to get back
to sleep."

Abe glanced up at the trapdoor again. It was still
closed. Even so, Abe's stomach clenched.

He took a deep breath and headed for the bedroom.
"Go ahead and turn off all the lights after I'm in bed,
please," he told the Bobbiedots.

"Okay," Rose called out.

"Good night," they all sang out.

Abe hurried to his bed, dived under the covers, and
pulled his blanket up to his chin. He stared at the darkened ceiling.

Was he really safer in this apartment than he had been
in his rubber tire fort?

★ ★ ★

Abe had to admit that he was kind of enjoying eating healthier food. He seemed to have more energy, and his head felt clearer. Consequently, he didn't mind that Rose had now prepared for him lists of acceptable foods, and she set out daily menus for him. Today's menu included an apple to go with his whole-wheat toast and two scrambled eggs.

Abe finished his breakfast while Olive wrapped up her reading of the day's current events against a backdrop of the music Gemini had started, which sounded like Celtic piano music. It was fine, but it wasn't something he would have chosen. Abe wasn't sure Gemini's parameters were set quite right. She seemed to be more interested in music and movies that she liked instead of what he preferred.

Although Rose provided all Abe's healthy food, she didn't limit herself to his nutritious choices. This morning, she was wolfing down two large cinnamon rolls.

Abe walked over to the sink and shoved his apple core down into the garbage disposal. As soon as he put his hand past the rubber cover, the disposal came on.

Abe yelped and whipped his hand up. "Hey!" he yelled.

Abe looked at the garbage disposal switch. It was on.

He hadn't touched it.

"Rose," Abe said, "why did you turn the garbage disposal on?"

Rose looked up. "Did I?" Her huge eyes looked even bigger than usual. She had cinnamon roll frosting on her upper lip.

"It came on," Abe snapped, "while my hand was in it."

Rose's lower lip quivered. "You're mad at me."

Abe immediately felt bad. He looked at his hand. It was fine. His fingers had been above the disposal's grinding mechanism.

"I'm not mad," Abe said.

And he wasn't. He was just . . . what? Worried? Scared?

Why had the disposal come on? Was it a short? Or was it a hiccup in Rose's programming?

Either way, there wasn't much Abe could do about it at the moment. He sure couldn't call anyone to look into the problem. He wasn't supposed to be in this apartment, so any issues it had were ones he had to deal with himself.

"You look upset," Gemini said. She touched her blue-tipped headset. "How about some soothing music?"

Something with a lot of violins started playing. Abe wanted to plug his ears.

"No music!"

The music stopped. Gemini's blue lips pursed into a pout.

"You're getting on his nerves," Olive said to Gemini. "Not everyone likes romantic stuff as much as you do." Olive flitted across the glass screen to get closer to Abe. Her green glow made Abe blink.

"I think what you need is a nice, long soak," Olive said.

Abe thought about the roof's hot tub. If only.

"Your tub is jetted," Rose said as if she'd read his mind.

The Bobbiedots couldn't read his thoughts . . . could they?

Abe hadn't noticed that his tub was jetted. He'd barely glanced at it; he'd only used the walk-in shower.

But a jetted tub bath was a good substitute for a soak in a hot tub. "That sounds good," Abe said.

"I'll get it going," Olive said.

Abe heard the sound of water running in the bathroom. "Thanks." He headed toward the bedroom.

The Bobbiedots followed Abe, moving from screen to screen. In the bedroom, they clustered on the screen next to the bathroom door.

Abe looked at the hovering Bobbiedots. "Some privacy, please."

"This means lunch will be late, doesn't it?" Rose asked, only the hint of a whine in her voice.

"Just a little," Abe said.

"I guess I'll survive," Rose said.

Gemini and Olive sighed.

All three Bobbiedots disappeared.

A few minutes later, Abe was soaking up to his shoulders. Still not interested in being alone with his thoughts, Abe had brought a paperback mystery novel into the tub with him. He stretched out and let the water beat the tension out of his muscles while he lost himself in the fictional detective's investigation.

Abe was so caught up in the whodunit that he didn't notice the water was getting hotter until sweat dripped off his nose and landed on the page he was reading. He frowned and put his hand in the water. It definitely felt hotter. Did it have a thermostat?

"Rose," Abe said, "could you please turn down the temperature of the water?"

Rose popped up on the nearest glass panel. "Oh good, are you getting out soon? The food is—"

"I'll be a little longer, I think. I just need the temperature lowered."

Rose sniffed, nodded, and disappeared.

Abe settled back, but then he squirmed. The water got even hotter.

"I said down, not up," he said.

Rose didn't appear.

And the water got hotter.

Too hot.

Way too hot.

Wincing in pain, Abe scrambled out of the tub. He'd barely gotten out of the water before it began to boil.

Feeling like his skin was on fire, Abe flopped onto the plush gray bath mat next to the tub. He stared in horror at his bright red lower body. As he stared, his feet swelled.

Beyond Abe's feet, the water in the tub bubbled violently. The water's agitation was far beyond any that the jets could create. The water in the tub was in a full rolling boil.

Abe quickly sprang up and reached into the shower enclosure. Turning on the cold water . . . and testing it to be sure it *was* cold . . . he jumped under the frigid spray. He shrieked at the shock of the cold. And he bellowed, "Rose!"

Rose appeared on the shower's glass enclosure. "What's the matter? Why are you in the shower?"

"The water in the tub started boiling!" Abe hissed through his clenched teeth, covering himself with a towel.

Olive popped up next to Rose. She leaned forward. Her green eyes were big behind her glasses as she studied Abe's skin. "It appears you have a superficial dermal burn. A topical application of aloe vera or an antibiotic ointment is recommended. Don't stay under the cold water for too long. It could bring on shock."

Rose fluttered her hands. "Oh dear. Your poor freckles are even pinker than my pigtails. There's aloe vera gel in the medicine cabinet."

Abe turned off the shower and got out. Doing his best to ignore his skin's screaming nerve endings, he crossed to the medicine cabinet. Sure enough, a large bottle of aloe vera sat on the top shelf. He grabbed it and began slathering it all over his legs and feet and lower torso. As he did, he heard the continued burble and pop of the boiling bathwater.

"Turn that off and empty the tub!" Abe yelled at Rose.

The jets immediately quieted. The water started to drain.

"You don't have to yell at me." Rose wiped one of her big pink eyes. "I need fudge," she said in a small voice. She disappeared.

Abe immediately felt like a jerk. It wasn't Rose's fault the water boiled. Right?

"I'm sorry," he called out.

"Oh, don't worry about her," Gemini said. "She's so sensitive."

Abe concentrated on rubbing in the aloe vera. The pain started to abate. He managed to pull on his robe, shuffle to his bed, and lie down. He stared at the ceiling, but he didn't see it. All he could see was the image of the boiling water in his tub.

"Rose!" Abe called out. "I'm sorry I yelled."

Rose popped into view on the panel by the bed. She was eating chocolate fudge. "It's okay," she said thickly.

"No," Abe said. "It's not. You're very sweet, and I appreciate everything you do. I was just in pain, and I was panicked, and I took it out on you."

Rose nodded. She licked chocolate off her fingers. "I understand."

Abe closed his eyes and took a deep breath. When he opened his eyes, Rose had a new piece of fudge in her hands.

"Can you tell me why the water boiled?" Abe asked.

Rose quirked her mouth. "I'm really sorry. It was the gen1s."

"But I didn't see a gen1," Abe protested. He hadn't had his eyes closed in the tub. He'd been reading. He'd have noticed if a robot had come in.

Olive appeared next to Rose. "The gen1s' cables occasionally get tangled with the power systems and plumbing lines in the apartment," Olive said. "They interrupt the apartment's proper functioning."

Abe frowned. No wonder the apartment was off-limits.

"What can be done about it?" Abe asked.

All three Bobbiedots shrugged.

Abe sighed. He pondered the notion of going up into the crawl space to see what he could do about the gen1s. He immediately shivered. The idea of facing damaged robots in a small, dark space wasn't at all appealing.

But . . . he had to do something.

"It seems like what we need is a system update," Abe said. "That might remove whatever is causing these glitches."

Olive fiddled with her glasses. "We aren't programmed for updates."

"What if I manually initiate a system update?" Abe suggested.

Gemini looked at Olive and Rose. All three Bobbiedots shook their heads.

"There aren't any updates available," Olive said.

Abe felt a headache coming on. The pounding warred with his stinging skin.

"Then what can I do?" Abe asked.

Rose polished off her fudge. She looked at Gemini and Olive. "How about we set up monitoring protocols to keep an eye on what the gen1s are doing?"

Gemini and Olive nodded. "We can do that," Olive said. She pointed at Abe. "And you can help by telling us in advance what you're going to do so we can make sure everything is functioning properly."

Abe nodded. "Sure."

"Yay," Rose said. "Can we start cooking now?"

Abe groaned. "In a bit. Let me just lie here for a while."

"Oh," Rose said. "Okay."

Abe closed his eyes. Trying to ignore his throbbing skin, Abe took comfort in knowing that the Bobbiedots would try to help protect him from the apartment's problems. But it wasn't a lot of comfort.

The truth was that Abe was more than a little freaked out.

What if he'd fallen asleep in the tub? He could have been boiled alive.

He opened his eyes and looked around the room.

"Even the greener grass has weeds," he whispered. His mom was right.

Speaking of his mom . . . Abe sat up and reached for his laptop. He opened his email. He stretched his fingers over the keyboard and typed, *Hi, Mom.*

Then he stopped. What was he going to tell her about his day? He sure wasn't going to tell her about what had happened. *Hey, Mom, I nearly had my hand chewed off by a garbage disposal and I was almost boiled alive* didn't seem like a good idea.

Abe thought for several minutes. Finally, he started typing.

> *Tonight was spaghetti night at the care center, right? I know you love spaghetti, like I do. Tonight was bath night, too, I think. I hope you had a nice relaxing bath. I had a good hot bath tonight, Mom. And when I got out, the Bobbiedots gave me something nice for my skin. They're really taking care of me.*

Abe rolled his eyes at the omissions in his story. But he didn't lie.

Abe ended his email and looked around his bedroom. He sighed. No matter what he told (or didn't tell) his mom, he had to admit to himself that the apartment that had felt like a sanctuary no longer felt safe. He couldn't help but wonder what was going to happen next.

Abe was teaching Preston how to fix a generator in the Pizzaplex day care. Or at least, that was what he was supposed to be doing. Unfortunately, Abe was so distracted that Preston was learning all the wrong ways to fix the generator.

"Why are the generators in the play structures?" Preston asked.

Abe looked up from the generator he was kneeling in front of. "Huh?"

The area around them was shrouded in darkness. Only their flashlights illuminated the generator.

"I mean, it just seems like a weird place to put a generator, here where the kids are playing," Preston said.

Abe shrugged. He gestured at the chaotic and colorful play area around them. "Does anything about this make sense?"

Preston shook his head, but he didn't say anything. He clearly thought criticizing his new workplace was a bad idea.

Filled with screaming kids, the day care was a carnival-like space filled with climbing structures, caves, rope bridges, ball pits, slides, and all manner of contraptions for kids to explore. That in itself wasn't so odd. What Abe thought was strange was that the entire day care was overseen by an animatronic attendant with a dual personality, sort of a (not) kid-friendly Dr. Jekyll/Mr. Hyde.

In its happy incarnation, the attendant was the Sun. That character had a somewhat deformed, round grinning face surrounded by yellow triangles clearly intended to mimic the "rays" of the sun. The Sun wore billowy red-and-yellow-striped pants and was clownlike in his appearance and demeanor. But he had a dark side called the Moon. And the dark side was literal. If the lights went out in the day care, the Sun morphed into a leering moonfaced "clown" wearing dark blue billowy pants dotted with yellow stars. The Moon would stalk around the day care admonishing the children: "You've been very naughty."

Abe handed Preston a wrench and pointed at a connection. "Tighten that."

Preston obeyed. As he did, he glanced around at the darkness that surrounded them.

"After the day care was completed," Abe said, "the designers realized there was a flaw in the lighting plan. The lights kept shorting out. It wasn't dangerous or anything. Not a fire hazard. Just a darkness issue. The easiest and cheapest fix was to install backup generators. They decided on five of them to be sure the area got full coverage. By then, all the installations were in place, and the climbing structures were the only locations that would conceal the generators."

Preston grunted and mumbled. "Doesn't seem very safe."

"Neither does an animatronic attendant that turns mean when the lights go out," Abe said.

"Yeah, what's up with that anyway?" Preston asked. He again checked the darkness that pressed in on them.

Abe sighed. "The Sun robot was an old stage animatronic. Part of its theatrical schtick was to turn evil when the stage lights went off. When it was reprogrammed to be the day care attendant, the performance functions were taken out, but the darkness trigger couldn't be removed.

That, combined with the occasional blackouts in the day care, created the Moon side of the attendant, which results in several undesirable behaviors." Abe shook his head. "Apparently, they had meetings about what to do, and they decided that fixing Sun was more trouble than it was worth. It's cheaper to just make sure the lights stay on."

Preston finished with the connection. "What about those wires?" He pointed.

Abe groaned. "Jeez. Sorry. We needed to reroute those before we tightened that connection I had you tighten. You have to undo what you just did."

Preston shrugged. "Okay."

"Sorry," Abe said again. "I'm a little distracted today."

Right as Abe spoke, the Moon's glowing eyes cut through the darkness. They peered into the climbing structure. "You've been a naughty boy," he said.

You don't know the half of it, Abe thought.

Abe had been naughty for sure when he'd inserted himself into the off-limits apartment. And now he was paying the price. When Abe had first checked out his apartment and found the hot sauce, he'd figured he could handle any issues the apartment had. When he'd heard the sounds in the night and then found out they were caused by malfunctioning robots, he was spooked, but he'd figured he could handle that situation, too. His job, after all, included dealing with animatronic break-downs. When his fingers had been very nearly mangled by the garbage disposal, he'd been rattled, but he'd decided, "No harm, no foul."

The boiling bath was another story. Abe was still sore this morning, despite the aloe. He couldn't downplay the boiling water. He couldn't delude himself anymore.

Abe was in danger. Serious danger.

But what could he do?

Any reasonable person would move out of the apartment. He knew that. Having a cushy place to live wasn't worth serious injury, or even death.

But having a cushy place wasn't the issue. The issue was having a place, period. If Abe moved out of the apartment, where would he go? Even with the raise that came with his promotion, he didn't have enough money saved up to rent an apartment, and now that he was sleeping in a real bed again and eating delicious food, he couldn't even imagine going back to being homeless and living on discarded pizza. No, he really didn't have an option. However dangerous his place might be, he had to stay there for now.

All he had to figure out was how to survive it. He'd been chewing on that problem throughout the morning, and all he could think to do was to stay alert and be prepared. That wasn't a very satisfying solution.

Preston finished undoing the connection and looked at the Moon warily. "How do I reroute the wiring?" he asked Abe.

Abe leaned in and showed Preston the little electrical trick he'd taught himself when he first took the Pizzaplex job. "It's a sort of bypass of the grounding wire," Abe explained. "See?"

The generator kicked in. The lights around them came on.

Preston noticeably relaxed as the Moon retreated. "That's pretty cool," Preston said.

In spite of his dark thoughts, Abe smiled. Yeah, it was pretty cool. Abe might have been naughty, but he was capable.

Abe's dark mood brightened.

He wasn't totally helpless. He had tech knowledge.

Whatever the apartment threw at him, he had the smarts to handle it. With the Bobbiedots helping him, he'd be okay.

Or at least he hoped he'd be.

Abe made it through the rest of his week without incident, and he was more than a little relieved when Saturday rolled around. Rodin had called that morning asking if Abe wanted to hang out, but Abe said he was busy. The day was dark and rainy, a perfect day to stay in and read . . . and maybe sip some tea. How much trouble could he get into with a book and a cup of tea?

After grabbing his novel, Abe wandered into the kitchen. The Bobbiedots, chatty as usual, followed him.

"I don't like rain," Olive said. "It causes SAD." She flicked her green pigtails.

"You mean it makes you sad?" Abe asked.

"No, I mean it causes SAD. Seasonal Affective Disorder. The lack of natural light dampens the mood."

Gemini's blue-lipped mouth opened wide as she laughed. "Dampens. That's a good one."

Rose giggled. "I get it. Rain. Dampens." She clapped her pink-tipped hands and squealed. "Oh, I know what you should do, Abe. You should bake cookies. Rainy days are great for baking."

"What do you care if he bakes cookies?" Gemini asked. "You can't eat any of them."

Rose stuck her tongue out at Gemini. "You're mean."

"Cookies actually sound pretty good," Abe said. "I'll make some tea to go with them."

"Yay!" Rose clapped her hands.

Abe smiled and headed to the kitchen.

A stainless-steel teakettle sat on the gas cookstove. Abe picked it up, crossed to the sink, filled the kettle with water, and returned to the stove. He reached across the stove to set the kettle on the largest burner.

The burner under his arm flared on—even though he was nowhere near the burner's knobs. Abe was wearing a long-sleeved hoodie, and his sleeve caught fire.

Abe's reaction was instant. He whipped the hoodie off and smothered the flames against the countertop. The fire was out a couple seconds after it started.

But still . . .

Abe looked at his arm. The hairs on his forearm were singed black, and his skin was pinkish. Not as pink as his legs had been after the tub incident, but pink.

"Run water over it!" Rose commanded.

The sink faucet came on. Abe stuck his arm under the flow of cool water.

"So much for a nice, safe tea party," Abe said.

"There's more aloe vera in the cabinet to your left," Rose said.

"In here?" Abe asked.

"I figured after the tub thing, you'd want it handy. Just in case." Rose clasped her hands and looked at Abe with earnest concern.

"Thanks." Abe reached for the aloe vera and spread it over his arm.

Abe looked at the hovering Bobbiedots. "Uh, I thought you were going to monitor things to stop these sorts of incidents. I did my part. I told you I was going to make tea."

The Bobbiedots exchanged chastised looks. "We're really sorry," Gemini said.

"We feel awful," Rose said.

"It's just that preventing problems isn't as easy as it sounds," Olive said.

"It's the gen1s," Gemini said.

"They have access to our displays," Olive said.

"Yeah," Rose said. "They can mess with our programming and make things turn on when they shouldn't."

Abe stared at the three Bobbiedots. Really? The damaged robots could get into the holographic systems?

"Great," Abe muttered. "That's just great."

"But we'll keep trying," Rose said eagerly.

"Yes," Gemini agreed. "We won't stop!"

"We'll do everything we can," Olive said.

"Thanks," Abe said. He didn't say out loud that he no longer had a lot of faith in the Bobbiedots' efforts.

Two blessedly uneventful days passed. Abe spent most of the next day, Sunday, in bed. His feet hurt. His skin was still sore. His mood was low. He read all day, and, to Rose's chagrin, he barely ate. Monday, he went to work and was so busy that he didn't have time to think about the apartment. For a brief interval, his life felt normal. Until he went home at the end of the day.

Abe had worked two hours late, and the sun was down before he got home. When he opened his door, he immediately requested, "Lights, please."

No lights came on.

Abe tried again. "Olive? Can you turn on the lights?" Nothing.

Abe sighed. Well, he wasn't so spoiled that he couldn't manage to switch on his own lights. Abe shut his door and reached for the light switch.

As soon as Abe's fingers touched the switch, electricity surged. Abe was thrown back away from the wall. He hit the sofa and tumbled head over heels onto the floor. His forehead hit the coffee table as he went.

Abe lay on the floor, moaning. His fingers felt like they were being stabbed by a million tiny needles. His head pounded and buzzed. He was nauseous.

Lying on his back, Abe carefully moved his arms and legs. Okay. He seemed to be okay. Besides the whack on the head and the painful tingles, he felt like himself and his body seemed to be working properly.

"Rose?" Abe called out.

The Bobbiedots appeared on the glass panel above Abe.

"What just happened?" Abe asked.

"I didn't know you were interested in gymnastics," Gemini said. "I can add that to your entertainment preferences if you'd like."

Abe took a deep breath. "Olive, what happened with the lights?"

Olive fiddled with her glasses. "I'm so sorry. It was my gen1 counterpart. She hijacked my control of the lights. I heard your command, but I couldn't respond."

"Okay," Abe said, even though it wasn't okay at all. He sat up. "What are we going to do about this?"

Olive pressed her green lips together. It looked like she was concentrating deeply. After a couple seconds, she nodded. "There. I rerouted the light controls so she can't get to them again."

"Great," Abe said. He managed to get to his feet. "I'm going to lie down for a bit. I'll have dinner later."

"Not too late, I hope," Rose said.

Abe didn't feel like eating a full dinner, so he ignored Rose's nutritional lecture and made himself a tuna sandwich. His mom had made him a lot of tuna sandwiches when he was a kid. He'd missed this comfort food when he was living solely on pizza.

Halfway through his sandwich, Abe looked at the Bobbiedots. "We need to have a household meeting."

"Meetings are good," Olive said. "It's a useful way to discuss strategies and make plans."

"I'm glad you approve," Abe said.

"We can't have a meeting with just a sandwich, can we?" Rose protested. "Can we have snacks, too?"

"Knock yourself out," Abe said.

Rose frowned and cocked her head.

"That means 'go for it,'" Abe explained.

"Oh goody! Let's have popcorn!" Rose said.

"That's the perfect snack for you," Gemini said to Rose. "It's as full of air as you are."

Rose ignored the jibe. She smiled in delight at the bowl of popcorn that suddenly appeared before her.

"Okay," Abe said. "Here's the deal. I think I need to take charge of what's going on here." He leaned forward and made sure the three Bobbiedots were paying attention. They were—even Rose, who ate her popcorn with her gaze fixed firmly on Abe.

"I'd like to talk to the gen1s directly," Abe said. "Maybe I can reason with them."

"They're too messed up to understand reason," Gemini said.

"Loony toony," Rose said.

"Well, maybe if I can get to them, I can reprogram them," Abe said.

The Bobbiedots shook their heads in unison. Their bright ponytails flapped around them.

"You can't get into their crawl space," Olive said. "It's locked."

"I could cut through the trapdoor," Abe said.

"It has a steel plate above it," Olive said.

Abe sighed. "Okay, well, why do the gen1s want to hurt me, anyway? What did I do to them?"

"I don't think they mean to hurt you," Gemini said. "It's just that they're inept."

Olive shook her head. "I think it's possible they may be acting with malice. The gen1s are close enough to human form that it's reasonable to assume they're envious of you."

"Envious?" Abe said.

"Envy is the personal pain that results when a being desires the advantages of someone else," Olive said.

"I know what envy is. But envy requires a level of self-awareness that I didn't think animatronics have."

"The gen1s are pretty advanced," Gemini said.

"Not as advanced as us," Olive said.

"Obviously," Rose said.

"I'd be glad to research the varying manifestations of envy if you'd like," Olive said.

Abe shook his head.

"I think the gen1s think you're Landon," Rose said.

Abe looked at her. "What makes you say that?"

Rose shrugged. "I don't know. It just popped into my mind."

"Why would the gen1s want to hurt Landon?" Abe asked.

"Landon didn't have freckles," Gemini said.

"Oh, well, that explains it," Abe said.

He chuckled. He shook his head, amazed that he was actually having fun, even in the midst of the serious circumstances. The Bobbiedots were a hoot, and he enjoyed them. At least he wasn't in this dire situation alone.

Abe reached for the last of his sandwich, but as he did, his stomach roiled. A wave of cramping gripped his intestines. "Whoa," he breathed. He pressed a hand to his belly.

"You're still hungry, right?" Rose said. "Are you sure you don't want to heat up enchiladas?"

Abe's stomach heaved at the very thought of enchiladas. He shook his head.

The cramping was replaced by a swell of nausea. It felt like the tuna sandwich was trying to come back up. Abe breathed slowly, but the nausea didn't abate. It got worse.

Abe shot out of his chair. "I'm going to be sick."

The Bobbiedots followed Abe, from glass panel to glass panel, as he dashed toward the bathroom. They all chattered at the same time.

"Nausea can be caused by a number of conditions," Olive said. "Bacteria and viruses are common causes, but others include vertigo, ear infections, intestinal blockages, liver failure, meningitis, and migraines."

"If you don't feel good, how about some music?" Gemini said over the top of Olive's laundry list of ailments. "Piano, maybe? Or some nice classical strings? Or would you rather have something more upbeat to distract you?"

What sounded like tribal drums began playing from the speakers. Abe couldn't open his mouth to protest.

"Are you going to eat the rest of your sandwich?" Rose asked while Olive and Gemini tried to be helpful.

Abe reached the bathroom just in time. He dropped to the floor in front of the toilet and violently ejected his tuna sandwich. The stink of the partly digested tuna and accompanying bile triggered another wave of vomit. Abe's stomach heaved, and his body gave up the last of the sandwich, the water he'd drunk with the sandwich, and more yellowish bile. A couple of dry heaves followed, and finally, Abe collapsed on the bathroom floor.

The toilet flushed. "Thanks, Rose," he managed.

"Poor baby," Rose said. "You lost your sandwich. I think you should make another one."

Abe's stomach lurched at the very thought. He groaned.

"Oh, shut up, you dolt," Olive said to Rose. "He doesn't need more food. He needs to hydrate. Humans require water to support their biologic functions. Water helps humans get rid of toxins."

The sink faucet came on. Abe didn't move.

"Peppermint can soothe the stomach," Olive said.

"Oh, mints," Rose said. "I like the ones covered in chocolate."

"I'm not talking about candy," Olive said. "He needs peppermint capsules. Or essential oils."

"I don't think the drums are helping," Gemini said. "Let's try jazz. That might perk you up."

The drums gave way to the sounds of trumpets and saxophones. Abe preferred the drums.

"How about silence?" Abe said.

Gemini emitted an exasperated huff. "Fine." The music stopped.

Abe managed to get to his feet. He stepped to the sink and put his hands in the still-running water. He splashed the water on his face and took a few sips of it. It didn't refresh him as much as he'd hoped it would. He turned off the faucet and left the bathroom. The Bobbiedots followed him. Gemini was sulking. Olive and Rose were still arguing.

"Can you please give me a few minutes alone?" Abe asked.

Gemini let out a "Harrumph" before she disappeared, storming off on the screen. Rose and Olive just went dark.

Abe lay down on his bed and pulled his comforter

up around him. He felt chilled and clammy at the same time. *It's just a touch of stomach flu,* he told himself.

An image of the tuna sandwich flashed through his mind, and his stomach cramped again. He pressed a hand to his stomach. Abe remembered getting food poisoning after he'd eaten some bad chicken a couple years before. What he felt now was similar to what he'd felt then.

No, this wasn't the flu. Something had made him sick. The tuna? Or something else?

Abe sat up. What if he'd been poisoned?

Could the gen1s have put something in his food?

Did the gen1s even exist?

If they didn't, and they didn't poison Abe's food, who did?

What if the Bobbiedots weren't being as helpful as they pretended to be?

Nausea gripped Abe again. He jumped up and ran for the bathroom.

A week later, Abe sat at the desk in his small home office, trying to write an email to his mom. It wasn't going well. Writing around what was really going on was getting harder and harder. He sure couldn't tell her the truth.

How has my apartment tried to kill me? he thought. *Let me count the ways.*

His shower had scalded him a few days before. A cord running to his bedside lamp had nearly strangled him. He'd been tripped by things left out and almost electrocuted multiple times. He'd started moving through his apartment in darkness because he was afraid to touch light switches when the Bobbiedots didn't turn on the lights for him. The tuna sandwich incident had been just the first in a string of similar experiences. He was so sure his food was being poisoned that three nights before, he'd started bringing home takeout for dinner and he only ate sealed packaged foods for breakfast (against Olive's nutritional advice).

Abe started typing. *Because I'm making more money now, I've been treating myself to take-out food. You remember how getting Chinese food in those cartons was always such a treat when I was little?*

Abe stopped and looked at the back of his hands. His skin was tender from the scalding. His head and his muscles and his joints ached. His stomach was skittish. He was a wreck.

Moaning, he sat back in his chair and looked around. He loved having an office in his apartment, and the one he now had in the Pizzaplex was great, too. Abe's new position had come with a larger desk in a semiprivate cubicle. He had a new plush desk chair that didn't squeak, and he had a better view of the Fazplex Tower, where he now lived. This was everything he'd been wanting.

He started typing again. *Mom, I can't believe I'm living the dream I had for so long. I have a nice desk now, with a view of my apartment building. I can't believe I actually live in the Fazplex Tower! It doesn't seem real.*

Abe stopped typing. He couldn't tell his mom what he was really thinking. The truth was that his ideal life had turned into a nightmare.

But what could he do about it?

Abe couldn't move out of the apartment. He had nowhere to go. He couldn't ask for help because he wasn't supposed to be in the apartment in the first place.

Abe's only source of help was the Bobbiedots. The Bobbiedots continued to be fun and attentive, and he *appreciated* them.

Abe typed another few words. *The Bobbiedots are such a big help.*

He stopped.

The Bobbiedots *were* trying to help him, weren't they?

The problem was that Abe was doubting his Bobbiedots more and more. He wasn't so sure they were on his side.

Thinking back over everything that had happened, Abe realized that he'd seen no evidence of the gen1s. For all he knew, the Bobbiedots had made them up.

The Bobbiedots were just so evasive. Abe didn't like the way they tried to distract him from certain questions.

The Bobbiedots also didn't seem to tolerate criticism very well. They got their feelings hurt way too easily. What if they were trying to punish him for his so-called lack of appreciation?

If the Bobbiedots were the ones causing all the problems, Abe was in a world of hurt. He couldn't move out, and without the Bobbiedots on his side, he didn't have any help to deal with the dangers.

Abe was stuck. And alone.

And terrified. How much more could he take?

Abe looked back at his email. *I need to get back to work, Mom,* Abe typed. *I have some planning to do. I love you. Abe.*

Abe hit SEND and closed his laptop. He took a deep breath. He wasn't lying about the planning. He had to find a way to get to the bottom of the Bobbiedots' malfunctions and stop them. The accidents were getting worse and worse. He might not survive the next one. Abe needed to catch the Bobbiedots in their lie and figure out a way to trap them . . . before they killed him.

Exhaling, Abe leaned back in his chair again and closed his eyes. He willed his mind to come up with a way to catch his Bobbiedots in an act of sabotage. How could he outsmart them?

Because his eyes were closed, Abe didn't notice the trailing end of a cable flit past the office doorway. He also didn't see that cable slither upward to disappear through the partly opened trapdoor. He did, however, hear the *click* of the door closing.

Abe's eyes shot open. He leaped out of his chair, hurried into the kitchen, and looked up at the trapdoor. Had he just imagined that sound?

Abe looked around at the darkened Bobbiedot screens. He rubbed away the goose bumps that suddenly covered his arms.

ABOUT THE AUTHORS

Scott Cawthon is the author of the bestselling video game series *Five Nights at Freddy's*, and while he is a game designer by trade, he is first and foremost a storyteller at heart. He is a graduate of the Art Institute of Houston and lives in Texas with his family.

Kelly Parra is the author of YA novels *Graffiti Girl*, *Invisible Touch*, and other supernatural short stories. In addition to her independent works, Kelly works with Kevin Anderson & Associates on a variety of projects. She resides in Central Coast, California, with her husband and two children.

Andrea Rains Waggener is an author, novelist, ghost-writer, essayist, short story writer, screenwriter, copywriter, editor, poet, and a proud member of Kevin Anderson & Associates' team of writers. In a past she prefers not to remember much, she was a claims adjuster, JCPenney's catalog order-taker (before computers!), appellate court clerk, legal writing instructor, and lawyer. Writing in genres that vary from her chick-lit novel, *Alternate Beauty*, to her dog how-to book, *Dog Parenting*, to her self-help book, *Healthy, Wealthy, & Wise*, to ghostwritten memoirs to ghostwritten YA, horror, mystery, and mainstream fiction projects, Andrea still manages to find time to watch the rain and obsess over her dog and her knitting, art, and music projects. She lives with her husband and said dog on the Washington Coast, and if she isn't at home creating something, she can be found walking on the beach.

We don't have time for this," Lucia whispered intently to Adrian.

Adrian looked up from where he knelt, next to Wade, who was doubled up, dry heaving, having already emptied his stomach over a decayed tangle of ripped-off arms and legs. The glistening, partially digested food painted yellow streaks along a mottled forearm crusted with dried blood. The sickening reek of acids and bile cut through the musty smell of the room.

Adrian, his eyes red, his face wet with tears that he was letting run unashamedly down his perfect cheeks, glanced up at Lucia. He nodded once, but he didn't move.

Lucia, struggling to keep her own stomach from unloading its contents next to Wade's, turned to watch the archway that separated the old pizzeria's dining room from its lobby. She winced when Jayce squeezed her hand so hard her knuckles cracked. Jayce had grabbed her hand as they had all ran down the hallway, away from the thing that had killed Hope. His hand was clammy and cold, but

...ear gave his fingers strength. He tugged at Lucia's arm, clearly sharing her desire to move on before the metal monster caught up to them.

Joel suddenly reached down and grabbed Wade by his upper arm. "Come on!" he hissed.

Wade, his six-foot athletic physique diminished by shock and grief, didn't resist as Joel yanked him to his feet. Wade wouldn't have stayed on his feet if Joel hadn't propped him up. And he wouldn't have moved if Joel hadn't started dragging him, like an oversize rag doll toward the back of the vast red-walled room.

"We need to get out of here," Joel said, unnecessarily.

Duh, Lucia thought. She had to stifle a giggle. The slight laughter would have given away how freaked out she was, and she was working hard to look and act like seeing someone ripped apart wasn't that big a deal. *Yeah, keep telling yourself that,* she thought.

Joel continued to half carry Wade past the piles of dismantled animatronic endoskeletons and detached human body parts. Their slapping, skirring footsteps sounded horribly loud, and they echoed through the large, stage-edged room.

Adrian, who had straightened when Joel began manhandling Wade, wiped away his tears. "Where are you going?" he called out softly to Joel.

"Away from here," Joel flung back over his shoulder.

Adrian looked at Lucia and Jayce. Then he stared past Lucia's shoulder, and his brows twitched in something that looked like surprise. Lucia whirled, shivers rippling down her spine, in the sudden conviction that the awful thing had snuck up behind her.

But it hadn't. Adrian was looking at Kelly, who was standing just a foot or so behind Lucia. Kelly's face was unexpectedly placid. She was alert, yes. He...

gaze was fixed on the lobby, but she didn't have the bug-eyed, pasty-skinned look that everyone else had.

Kelly, shy and quiet Kelly, didn't look like someone who had just seen her best friend violently dismembered. *Maybe Kelly was disassociating,* Lucia thought. It was a realistic way to handle severe trauma. But was it one that would keep her alive?

A *crunch* came from the hallway. Not too close. But close enough.

Adrian motioned for Lucia, Jayce, and Kelly to follow him, and he in turn trotted after Joel and Wade, who were heading toward the doorway to the back hallway. As she hurried past a tangle of bar-height stools, Lucia kicked up a cloud of old red confetti. Watching the tiny pieces of paper waft into the air, Lucia tried to tell herself that she and the others would be able to hide from the deadly thing that killed Hope until they could find a way to get out of the abandoned restaurant. But she had a feeling she was lying . . . big time.

Joel hauled Wade into the back hallway. He propped his friend against the wall and held him there with the flat of his hand. He leaned in and got in Wade's face. "Dude! You need to get a grip. You want to die, too?"

Wade, his face smeared with tears, his breath rank and sour, blinked red eyes at Joel. Joel sighed and gave Wade a light head slap. Wade grunted and frowned.

But the head slap worked. Wade shook off Joel and pushed away from the wall. His legs held him. He wiped his face.

Joel exhaled. Good. A sniveling friend wasn't going to be a helpful friend. And Joel knew he would need help if he was going to get out of this hellhole.

Joel was *definitely* going to get out. No way was he going to end up like Hope or like Nick. Before Hope was attacked by the massive metallic creature, she'd told them that the thing had pulled Nick's head off. At the time, Joel had thought she was hysterical. But then he'd seen the creature do the same thing to Hope.

That was *not* going to happen to Joel. No way.

The taps of several footsteps made Joel turn toward the dining room doorway. He wasn't scared. They weren't the creature's footsteps. Those were distinctive. These steps belonged to the others.

Adrian, Jayce, and the two girls clustered together as they joined Joel and Wade. "You okay?" Adrian asked Wade.

Wade nodded. "Sorry, I . . ."

"Forget it," Adrian said. "We're all . . ." He stopped and swallowed hard.

Joel was relieved that was all they said. What good would it do to talk about what just happened?

"What now?" Jayce asked.

The nerdy little artist's voice was squeaky. Joel suppressed an eye roll. He didn't like Jayce and had no idea why Adrian hung out with him. It was embarrassing.

"When Lucia and I were in the office," Kelly spoke up, "we saw an old radio. We might be able to get that working and call for help."

Joel raised an eyebrow. He'd never heard Kelly say more than three or four words at a time. And whenever he'd heard her talk, her voice had always been soft and breathy. Now her voice was strong and smooth . . . confident.

"That's a good idea," Lucia said. "I might be able to jerry-rig it to call out."

"But the office is right next to Parts and Service," Jayce squeaked again.

"That's a good point," Joel said. He hated to agree with the mouse, but Parts and Service was where Hope had died. "And besides," Joel added, "I think it's a better idea to just get out of here. We haven't thoroughly explored that room at the end of the hall. Maybe there's an exit through there." He gestured toward the far end of the hallway.

Adrian shook his head. "We saw that room when we were running around the first time, trying to find a way out. But it's just the systems room. The furnace and all that. There's no way out in there."

Joel scowled. "We didn't try that hard to find a way. We just ran on to the next room, looking for a window that would open. Maybe we missed a crawl space or something."

Adrian pressed his lips together, thinking. Joel thought Adrian looked like a priss when he did that, like stuck-up royalty or something.

A thud sounded from the dining room.

Discussion was over. The whole group began scampering down the hallway, away from the dining room.

The first room off to the right of the hallway was the employees' lounge and locker room. Adrian turned into that room. Lucia, Kelly, and Jayce followed him. Wade started that way, too, but Joel grabbed his arm again.

Wade made a little sound of protest, but he didn't say anything as Joel jerked him away from the employees' lounge and pulled him farther down the hall.

A short way behind him, Joel heard heavy taps interspersed with a hissing rasp. The taps were nearing the hallway's entrance.

"Joel!" Adrian called out.

Joel didn't answer. He kept running, dragging Wade along with him. They had to get to the little room at the end of the hall before the killing thing got to the hallway and spotted them. The others could do whatever they wanted. Forget the stupid old radio. Joel wanted out *Now*. And he was going to find a way.

Lucia grabbed Adrian's arm and pulled him into the employees' lounge. "Let them go," she whispered as she quickly pushed the door closed.

Adrian didn't protest as Lucia led him away from the door. Adrian's self-assurance had left him, she realized. She didn't fault him for that. He had, after all, just watched his girlfriend get murdered by . . . what was the thing anyway? A robot? No, more than that. A monster? No, a creature. Lucia settled on *creature* because it sounded less formidable. She doubted her brain would go for that word trick, but it was worth a try.

But she didn't have time to ponder what to call their adversary. And they didn't have time for shock and grief. They needed to think.

Lucia flicked a couple of dusty, sweaty curls from her eyes. She could only imagine how wild her hair looked. She glanced down. Her long patchwork velour skirt, one of her favorites, was torn and filthy. But that was the least of her problems.

Lucia turned toward Kelly, who was already weaving her way around overturned tables and chairs, kicking up discarded papers that looked like time sheets and shriveled packages of napkins. She headed toward the door on the far side of the room. That door led to the restaurant's front hallway, at the end of which was the office.

Jayce, thankfully, had let go of Lucia's hand when they'd run down the hall. Now he huddled against one of the metal lockers. He hugged himself. His black-rimmed glasses were askew and his mouth hung open, slack. He blinked several times as he fussed with the collar of his checked shirt and straightened the pens in his pocket protector. Nervous twitches.

Outside the closed door, the hissing, rasping taps moved down the hall. The already-dim lights in the staff room went out. Lucia froze and held her breath. She could tell that the others were doing the same thing.

The blackness was so fully complete that Lucia could almost feel it physically, like a viscous cloak enfolding itself around her. A scream tried to claw its way up her throat, but she tamped it down.

And the lights came back on. They flickered, but they didn't go out again.

Kelly made a small *psst* sound. Lucia looked toward her.

Kelly gestured toward the front hall. She pantomimed using a radio. Lucia nodded. She stepped carefully toward Adrian and touched his hand. He startled, but he remained silent. Lucia pointed toward Kelly and gestured for Adrian to follow her as she picked her way over the debris littering the white-and-black-checked floor. The floor was covered with filthy plastic plates and cups and several rusting robotic parts. Lucia avoided them as she approached Jayce and took his arm. He was totally malleable; she easily led him toward where Kelly stood by the doorway to the front hall.

Lucia didn't look back to see if Adrian was following them. As much she liked Adrian, she wasn't going to let him keep her from getting to the radio. The need to survive trumped an unrequited crush any day.

"We should have gone with the others," Wade said as Joel shut the door to the systems room.

"Shh," Joel said. He gazed around and spotted what he was looking for. A heavy wood crate was sitting against the far wall of the small L-shaped room. He hurried over, lifted it, and carried it back to shove it in front of the closed door.

Joel knew that if he could lift it, the crate wasn't heavy enough to stop a metal monster capable of popping off human heads and limbs, but maybe it would slow the thing down. And maybe the creature followed the others. As terrible as the thought was, Joel really hoped it did.

Joel turned and looked around the crowded room. He stifled a sneeze and lifted the hem of his purple-and-yellow team shirt to wipe sweat from his face.

Like all the other rooms in the old pizzeria, this one was filled with dust. It also held a rusting old furnace bulging with pipes and chutes that extended in several directions and were entangled with broken-down scaffolding. This room, unlike the rest of the rooms in the abandoned restaurant, was two stories tall. A couple of the furnace chutes extended up to the top of the room's high ceiling; the rest of them bent around the corner of the room's L.

The room smelled faintly of rotten eggs. Joel didn't know much about furnaces, but he remembered that smell coming from his grandpa's old one when it was going bad. This particular one wasn't functioning, Joel didn't think, but something in this room was running. He could hear a humming sound that alternated with a rapid rhythmic *whoosh*. It sounded like a fan.

Joel glanced at Wade, who had slumped to the dirty floor. He sat with his back against the room's cement wall. His knees were bent, and he had his arms wrapped around them. He stared into space; his long, usually shiny hair hung in strings over his face.

Joel shook his head. Who knew Wade was so fragile?

Joel and Wade had been friends ever since Joel had made it onto the football team. Already the star center on the school's basketball team, Joel had thought that also being the football team's star offensive lineman, the "mountain" who protected Wade from the opposing team's defensive line, would have gotten him more credit than it did. He knew he wasn't the brightest guy in the world, but he was strong. And he was in great shape. These qualities, however, didn't win him many friends. Not that it mattered. But having Wade as a friend did have its perks. Because of Wade, Joel dated popular girls and got invited to the big parties. Because of Wade, some of the teachers cut Joel slack when he didn't bother with his schoolwork. Wade was useful. Usually.

Joel turned his back on Wade and started poking around the old furnace. It didn't take him long to check it out. The bulk of it sat in a fifteen-foot-square space, but its chutes reached beyond that space. Joel was particularly interested in the ones that stretched upward.

Joel tilted his head back and squinted up at the ceiling. The light in this room was as pitiful as the light in the rest of the pizzeria, but Joel was pretty sure that one of the furnace chutes disappeared into a venting system on the ceiling. What if there was a way out through that system?

Wade moved his foot. The slight *shh* sound made Joel turn around. He watched Wade push himself to his feet.

Wade looked toward Joel as a *clank* emanated from down the hallway, from a pretty good distance. Both Joel and Wade cocked their heads and listened. The *clank* was followed by silence. They waited a few seconds. Then

Joel motioned for Wade to follow him around the corner of the room's L.

Wade hesitated but then complied. Joel led Wade to the base of the furnace's longest chute.

Joel pointed upward. "I want to climb up there and see what's beyond the end of the chute. I think it's a venting system."

Wade frowned but then nodded. He poked around the furnace's corroded pipes and chutes. Joel started to turn away, but Wade nudged him. "I think this panel comes off," Wade whispered. He pointed.

Joel saw what Wade was looking at. There was an oxidized metal panel on the furnace wall beneath the main chute. It was held on with bolts, but the bolts were crumbling.

Joel saw a gap at the edge of the panel. He managed to stuff his thick fingers into the opening. He took a breath and tugged. As he'd hoped it would, the panel fell away from the furnace with a metallic pop. Wade quickly reached out and caught it before it could clatter to the floor.

"Good hands," Joel whispered.

Wade didn't respond.

The panel wasn't all that big, but its removal exposed an opening big enough for Joel to shove his shoulders through. He immediately pushed in through the opening and looked up.

"All right!" His voice echoed in the enclosed chute.

"What?" Wade asked.

"There are metal handholds and footholds in here. I think this is a maintenance chute. I'm going to check it out."

Wade again didn't answer. So, Joel squeezed inside the chute and began climbing upward.

The interior of the chute was nearly dark, but the glow of an exposed bulb on the wall near the chute managed to creep in through cracks in the chute's decaying metal. Joel could see well enough.

It took just a minute or so for Joel to climb high enough to get a better view of what lay beyond the top of the chute. As he suspected, it was part of a ventilation system. The maintenance chute ended in front of a huge metal fan. The fan's blades were rotating quickly and steadily. That was the sound Joel had heard earlier. Joel peered at the blades. Frowning hard, he concentrated on seeing beyond the fast-moving curved metal. Yes! Just as he'd hoped. He could see light, bright light. Just a slice of it. But it was unmistakable. Joel could see sunlight. This was their way out!

All they had to do was figure out how to turn off the fan. Then they'd be able to slip through the openings between the blades and climb out through a vent in the roof.

Grinning, Joel backed down the chute and crawled out of the furnace. Wade was slumped against the wall, once again, staring into space.

"I found the way out," Joel said, catching his breath.

Wade blinked. His slack face regained a little color. "Really?"

Joel nodded. "There's a fan at the top of the chute. Beyond the fan, I can see a little sunlight coming through a vent in the roof, I think. All we have to do is figure out how to turn off the fan."

Wade straightened. He was looking a little more like his usual self. "We need to go get the others," he said.

Joel shook his head. "There's no time. That thing is out there, and it's not going to be long before it checks in here. The best thing we can do is get ourselves out and—"

"But we can't leave."

"We'll get help for the others once we're out," Joel interrupted. He put as much sincerity in his voice as he could.

The truth was, Joel couldn't have cared less about the others. Adrian was a pretty boy who was too big for his britches. Jayce was a sniveling nerd. Lucia was a weirdo, and Kelly was . . . Well, admittedly, Kelly was pretty, but she wasn't pretty enough to come before Joel's right to get out of this place alive.

"What if that thing gets them before we can get help back here?" Wade asked.

"What if it gets *us* before we can tell them about the way out?" Joel countered. "That thing could be right outside the door for all we know."

Wade sucked in his breath. He turned toward the closed door. And he nodded.

"Good," Joel said. "Let's find a way to shut off that fan."

Adrian closed the office door as quietly as he could. He felt the tension bunch in his shoulders when the latch made a clicking sound. He put his head to the door and listened.

He and the others had heard the huge creature coming down the back hall as they cut through the employee lounge to exit out the other door. It sounded like the creature went on down the hall, but Adrian couldn't be sure. It could have passed through the lounge after them and be coming for them.

Adrian turned to look at Lucia and the others. "Are you sure you can figure out how to get that radio working?" he asked Lucia.

Lucia stepped around a battered gray metal desk and headed toward the dusty wood credenza sitting against the wall. The credenza held a black rectangular box with silver metal knobs. A coiled cord attached to a microphone lay next to the box. "I can try," she said, glancing over her shoulder at Adrian. "Just see if you can keep that metal monster from getting in here while I do."

Adrian nodded. He stepped over to the desk. "Jayce, can you help me lift this so we can put it in front of the door?" Adrian wasn't sure Jayce would be much help, but without Jayce, Adrian would have to drag the desk. He didn't want to make that much noise.

Jayce, who looked even smaller than usual, sniffed, but he nodded. He did his best to lift one end of the desk while Adrian took the bulk of the desk's weight. Between them, they managed to position it in front of the door without creating a sound.

As soon as the desk was in place, Adrian pointed at a black metal filing cabinet. "Let's see if we can put that on top of the desk."

Jayce nodded again.

The contents of the filing cabinet rattled when they turned it on its side. Adrian tensed, but he didn't hear anything moving in the hallway. He motioned for Jayce to lift his end, and they managed to set the cabinet on top of the desk.

Adrian immediately looked around the room. He spotted a vent cover near the floor under the credenza.

While he and Jayce had been moving furniture, Lucia and Kelly had huddled over the radio. They were whispering to each other now. Adrian couldn't hear everything they were saying. He caught the occasional words: frequency, wire, reroute, splice. Kelly seemed to be following what Lucia was telling her. She ever offered her own ideas.

Adrian was beginning to realize that there was fa more to Kelly than she'd ever let on.

Adrian motioned for Jayce to come with him as he crossed the office to the credenza. Adrian was pretty sure their barricade wouldn't be enough to stop the thing i it wanted to come into the room. He didn't want Jayce anywhere near the door in case that happened.

Nearing the two girls, Adrian whispered, "Can you two move down just a little? I want to see if we can ge that vent cover loose." He pointed at it. "That way if the thing comes through the door, we'll have an escape route.'

Lucia froze in the middle of fiddling with a couple o the radio's wires. Her face paled.

Kelly looked down at the vent cover. "What's to stop the thing from using the ductwork to get in here? Maybe by taking off the cover, you're playing right into it hands."

"You think that thing has a plan?" Jayce asked, his voice pitched even higher than usual.

Kelly shook her head. "Not in the way you're thinking No. But from what I saw, admittedly briefly, it's at leas in part mechanical. That means someone programmed it and so it has some kind of protocol it's following. If tha protocol includes removing all intruders, it probably also has the programming necessary to complete the task. I'c guess that would include being able to use any way pos- sible of moving through this place."

Adrian gazed at Kelly with ever-rising respect. He found himself noticing how pretty her eyes were, hov pretty *she* was. No, not just pretty. Kelly was beautiful Even now, with her long brown hair tangled and he clothes filthy, she was stunning.

How strange is that? Adrian thought. Had he been so blinded by Hope's looks and vivacious personality that he'd failed to see Hope's friend?

"Adrian, are you okay?" Lucia asked. "You look freaked out."

Adrian blinked and shook his head. "Sorry."

Lucia stepped away from the radio. She put a hand on his arm. "It's okay. I know you're . . . I'm sorry about Hope."

Adrian swallowed hard and nodded. He shifted his gaze away from Lucia and Kelly, and he noticed Jayce frowning at Lucia's hand on Adrian's arm.

Adrian stepped back. He looked at the vent grate. "I still think we should try to get the cover loose. If we get it off, we can prop it into place with something. I think we'll hear the thing coming if it comes through the vent duct. But if it comes through the door, it could take us by surprise."

Lucia and Kelly exchanged a glance. They were bonding, Adrian realized. Two brainy girls in a situation that had nothing to do with being popular or fitting in. Strangely, they were in their element.

Kelly finally nodded. "That sounds like a plan," she said.

She and Lucia returned their attention to the radio. Adrian dropped to his knees and pulled out his pocketknife.

Wade looked at Joel and shook his head. "It's no use," he said.

After turning every knob and pushing every button on the room's control panel and on the furnace itself, he and Joel still hadn't been able to get the fan to stop turning. Even flipping all the switches in the fuse box they'd managed to find behind the furnace didn't do any good.

It must be on another circuit," Wade said. "Its own circuit. And who knows where that is."

Joel let out a growl. Wade was familiar with the sound. Joel always growled like that when he missed a tackle.

Wade understood Joel's frustration, but he didn't share it. He wasn't about to tell Joel, but Wade really didn't care whether they found a way to stop the fan. He couldn't summon up the motivation. The truth was that he was numb. He'd been numb ever since he'd thrown up in the dining room. That was when he'd accepted that he really had just watched some kind of monstrous creature rip apart the girl he loved.

Okay, so maybe he wasn't totally numb. He was finally facing the truth that he'd loved Hope. Because Hope had been with Adrian and clearly didn't feel anything for Wade, Wade had been trying to convince himself for a long time that he just had the hots for her. But it wasn't "the hots." It was love. And now she was gone.

"Hey!" Joel shook Wade by the shoulder.

Wade frowned and pushed Joel away.

Joel didn't protest. He bounced on the balls of his feet like an excited little kid. "I have an idea."

Wade waited for what he assumed would be some-thing boneheaded.

"Remember how the lights went out when the crea-ture showed up, before it killed Hope?" Joel asked.

Wade didn't want to remember anything about watch-ing Hope die. But he nodded anyway.

"Something about that thing affects electricity, right?" Joel said.

Wade shrugged.

"If we could lure it in here," Joel continued, "get it close, the power to that fan should shut off. Shouldn't it?

Wade raised an eyebrow. "You mean after it tears us apart? I bet we'd fit through the fan just fine in pieces."

Joel snorted and punched Wade in the bicep. "Funny. But I'm not joking around. If the creature shorts things out, it could short out the fan. We just need to make sure it's close and then get up the chute before it grabs us."

Just as Wade suspected. Something boneheaded.

Joel rubbed his pug-like jawline and looked at Wade. "All you have to do is go out there and get the robot's attention and then get it to chase you back in here."

"Me?" Wade glared at Joel. "Why me? It's *your* stupid idea."

Joel made a face and gestured at his fireplug-like body. "I'm the center on the basketball team, not the forward. Power. Not speed." He tapped his chest. "Linebacker." He poked Wade's chest. "Quarterback. You're the king of scramble, remember? No one outmaneuvers tacklers like you do."

Wade opened his mouth to protest, but he didn't get any words out. Joel actually had a point. And his plan, although stupid and dangerous, wasn't half-bad.

Wade made himself remember how the creature had moved in the Parts and Service room. Was it fast? Not really. It was crazy strong, yeah. But when it moved, it was cumbersome. He could outmaneuver it.

"The only way we're going to get out of here," Joel said, "is to get past that fan."

"Okay," Wade said.

Joel raised both eyebrows. "Really?"

"Why not?" Wade meant that. Why not? It would give him something to do besides wallow in grief and

Lucia snatched her hand back when the radio's wire sparked for the third time. "Crap!" She resisted the urge to put her head in her hands.

It wasn't working. She and Kelly had rewired the radio and reconfigured its frequency, but it wasn't receiving anything but static. And the wires were so old that they wouldn't hold together.

Lucia looked up at Kelly and shook her head. Kelly gently nudged Lucia aside. "Let me try again."

Lucia stepped back. While Kelly started manipulating the wires, Lucia turned to watch Adrian and Jayce. Adrian was pacing back and forth in front of the desk and filing cabinet barricade, and Jayce was sitting cross-legged in front of the vent cover Adrian had removed and propped back into place. Jayce was supposed to be watching and listening for the robot's approach through the ductwork, but he was hunched over his sketch pad drawing cute bunnies cavorting in a forest meadow. Lucia couldn't help but smile. Everyone had their own coping mechanism.

Lucia wanted to say something to Adrian, something comforting, something more than her "Sorry about Hope" from earlier. But she wasn't any good at that kind of thing. And what would be comforting anyway? "It's horrible that your girlfriend lost her head." "Do you want to talk about how you feel about Hope being brutally murdered?" No. And no.

And *was* Hope murdered? Could a machine—because she was pretty sure the creature was some kind of horrible machine—commit murder? Murder required premeditation. Could something that was built do that? Lucia doubted it. The thing was following its programming, however messed up that was.

In another place, another time, Lucia might have

enjoyed kicking around these questions. She might even have liked discussing the ideas with Kelly. The more time Lucia spent with Kelly, even in this totally wacked-out situation, the more she liked her. For the first time in her life, Lucia might have been making a friend, a good friend.

While they'd worked on the radio, Kelly had chattered. Lucia was pretty sure it was nervous chatter, but it wasn't your typical girly nonsense. Kelly talked about her feelings, about how she always felt "less than" when she was around Hope. That was why she was so shy, she explained. She never felt like she had much to contribute in a group. She was overshadowed.

It didn't escape Lucia's awareness that this budding friendship with Kelly wouldn't have been possible if Hope was still alive. The Kelly-Hope dynamic wouldn't have had room for Lucia.

This explained what Lucia had been feeling for the last half hour, she realized. Even under the horror of what they'd seen and the terror of what might happen next, Lucia felt guilty. Now she knew why. She felt guilty because Hope's death benefited her. No more Hope meant Adrian was now available (not that he'd shown any interest in Lucia, in that way), and it meant a super-cool girl could come out into the light and be herself.

Kelly sighed loudly.

"Nothing, huh?" Lucia asked. She frowned at the radio. Then she snapped her fingers. "Maybe there's a manual or something."

Lucia rushed over to the filing cabinet. Even though it lay on its side, she could still get to the folders stuffed in its drawers. She began rifling through them.

Although she sorted quickly, at one point, her hand

came to an abrupt stop. Reaching into a file, she yanked out what looked like an old, yellowed operator's manual. She turned to the page she'd just glimpsed as she'd flipped through the file.

"Whoa," Lucia said. She waved the manual in the air.

Kelly came over to her. Jayce and Adrian remained where they were.

"What's that?" Kelly asked.

"It's an operator's manual," Lucia said, skimming its pages quickly. She opened the manual to the last page and tapped the drawing she'd seen there.

"That's the thing," Kelly breathed.

Lucia nodded.

"What'd you find?" Adrian asked.

Lucia flipped the page and read some more. "It's an old user's manual," she said. "It describes a bunch of different kinds of robotic endoskeletons. The one we saw is either a Mimic Model 1 or 2." She ran her finger down the page. "These things are pretty creepy; they have retractable and expandable limbs and a contracting torso so they can fit into pretty much any mascot costume." Lucia frowned and read some small print under the sketch of the thing that had killed Hope. "Oh jeez," she gasped.

"What?" Kelly asked.

Lucia looked up from the manual. "Apparently, the tech in the Mimics was pretty clunky. It says that if you encounter one of these things, you should immediately disconnect its power source and disassemble it." She looked at the others. "That's not good. We need to get out of here."

Lucia hurried back to the radio and spent the next few minutes frenziedly moving around wires and turning dials. Kelly put her hand on Lucia's arm.

Stop," Kelly said. "We need to get a grip on our- selves." She glanced down at Jayce. "Maybe he has the right idea. Maybe we need to clear our heads for a few minutes."

Lucia rolled her shoulders to release her pent-up ten- sion. "Okay."

Kelly sat down on the floor next to Jayce. She put her hand on Jayce's knee. He flinched but kept drawing.

"What's your favorite color?" Kelly asked Jayce. "And why?"

Jayce blinked several times and then frowned. Without looking up from his sketch pad, he said, "Yellow, because it makes me think of fuzzy chicks." He glanced up at Kelly through his messy, thick black bangs and gave her a half smile.

She smiled back. "Good. Mine's green, bright green, because it's the color of seedlings. That makes me think of how things can grow, how people can grow." She looked up at Lucia. "How about you?"

"Purple. It's the color of a really good, deep bruise. Something painful and real." The words had just tumbled out, and Lucia regretted them immediately. That might have been a little too raw. Did she really want Adrian to know how dark her mind was?

Lucia looked toward Adrian as Kelly repeated the question to him.

Adrian, his face expressionless but still as model gor- geous as ever, said flatly, "Blue. Like the sea. It makes me think of freedom."

Out of the corner of her eye, Lucia noticed Jayce glance up at her and then look over at Adrian. A muscle twitched along his jawline. His eyes narrowed. He knew, Lucia realized. He knew how she felt about Adrian. And

"Speaking of blue," Lucia said. "I have an idea." She turned back to the radio and began fiddling with it.

Lucia didn't really have an idea. She just needed to put her back to Adrian and Jayce. As sweet as Jayce's love of cute fuzzy things was, Lucia just plain and simply wasn't attracted to him. She might have looked like she paired well with nerds, but apparently she was all about heart-palpitating good looks like Adrian's.

Joel stood by the door to the hallway. He listened intently.

At least sixty seconds had passed since Wade had gone through the door. Obviously, the creature wasn't outside in the hallway because the only sound Joel heard as he closed the door was Wade's soft footfalls heading down the hallway.

The systems room's lights, though abysmally murky, were still on steady. The creature wasn't nearby.

Okay. Now.

Joel strode away from the door and trotted to the bottom of the chute. Shoving his bulk through the barely-wide-enough opening, he began shimmying up the shaft.

As he climbed, he thought about Wade. Would he be able to get the creature close without getting killed?

Joel sure hoped so.

In the back of his mind, Joel was aware that they were in this mess because of him. It had been his idea to come check out the construction site. But Wade had his part in it, too. He was the one who'd spotted the way into the old pizzeria. Served him right to be the bait that would get Joel out of here.

Joel had to look out for number one. It was a dog-eat-dog world. Every person for themselves.

Joel stopped thinking and concentrated on climbing.

★　★　★

Every little hair on the back of Wade's neck stood on end as he eased down the hallway toward the dining room. Looking left and right, rotating regularly to glance down the hall, Wade was aware the creature could appear at any moment.

He really hoped that flickering lights would give him enough warning to run. He just needed a head start. He figured if he had that, he could stay ahead of the mammoth animatronic killer.

That was why he was heading toward the restaurant's main room. Even though it was littered with mangled tables and chairs, old party debris, and construction supplies—not to mention body parts—it was still the largest area in the old building. He wanted space to maneuver.

But he wasn't going to get it.

The lights started to flicker just as Wade was passing one of the swinging doors that led into the kitchen. Wade whirled.

Where was it?

Over the deafening sound of his pounding heart, Wade heard the *tap-hiss-rasp* of the robot's footsteps. They were coming from the employees' lounge.

Wade shot to the right and flung himself through the kitchen's swinging door. He immediately turned right again, heading toward the other kitchen door. He hoped he could get through the kitchen and come out in the hallway, behind the creature, while the thing searched for him.

The kitchen went black.

The scratching taps entered the kitchen. Too soon. Wade didn't have time to get to the other door. Not in the dark.

Wade ducked behind the boat-size stainless-steel kitchen island. As he crouched, his hand slid over a stack of pizza pans. They cascaded to the ground and scattered with clangs and jangles anyone—human or not—would have noticed.

The taps stopped. A heavy vibration shuddered through the kitchen. A long hiss came from the opposite side of the island.

The thing was *right there.*

Scrambling on his hands and knees, Wade gathered pizza pans as he crawled as fast as he could around the island, back in the direction he'd come from. The floor's reverberations told him the creature was following him.

Wade shot to his feet. And he ran. At full speed. He raced around the island and blasted back through the door he'd just come through. As he surged into the hall, its lights flickered on.

Wade glanced over his shoulder. The creature was nothing more than a hulking shape in the kitchen's continued darkness. Watching it move was like watching the undulating motion of a shadow monster. Its progress wasn't fast, but it was steady.

Without thinking about why he was doing it, Wade started firing pizza pans toward his pursuer. He flung them as if they were Frisbees, whipping them toward the robot's neck.

Wade didn't have any delusions that a pizza pan could take out a monster made of metal, but he thought they might be enough of a nuisance to slow the thing down. And he might even get lucky and dislodge a cable to disable the thing.

Or maybe not. Even in the kitchen's blackness, he could see the pizza pans bouncing off the robot's shoulders and chest.

Wade started toward the dining room, but he lost his footing. He stumbled and fell, skidding down the hallway floor, away from the dining room.

The creature exited the kitchen. The kitchen's lights came on as the swinging door closed behind the thing.

The hall lights flickered and went out, but not before Wade was able to see that the creature was now between him and the dining room. Wade tore into the employees' lounge and galloped through the room.

As he ran, Wade formed a plan.

Wade had briefly considered running down the hall toward the systems room when the creature pursued him into the hall. But running the length of the hall in the dark, the thing right behind him, wasn't something he wanted to do. He needed more of a head start to get into the chute. What he had to do was get out ahead of the creature before he let it spot him.

Wade thrashed over a pile of chairs, once again losing his balance. He went down hard, cracking his knee on the edge of a metal locker. He didn't let the pain stop him, though. He got back on his feet instantly, and he careened out of the room, into the front hallway. Turning right, Wade dashed toward the lobby.

It took only a couple seconds to get to the archway between the lobby and the dining room. There, Wade paused and looked back. The hallway behind him was empty. Its lights were weak, but they weren't flickering.

Where did the thing go?

Wade frowned and concentrated on catching his breath so he could hear something besides his own heavy panting. He listened hard.

Wade took a few tentative steps toward the dining

Then he heard it. The hissing steps were close. Too close. The creature hadn't followed him; it had gone back the other way, into the dining room.

The lights flickered. The room went dark.

Wade turned to run, but before he could, metal grazed his forearm. It dug into his skin. He felt wet warmth flow down over his wrist and palm. The robot's hissing rasp was closer now. Wade couldn't see the thing, but he could sense it reaching for him. He could imagine its metal fingers extended toward his throat.

Wade juked to the left and then dropped to his knees and rolled. As he came back up to his feet, burning hot pain shot through his right shoulder. The creature had tried to grab him and missed. But it's razor-sharp fingers had scored Wade's flesh. Deep. Blood was rushing down Wade's side. He ignored it.

Wade began darting left and right as if trying to avoid being sacked on the football field. Joel had been right. Wade was good at scrambling. So, he scrambled. He bobbed and weaved, and he scuttled toward the arcade.

Slipping between a couple of pinball machines, Wade crouched and listened. The arcade's lights were still on, so the creature wasn't there yet. But the thing's steps were steady . . . and approaching.

The arcade went dark.

Wade held his breath, stayed low, and circled around the arcade's perimeter until he was back in the dining room. The dining room's lights came on, and Wade found himself standing next to an overturned table that lay in the puddle of a torn purple-striped tablecloth. Clutching his forearm and trying not to think about the gash on his back, Wade scanned the area.

He didn't have a big enough head start yet, especially now that he was injured. He was losing a lot of blood.

and he could feel his legs weakening. He needed to hide until the creature moved farther off. But where?

Wade looked toward the stage. No. Too far.

He glanced at the overturned tables and chairs. Not enough cover.

He turned and looked at one of the piles of decaying body parts. His stomach flipped over. His skin crawled. Every fiber of his being yelled, *No!*

He ignored the advice.

Getting a running start, Wade leaped over a couple of chairs, and he dived right into the pile of dismembered arms, legs, heads, and torsos. Not allowing himself to think about what he was doing—*It's just a pile of sweaty football players*, he told himself—Wade buried himself under the grotesque deconstructed remains of the robot's old victims. Like an animal, he burrowed beneath the spongy flesh and brittle bones.

Keeping his eyes closed, Wade breathed as little as possible as he flattened himself to the floor. Then he lay still and listened.

Even with his eyes closed, Wade knew when the dining room lights went out. The thing was nearby.

Wade held his breath. Blood continued to flow from his wounds. He could feel the thick warmth track across his skin.

The robot's scraping taps came closer . . . and closer. Then they stopped.

Wade continued to hold his breath. He willed himself not to think about where he was.

The robot's footfalls started up again. They began moving away.

Wade allowed himself the tiniest bit of an inhale. He ignored the fetid smell that assaulted his nostrils. He was thankful that he'd emptied his stomach earlier. Even though it roiled now, it didn't heave.

The robot's footfalls continued to move off. It sounded like it was heading toward the stage.

The dining room's lights came back on.

Wade waited.

He remained still until he heard a break in the foot-falls' cadence. Wade was pretty sure the creature was heading up the steps to the stage.

That was far enough. Now was Wade's chance.

Bursting up through his revolting hiding place, Wade batted aside a claw and steadied himself on his feet.

Then he ran.

Wade ran hard. Harder and faster than he'd ever run before.

Wade made it to the doorway to the back hallway in seconds. As he headed down the hall, the dining room lights went out behind him.

The creature was in pursuit.

Joel wasn't sure how long he waited, clinging to the handholds in the chute, just below the fan. It probably wasn't long, but his muscles were starting to spasm when he finally heard the sound he'd been waiting for.

Pounding footsteps. Heading this way.

Joel shifted so he could look down the chute.

The pounding paused for a nanosecond, and then the door to the systems room banged open. More pounding.

Joel looked down. Wade's head appeared at the bottom of the chute. Wade looked up and quickly started scrambling into the chute.

The lights in the systems room started flickering. Wade was fully in the chute now. His face, covered in sweat, stark white, looked upward. His gaze met Joel's.

Then the chute went black.

Wade screamed.

Thudding. Pounding. Clanging. Metallic rat-a-tat-tats. Another scream.

This was all going on below Joel, but he didn't focus on that. He knew what it meant.

"Joel!" Wade cried out. "Help me!"

Joel looked down into the darkness. He couldn't see Wade, but he didn't have to see to know what was happening. The creature was killing his friend.

But Joel was more interested in what was going on above him. He looked up. Between the sounds of struggle and violence, he listened for what he wanted to hear. And he heard it.

The fan had stopped whirring. Its rhythmic *whoosh* was winding down. Slower and slower.

Wade wailed. A squelching wet grinding sound filled the chute. Then a *thud*.

Joel reached up in the dark and his knuckles encountered one of the nearly motionless blades. He caught it and stilled the fan. He pushed himself upward, shoving his bulk through the narrow opening between the blades.

The opening was a lot tighter than Joel had thought it would be. He'd never gotten a good look at the fan. It was hard to visualize it while it was spinning. It was a big fan, though, and he'd hoped he'd be able to squeeze through it when it was stopped.

He was wrong.

Although Joel was able to get his head and neck through the opening easily, his shoulders were another story. He had to squirm to shove himself upward.

He finally got his chest between two of the blades. But he was too big to get through. Although he grunted and strained, Joel couldn't move any farther.

He couldn't back up, either. He was stuck.

Going as limp as he could, hoping that relaxing his

muscles might get him free, Joel listened to the clunking and clanking going on below him. He still couldn't see, but it sounded like the creature was pulling Wade's body out of the chute.

Joel had no doubt Wade was dead. Wade hadn't made a sound in several seconds. And the other sounds had made it pretty clear the creature was doing to Wade the same thing it had done to Hope.

Now it sounded like the creature was gathering Wade's parts. Maybe it was going to take them back to the dining room to put them with all the other cut-up bodies.

Joel twisted his shoulders and tried to free himself from the blades. He idly wondered what programming made a metal creature dismember a human and pile up its pieces.

And that thought was the last coherent one he had.

The lights in the systems room came back on. The fan reactivated. Its sharp blades immediately began chewing through Joel's arms.

Joel howled, his consciousness assaulted by the most pain he'd ever felt. It was worse than he could even have imagined.

The fan's blades picked up speed. They cut through Joe's arms and chest, cleaving him in two. As the bottom half of his body thumped its way down the chute, Joel's brain continued to process the pain just for another couple seconds as the fan began chopping the rest of him into bloody bits.